PILGRIM'S PROGRESS
REWALKED

From This World to That Which Is to Come

By
Shawn P. Robinson
A Modern Day Retelling of
John Bunyan's Classic

BrainSwell
PUBLISHING

BrainSwell Publishing
Ingersoll, Ontario

ISBN: 978-1-989296-82-0

Dedication and Thanks

*To Juanita, who is such an encouragement to me as I
follow this path of writing for God's glory.
To my family who still manages to get excited about the
new books I write.
To John Bunyan for writing a book that has captivated
my heart since I was a small boy.
And to all of you! I hope you are blessed and
encouraged by Pilgrim's Progress Rewalked!*

This book is a work of allegorical Christian fiction. Characters and places and such are fictional and have been laid out by John Bunyan and rewritten in a contemporary narrative form as an allegorical picture of the Christian walk.

Table of Contents

John Bunyan's Apology[1] for His Book

When at the first I took my pen in hand[2]
Thus for to write, I did not understand
That I at all should make a little book
In such a mode; nay, I had undertook
To make another; which, when almost done,
Before I was aware, I this begun.
And thus it was: I, writing of the way
And race of saints, in this our gospel day,
Fell suddenly into an allegory
About their journey, and the way to glory,
In more than twenty things which I set down.
This done, I twenty more had in my crown;
And they again began to multiply,
Like sparks that from the coals of fire do fly.
Nay, then, thought I, if that you breed so fast,
I'll put you by yourselves, lest you at last

---

[1] The word *Apology* in this sense carries with it the meaning of *argument* or *reason*.
[2] I have left Bunyan's *Apology* in its original language. I am not a gifted poet, and I know it. If I were to try to rewrite this poetry in modern English, you would also quickly come to "know it".

Should prove ad infinitum, and eat out
The book that I already am about.
Well, so I did; but yet I did not think
To shew to all the world my pen and ink
In such a mode; I only thought to make
I knew not what; nor did I undertake
Thereby to please my neighbour: no, not I;
I did it my own self to gratify.
Neither did I but vacant seasons spend
In this my scribble; nor did I intend
But to divert myself in doing this
From worser thoughts which make me do amiss.
Thus, I set pen to paper with delight,
And quickly had my thoughts in black and white.
For, having now my method by the end,
Still as I pulled, it came; and so I penned
It down: until it came at last to be,
For length and breadth, the bigness which you see.
Well, when I had thus put mine ends together,
I shewed them others, that I might see whether
They would condemn them, or them justify:
And some said, Let them live; some, Let them die;
Some said, JOHN, print it; others said, Not so;
Some said, It might do good; others said, No.
Now was I in a strait, and did not see
Which was the best thing to be done by me:
At last I thought, Since you are thus divided,
I print it will, and so the case decided.
For, thought I, some, I see, would have it done,
Though others in that channel do not run:
To prove, then, who advised for the best,
Thus I thought fit to put it to the test.
I further thought, if now I did deny
Those that would have it, thus to gratify.
I did not know but hinder them I might
Of that which would to them be great delight.

For those which were not for its coming forth,
I said to them, Offend you I am loth,
Yet, since your brethren pleased with it be,
Forbear to judge till you do further see.
If that thou wilt not read, let it alone;
Some love the meat, some love to pick the bone.
Yea, that I might them better palliate,
I did too with them thus expostulate:--
May I not write in such a style as this?
In such a method, too, and yet not miss
My end--thy good? Why may it not be done?
Dark clouds bring waters, when the bright bring
none.
Yea, dark or bright, if they their silver drops
Cause to descend, the earth, by yielding crops,
Gives praise to both, and carpeth not at either,
But treasures up the fruit they yield together;
Yea, so commixes both, that in her fruit
None can distinguish this from that: they suit
Her well when hungry; but, if she be full,
She spews out both, and makes their blessings null.
You see the ways the fisherman doth take
To catch the fish; what engines doth he make?
Behold how he engageth all his wits;
Also his snares, lines, angles, hooks, and nets;
Yet fish there be, that neither hook, nor line,
Nor snare, nor net, nor engine can make thine:
They must be groped for, and be tickled too,
Or they will not be catch'd, whate'er you do.
How does the fowler seek to catch his game
By divers means! all which one cannot name:
His guns, his nets, his lime-twigs, light, and bell:
He creeps, he goes, he stands; yea, who can tell
Of all his postures? Yet there's none of these
Will make him master of what fowls he please.
Yea, he must pipe and whistle to catch this,
Yet, if he does so, that bird he will miss.

If that a pearl may in a toad's head dwell,
And may be found too in an oyster-shell;
If things that promise nothing do contain
What better is than gold; who will disdain,
That have an inkling of it, there to look,
That they may find it? Now, my little book,
(Though void of all these paintings that may make
It with this or the other man to take)
Is not without those things that do excel
What do in brave but empty notions dwell.
'Well, yet I am not fully satisfied,
That this your book will stand, when soundly tried.'
Why, what's the matter? 'It is dark.' What though?
'But it is feigned.' What of that? I trow?
Some men, by feigned words, as dark as mine,
Make truth to spangle and its rays to shine.
'But they want solidness.' Speak, man, thy mind.
'They drown the weak; metaphors make us blind.'
Solidity, indeed, becomes the pen
Of him that writeth things divine to men;
But must I needs want solidness, because
By metaphors I speak? Were not God's laws,
His gospel laws, in olden times held forth
By types, shadows, and metaphors? Yet loth
Will any sober man be to find fault
With them, lest he be found for to assault
The highest wisdom. No, he rather stoops,
And seeks to find out what by pins and loops,
By calves and sheep, by heifers and by rams,
By birds and herbs, and by the blood of lambs,
God speaketh to him; and happy is he
That finds the light and grace that in them be.
Be not too forward, therefore, to conclude
That I want solidness--that I am rude;
All things solid in show not solid be;
All things in parables despise not we;

Lest things most hurtful lightly we receive,
And things that good are, of our souls bereave.
My dark and cloudy words, they do but hold
The truth, as cabinets enclose the gold.
The prophets used much by metaphors
To set forth truth; yea, who so considers Christ,
his apostles too, shall plainly see,
That truths to this day in such mantles be.
Am I afraid to say, that holy writ,
Which for its style and phrase puts down all wit,
Is everywhere so full of all these things--
Dark figures, allegories? Yet there springs
From that same book that lustre, and those rays
Of light, that turn our darkest nights to days.
Come, let my carper to his life now look,
And find there darker lines than in my book
He findeth any; yea, and let him know,
That in his best things there are worse lines too.
May we but stand before impartial men,
To his poor one I dare adventure ten,
That they will take my meaning in these lines
Far better than his lies in silver shrines.
Come, truth, although in swaddling clouts, I find,
Informs the judgement, rectifies the mind;
Pleases the understanding, makes the will
Submit; the memory too it doth fill
With what doth our imaginations please;
Likewise it tends our troubles to appease.
Sound words, I know, Timothy is to use,
And old wives' fables he is to refuse;
But yet grave Paul him nowhere did forbid
The use of parables; in which lay hid
That gold, those pearls, and precious stones that were
Worth digging for, and that with greatest care.
Let me add one word more. O man of God,
Art thou offended? Dost thou wish I had
Put forth my matter in another dress?

ʋ

Or, that I had in things been more express?
Three things let me propound; then I submit
To those that are my betters, as is fit.
1. I find not that I am denied the use
Of this my method, so I no abuse
Put on the words, things, readers; or be rude
In handling figure or similitude,
In application; but, all that I may,
Seek the advance of truth this or that way
Denied, did I say? Nay, I have leave
(Example too, and that from them that have
God better pleased, by their words or ways,
Than any man that breatheth now-a-days)
Thus to express my mind, thus to declare
Things unto thee that excellentest are.
2. I find that men (as high as trees) will write
Dialogue-wise; yet no man doth them slight
For writing so: indeed, if they abuse
Truth, cursed be they, and the craft they use
To that intent; but yet let truth be free
To make her sallies upon thee and me,
Which way it pleases God; for who knows how,
Better than he that taught us first to plough,
To guide our mind and pens for his design?
And he makes base things usher in divine.
3. I find that holy writ in many places
Hath semblance with this method, where the cases
Do call for one thing, to set forth another;
Use it I may, then, and yet nothing smother
Truth's golden beams: nay, by this method may
Make it cast forth its rays as light as day.
And now before I do put up my pen,
I'll shew the profit of my book, and then
Commit both thee and it unto that Hand
That pulls the strong down, and makes weak ones
stand.

This book it chalketh out before thine eyes
The man that seeks the everlasting prize;
It shews you whence he comes, whither he goes;
What he leaves undone, also what he does;
It also shows you how he runs and runs,
Till he unto the gate of glory comes.
It shows, too, who set out for life amain,
As if the lasting crown they would obtain;
Here also you may see the reason why
They lose their labour, and like fools do die.
This book will make a traveller of thee,
If by its counsel thou wilt ruled be;
It will direct thee to the Holy Land,
If thou wilt its directions understand:
Yea, it will make the slothful active be;
The blind also delightful things to see.
Art thou for something rare and profitable?
Wouldest thou see a truth within a fable?
Art thou forgetful? Wouldest thou remember
From New-Year's day to the last of December?
Then read my fancies; they will stick like burs,
And may be, to the helpless, comforters.
This book is writ in such a dialect
As may the minds of listless men affect:
It seems a novelty, and yet contains
Nothing but sound and honest gospel strains.
Wouldst thou divert thyself from melancholy?
Wouldst thou be pleasant, yet be far from folly?
Wouldst thou read riddles, and their explanation?
Or else be drowned in thy contemplation?
Dost thou love picking meat? Or wouldst thou see
A man in the clouds, and hear him speak to thee?
Wouldst thou be in a dream, and yet not sleep?
Or wouldst thou in a moment laugh and weep?
Wouldest thou lose thyself and catch no harm,
And find thyself again without a charm?
Wouldst read thyself, and read thou knowest not

what,
And yet know whether thou art blest or not,
By reading the same lines? Oh, then come hither,
And lay my book, thy head, and heart together.

John Bunyan

Shawn P. Robinson's Apology for This Book

I'm so glad to share this book with you, and I am glad to share this brief apology with you.[3]

Pilgrim's Progress has always been a favourite of mine. Even as a child, this book fascinated me. Over the years, I have read it countless times, and despite how often I've read it, I continue to learn and grow each time!

Now, this book has been rewritten into modern English many times, and these rewrites have often resulted in quality works. However, I wanted to do this myself for many reasons. One of the main reasons is because I wanted to do something a little different from what I have seen out there in some contemporary versions, but as I worked through it, another motivation grew in me.

What surprised me most was how much more I got out of the book as I worked through "translating" it

---

[3] The word *Apology* in this sense carries with it the meaning of *argument* or *reason* as in, "This is Shawn Robinson's reasoned argument for writing this book." I kept this language (rather than use the word "Introduction") because Bunyan gives an *Apology* for his book.

into modern English, so much more than in any of my countless readings over the years. As such, if you wish to go much deeper in this allegorical treasure, I recommend you do a rewrite yourself! Get a hold of an old, original version of it… and work through it! The original is no longer copyrighted (as opposed to modern rewrites, which are), and I think you'll find the book opens up to you in brand new ways as it will force you to seriously think through the meaning, not only of the story, but also of the words and phrases!

I'm also motivated by a desire to encourage others to experience this book. As a result, I have created study guides to walk people through this story. I hope the *Rewalked* version, in an easy-to-read format, will help a generation of people who have not read the book to enjoy this beautiful story which has impacted millions of Christians over the centuries!

Now, if you dive into the study guides,[4] they have been based upon a series that I did with my own church when I was pastoring a few years back, prior to a personal illness that has prevented me from doing such kinds of things in recent years. A portion of the church worked through the story as a means of discipleship, asking questions and talking through it together.

For this contemporary version, the following will explain how I approached the writing of this *Rewalked* edition.

1. I tried to keep the *Rewalked* edition as close to the original's intent as possible but added in some emotion and description to make the story flow a little better. Unfortunately, in some places, the specific details of the book did not *translate* well to contemporary English. If I

---

[4] The Study Guides are available for both the Rewalked edition and the Original edition.

had to change the sense of it for the sake of flow, I made a footnote for it. Otherwise, I stuck to the same concepts as much as possible. These occasional changes, however, are minor.

2. Whenever I dealt with names of God, people, or locations, I kept the wording the same. For example, if the original referred to Jesus as the Lord of the hill or as the Lord Jesus, that is what you will read in this rewrite.

3. For idioms, it is important to understand that not all idioms make sense in a modern context. When possible, I kept the idioms the same and only changed what I felt was necessary, but in some places, the idiom needed to be changed entirely. Whether with a small or large change, I included a footnote to explain the wording.

4. I have also put the occasional footnote in the text to point out the specifics of what the original said for no other reason than to clarify something that might have a subtle difference between the older English and the modern English. I have also tried to point out some theological concepts that are easy to miss or explain certain things that are not commonly understood.

5. Historically, or at least in the versions I have read, there are countless Scripture references inserted in the text. I have, throughout the book, taken these and put them into footnotes, rather than in a bracket included in the text (as you'll see in older versions). Since there were often multiple Scripture references within a single paragraph, I have typically grouped those references together into one footnote, attached to the end of the paragraph. The exception to this is when Bunyan had a massive paragraph, and I broke it into smaller paragraphs for the sake of readability. In those cases, Scripture references will apply to that general area, rather than for that specific paragraph.

6. In addition, I found a couple of spots in the story where references do not appear in the original text, and beta readers identified some others. In those situations, I have added the Scripture reference into the footnotes.

7. For the actual wording of Scripture, I have changed it from the King James Version to the English Standard Version. This created a challenge in at least one spot where the different translations were *quite* different, but I did my best to reconcile that matter.

8. I wrote the *Rewalked* version primarily in British English. First, Bunyan wrote in British English, so if you are used to American English, this may be jarring for you. Second, I am Canadian. Though I typically, as an author, write my books in American English since that tends to be where I sell the most books, I enjoy writing in British English as it is what Canadians use.

9. One of the biggest changes I faced comes with the book's point of view. I wrote the *Rewalked* version in a first-person narrative style rather than the third person script format used in the original. I did this out of a desire to create a story which flows better with contemporary writing styles, hoping to help readers to better immerse themselves in the story. Because of this change (from third person script to first person), it means the dreamer doesn't always speak in the book[5] in the same way, but I have tried to adjust those sections to make it flow with this style.

10. I've also written most of the book in past tense as though the protagonist, named Christian, was writing his story out in a journal or his own autobiography, and even added in points throughout the story to refer to this journal. At the end of the book, I have Christian hand the journal off to someone else, and Christian himself does not record the last section. As a result, the final pages are not

---

[5] As in "I saw in my dream..."

in past tense, telling the story that he *had* experienced, but rather present tense as though he's experiencing it at that moment, simply living through the last days of his life. The purpose of this is to, Lord willing, bring the reader into the moment. I hope this is especially helpful at the end of the book, considering the final events of the allegory.

11. With Bunyan's use of the word "way" to refer to the Christian journey, I changed the wording to the "path" in each instance, as long as it flowed with story and style. For those asking "Why? Why would you do such a thing???" It was just a stylistic change. In contemporary Christianity, we use both terms "the right way" and "the right path", and I felt "path" flowed better in the *Rewalked* version.

12. Now, for the poems… this is where it gets difficult. Although I love to write stories, I am not a poet. As such, when Bunyan wrote short poems in his text, I left them in the original English, rather than translate them into modern English and cause grief in the hearts of anyone with any poetical sense whatsoever. If you were to see my poetry, you would find yourself filled with gratitude towards me for my considerable kindness in leaving the poetry alone.

I think that pretty much sums up the approach to this book. I just have two things left to say.

First, if, when reading, you come across places where you feel I reworded the story in a way in which some of the original intent was lost, or if you feel I reworded it in a way that changed the theology, please, contact me.[6]

---

[6] Please contact me with issues rather than take the approach of, "Look how this guy messed up! I could tell him with grace and kindness… but I think I'll just complain about it instead!" Don't do that. If there's one thing Christ has taught me in writing twenty plus books is to listen to constructive criticism with an

Contacting me and pointing out something is far kinder than grumping about it. I truly want this rewrite to be accurate to the original's intent, even when it makes me uncomfortable, so if you find something that is off, I want to know so I can fix it. If it's a matter of opinion or interpretation, then I may not make the adjustments, but I will receive all critique offered in love in like manner.

Second, please understand the purpose of this book is to, in Bunyan's words, "make a traveller of thee," and "make the slothful active be; The blind also delightful things to see."

So, my friends, take this book and let it inspire you to be a traveller on the path to the Celestial City!

Shawn P. Robinson

appreciative heart. I ain't perfect. Contact me when you find issues. Perhaps Bunyan put it best when he says in his conclusion, "Nor let my figure or similitude, put thee into a laughter or a feud. Leave this for boys and fools; but as for thee, do thou the substance of my matter see."

1. The Beginning

In the Similitude of a Dream

In the heart of a dreamer, a man found a den, a place to rest his weary soul. And in that place, he found his rest and dreamed a dream. A dream of travellers, pilgrims, a journey, a path. A journey to take him from this world to that which is to come. A journey, which I now share with you.

I stood hunched over, my back to my home. My only clothing, rags, hung on my body, and the burden weighed heavily on my shoulders as I gripped the worn, leather-bound book in my hand.[1] With shaking fingers, I slowly opened the book and read the ancient words in the mid-afternoon light, desperately seeking, hoping, searching.

Once again, the words filled my heart with dread and drove me to weep. My body convulsed under the weight of my own grief.

---

[1] Isa. 64:6; Luke 14:33; Ps. 38:4; Hab. 2:2; Acts 16:30-31.

Unable to hold it in, I cried out, "What can I do?"[2]

With all this weight heavy on my heart, I turned back to my home, forcing a smile onto my lips and doing my best to brighten my expression. Climbing the steps to my door, I reached our small wooden porch, the boards creaking under my weight and paused. With a final deep breath, I composed my face and turned the handle on the door, doing all I could to keep the grief inside, unwilling to allow my wife and children to see my pain.

But try as I might, I could not hold it in for long. Every moment I lived, every step I took, every smile I tried to offer, my grief only grew worse.

It was in this state of agony, of such deep conviction, that I finally laid it all out for my wife and children.

With a loud shout, I called them to come into our kitchen, the only room in the house with enough seats for my wife, my four sons, and me. I invited them to sit, my hands sweating and even shaking, as I considered my words and what I had to tell them.

Turning to my wife, I addressed her the way I always had. "My love?" To my sons, I added, "My children?"

Taking a slow, deep breath, I pulled my own chair out from under the table and settled into the seat before them at the head of the table. "I… I must tell you what's been going on inside. In my heart. I have to share with you what I feel." Deciding to just lay it all before them, I explained, "Family, I'm falling apart because of a great burden on my shoulders. I've learned something terrible. Fire from heaven will burn this city to the ground, and there's no way to protect ourselves from this judgement.

---

[2] Acts 2:37.

Not unless we can escape, not unless we can find some deliverance!"

I shook my head, and tears streamed down my cheeks as I stared at my clenched fists on the table before me. "My family… I've tried… I've searched. I've looked high and low, everywhere I can think of, but no matter where I look, I can't find a way out!"

When I raised my eyes, I saw my wife's mouth hanging open, and my children's faces filled with shock. I could see as clear as day, they didn't believe me. I'd seen that look before when insanity had gripped the minds of others in our city, even shown it myself. Now that look was turned on me. Perhaps they thought I was sick. A fever, maybe. Or something worse. But whatever they thought, my words sounded like nonsense to them.

My wife put her hand gently on my arm and leaned close. "It's getting late, dear." Her face filled with a sad smile as she and my four sons gathered around. "Let's get you to bed. That might help calm you a little."

My wife led me to our room, and I settled in, pulling the blankets up and over my head, hoping to find some rest. But as the hours wore on, I found the night was as bad as the day. I couldn't drift off to sleep, no matter how hard I tried. I spent the entire night tossing and turning, trying to cry myself to sleep, but in it all, I found no relief.

The next morning, all six of us sat around the table for breakfast. I poked at the food on my plate, my appetite as impossible to find as the peace I so desperately craved.

"How are you today?"

Raising my eyes, I tried to bring myself back to the moment, back to my family, to leave the dark thoughts behind. The voice… my oldest son. It must have been him.

I shook my head, and when I answered, it took all my strength to keep my voice steady. "Worse every moment."

I tried again, trying to warn them, desperate to help them understand, but the more I pushed, the more it drove them to stubbornness. We finished our breakfast, and everyone left to go about their day, but I couldn't let it go. I had to get through to them, to warn them of the coming destruction!

This desperate attempt to alert them to the danger was all I had, and as the days wore on, their compassion faded. I watched as everyone I loved, one by one, grew cold and harsh towards me, sometimes ridiculing me, telling me off, and sometimes just outright ignoring me.

Their disdain drove me to spend a lot of time in my room, by myself, sitting on the edge of my bed. I prayed for them, pitied them, longed for them. Hoping to find some relief, some help amid the struggle, I regularly left the house to walk by myself in the fields. On my walks, I would read from my book and pray.

And this was how I spent my time for many, many days.

Until one such day, out in the fields, desperate to find some relief, I found myself once again reading my book, but this time, the pressure, the stress, the fear... it all became too much. In a loud voice, I cried out, "What do I have to do to be saved?"

My breathing came in ragged gasps, and my vision blurred, fear and anguish overtaking me. I spun around, looking for somewhere to run, somewhere to flee from the coming judgement. I had to find some escape, but there was nowhere to go!

"Why are you upset?"[3]

I stumbled backwards, away from the voice, and landed hard on the ground. Not much more than ten steps away, a man stood before me, tall, well-built, confident. I had never seen him before, but I felt so anxious to find anyone, anyone at all who could help me, maybe give some answers, that I scrambled to my feet and ran right up to him, hoping he might have some deep wisdom or secret solution to my desperate problem. Grabbing him by the shoulders, I hollered, "Sir!" hoping to find some relief from my agony. "Sir! Help me!"

The man tilted his head and smiled. "My name is Evangelist," he said kindly, his voice soft and without the disdain to which I'd grown accustomed. "I wander these parts, seeking those in need of help, and thought I might be of assistance to you."

My tears flowed down my cheeks, and I gripped his shoulders even tighter, desperately hoping he had something to offer, some way out of this mess! Holding up my book, I said, "Sir! If you are here to help, help me! I've learned in these writings that I'm condemned to die, and after that, I'll face judgement! I'm not willing to die, and I'm not able to endure judgement.[4] I don't know what to do!"

"Is that so?" he said, his eyes boring into mine. "Tell me, why are you so unwilling to die since this life is filled with so much evil?"

I closed my eyes and shook my head, fearful of pouring out my true thoughts, but I took the risk. "Because… I fear this burden I carry on my shoulders will weigh me down, and when I die, I'll sink lower than the

---

3 Job 33:23.
4 Heb. 9:27; Job 16:21; Eze. 22:14.

grave and fall into hell.[5] And Sir, I'm sure I can't handle prison! How am I supposed to endure judgement and then execution? These thoughts drive me to tears!"

"If this is the way you feel," Evangelist asked, "why are you still standing *here*?"

I shook my head yet again. "I don't know where else to go."

Evangelist smiled and reached into an inner fold of his cloak. Pulling something out, he handed it to me, and when I took it from his hand, I saw it was a scroll. My hands shook with fear, with anticipation, and with hope as I untied the leather strap binding it closed and unrolled the parchment. In large, simple writing, I read the words out loud, "Flee from the wrath to come!"[6] I rolled it back up slowly, and then raised my eyes to Evangelist, forcing myself to take slow breaths, hoping to keep myself from weeping so hard I could no longer speak. "Please, Sir! Where do I go?"

With a kind smile, Evangelist raised his arm and pointed. "Do you see in the distance the Wicket-gate?"[7]

I strained to see, standing on my toes, hoping the little extra height would help, but nothing. Dropping back down, I confessed, "No, I can't see it."

"Then do you see in the distance the shining light?"[8]

As I squinted, straining as hard as I could, I replied, "I… I think so."

---

[5] Isa. 30:33.
[6] Matt. 3.7.
[7] Matt. 7:13,14. The word *wicket* refers to a small gate.
[8] Ps. 119:105; 2 Pet. 1:19.

"Then," said Evangelist, "keep that light in your eye and go directly there. When you reach it, you will see the gate. Knock, and he will tell you what to do."

Without another word to Evangelist, I ran.

I ran, and I ran, and I ran. I ran as hard as I've ever run in my life!

On my way, I passed my home, not even glancing at it. I had my hope, my salvation from the coming destruction! But as I passed by, my wife and children saw me and ran out from within the house. They called out for me to return, but I couldn't look back. Not now. Not anymore! There was nothing but death and destruction behind me. I covered my ears instead and cried out, "Life! Life! Eternal life!"[9] All the while, I refused to look behind me but ran for my life towards the middle of the plain.[10]

Running by more houses, some of my neighbours came out to see me flee.[11] Some mocked me; some called out threats; and some cried out for me to return, but I wouldn't listen to anything they said.

Out of those among my neighbours who shouted, two chased after me, hoping to take me back by force. The name of the one man was Obstinate, the name of the other, Pliable.

By that time, I'd put a lot of distance between us, running as though chased by hell itself. Those two men, however, were determined to catch me, and in a little while, they overtook me.

Catching sight of the two men coming up beside me, I asked between breaths, not daring to slow down, "Why have you come?"

9 Luke 14:26.
10 Gen. 19:17.
11 Jer. 20:10.

The one man, Obstinate, snarled at me as he ran. "To persuade ya to go back with us!"

I shook my head, more determined than ever. "I won't do it! You live in the City of Destruction, the place where I was born. When you die there, you'll sink lower than the grave into a place that burns with fire and brimstone!" Taking the chance, hoping perhaps to persuade these two men, I slowed down just a little so I could talk to them. "Why don't you come with me?"

Obstinate, a man of medium height, but solid build, laughed at me. "What? Leave our friends and comforts behind?"

"Yes," I said, hoping they'd listen.[12] "Everything you could give up here is so small it's not worthy to be compared with even a little of what I'm looking forward to! If you come with me and along this path, you'll receive the same. The place I'm going to has more than enough to go around. Come and see for yourself!"[13]

Obstinate frowned at me but cocked his head to the side just a bit in his curiosity. "What kinds of things ya after? What d'ya expect to receive since ya're leaving everything to get it?"

"I'm after an inheritance! I'm looking forward to one that's incorruptible, undefiled, one that'll never fade away! My reward waits for me in heaven, and it's safe there! This gift is given at the right time to anyone who diligently seeks it!" Coming to a halt, I stared Obstinate right in the

_____

[12] In the original version of Pilgrim's Progress, this is the first time in the book that our character is called, "Christian." Since the version you are reading is written in first person, we'll rarely read his name, but from now on in the book, he goes by the name, "Christian."
[13] 2 Cor. 4:18; Luke 15:17.

eyes and met his frown with an enormous smile. "You can read about it yourself in my book!"[14]

Obstinate scowled back at me. "Forget yar book! Are ya coming back with us or no?"

"No!" I replied. "I've already put my hand to the plow."[15]

Obstinate growled to himself, his eyes filling with disdain as he stared at me. Turning to his friend, he shook his head and said, "Come on, Pliable. Let's turn around and head back without 'im. There're a lot of these fools. When they get an idea in thar heads, they think tha're smarter than seven geniuses."[16]

I expected Pliable to just turn and go with Obstinate, but he didn't move right away. Instead, he looked from Obstinate, back to me, then back to Obstinate again. After a moment, he shrugged awkwardly. "Don't be so critical, Obstinate. If what Christian says is true, the things he's after are better than anything we have now!" He paused for just another second or two before adding, "I'm… I'm inclined to go with him!"

"What?" Obstinate hollered. "What? Another fool! Listen to me, Pliable! Ignore this moron and come back with me. Ya don't know where this fool is leading ya. Get your head on straight and let's go 'ome!"

I couldn't just let Obstinate bully my neighbour. "No, Pliable," I said, reaching for his arm. "There's so much to gain! Sure, there are the wonderful rewards I mentioned, but there's also much more! If you don't believe me, you can read it all here in this book! And if you

---

[14] 1 Pet. 1:4; Heb. 11:16.
[15] Luke 9:62.
[16] Prov. 26:16.

9

doubt the words you read, it's all confirmed by the blood of the One who wrote it!"[17]

Pliable nodded slowly and a smile spread across his face before he turned back to his companion. In a confident voice, he said, "Obstinate, I'm sorry, but I've made my decision. I'm going with Christian. I want to be a part of this." To me, he then asked, "Do you know the way to this place?"

My face broke out in a grin as I answered, "A man named Evangelist showed me the way!" Turning towards the light, I pointed and said, "We have to reach a little gate. Once there, we'll receive instructions about the path."

"Well, Christian," replied Pliable with a laugh, "let's get going!"

With that, we turned away from Obstinate and moved on together.

Behind us, I heard Obstinate growl again. With a huff, he said, "Well, I'm goin' back 'ome! I won't 'ave anything to do with delusional people," before he turned and stormed away.

But Pliable and I continued forward, talking as we made our way across the plain.

"Pliable! Uh… how are you?" I began awkwardly, then added, "I'm glad you joined me. If Obstinate had felt what I felt of the power and terror of what's coming, he wouldn't have been so quick to turn around."

Pliable nodded, the smile still on his face. "Christian, since we're the only ones here, tell me more of what we'll enjoy when we get to that place… the one with all the rewards."

---

[17] Heb. 9:17-22; 13:20.

I nodded. I understood the curiosity about what was to come. "It's hard for me to describe what I see and understand in my head, Pliable," I replied with a laugh. "The things of God are impossible to describe, but since you really want to know, I'll read them to you from my book."

"And do you really think the book is telling the truth?"

"Oh, for sure! The One who wrote it can't lie!"[18]

"Well, that's good!" He then paused for a moment before asking, "And what things are in the book?"

"It tells us," I explained, "of an eternal kingdom where we can live, and everlasting life for us so we can live in that kingdom forever!"[19]

"Oh, wow! What else?"

My face filled with the wonder I felt in my heart as I continued to tell of what we'd receive. "There are crowns and glory for us and clothes that will make us shine like the sun!"[20]

"That sounds pretty great! What else?"

"There won't be any more crying. No more sorrow or sadness. In fact, the One who owns the place will wipe all the tears from our eyes."[21]

"And who else will be there?"

"Well, we'll be there with seraphims and cherubims, creatures that will dazzle your eyes to look at. And you'll meet thousands and ten thousands who have reached that place before us. Not one of them is cruel, but

---

[18] Tit. 1:2.
[19] Isa. 45:17; John 10:28, 29.
[20] 2 Tim. 4:8; Rev. 3:4; Matt. 13:43.
[21] Isa. 25.6-8; Rev. 7:17, 21:4.

they're all loving and holy, every single one walking with God and standing in his presence—even accepted by God himself for all eternity! We'll see there the elders with their golden crowns; and there we'll see the holy virgins with their golden harps; and there we will see men who were cut to pieces by the world, or burned, or eaten by wild animals, or drowned in the sea—those who suffered because of the love they have for the Lord of the place. There, they will all be healed and dressed with immortality!"[22]

Pliable laughed again and said, "This is enough to get me really excited! But," he said, pausing, concern on his face, "can we really have it too? How do we get to be a part of it?"

I smiled at that and answered, "The Lord, the Governor of that country has promised in his book that if we are truly willing to have it, he'll give it to us freely."

"That's good to hear!" Pliable said to me. "If that's the case, let's speed up!"

"As much as I want to move faster," I replied, "I can't because of this burden on my shoulders."

Pliable furrowed his brow, examining me as if seeing the burden for the first time. He said nothing about it, however, but merely turned back to the path and continued on.

We talked some more of what was to come, looking forward to the wonderful future we had! However, our minds and hearts were so focused on our conversation that we failed to see what lay just ahead. Not until the ground gave out beneath our feet did we realize the danger we were in!

_____

[22] Isa. 6:2; 1 Thess. 4:16-17; Rev. 5:11; Rev. 4:4; Rev. 14:1-5; John 12:25; 2 Cor. 5:4.

I dropped like a stone, sinking into wet, thick mud, with Pliable right beside me. Struggling and pulling and twisting, I fought as hard as I could to force my way out, but the thick sludge held me fast.

Pliable grunted beside me. As we both struggled in the thick mud, we drifted farther apart, his voice and grunts growing quieter with every second. I tried to reach out to him, call out to him, but with the weight of the burden on my back, I could barely keep my head above the surface, let alone find anyone else!

At the time, I didn't know that this bog had a name—and it was well named! It was called the Slough of Despond, and in this swamp, we floundered for a long time.

"Christian! Christian!" Through the mist and the thick, barely breathable air, I heard Pliable call out, only just audible in that terrible place. "Christian! Where are you?"

"I… I don't know!" My heart filled with despair, leaving me with nothing else to say.

"What?" Pliable shouted back. Although his voice was faint and I could see nothing much beyond the reach of my own hands, his anger, his rage, it was all as clear as the sun. "Is this the happiness you told me about? If we're having such a hard time at the beginning, what can we expect between here and the end of the journey? If I can get out of here alive, Christian, you can have that country you spoke of all to yourself!"

And with that, I heard splashes and grunts and more, and somehow, Pliable reached dry land on the same side on which we fell in, the side closest to his home. Pulling himself out of the mud, he climbed back onto solid ground and rushed away without another word, leaving me lost in my despair. From that day on, I never saw poor Pliable ever again.

But for me, there was no safety, no hope back that way. Only death. To move forward... *that* was where my hope lay. I pushed on, struggling in the Slough of Despond all by myself, fighting, kicking, reaching, and more. It was all I could do just to move in the direction of the wicket-gate, for I had nowhere else to go.

When I finally reached the far side of the Slough, I grasped the edge, but my fingers, covered in the slime and muck of the bog, couldn't grip the wet grass or weeds on the bank. I grasped for anything I could until I finally wrapped my fingers around a solid root. With all my strength, I pulled on it, hoping to force my way up onto dry, solid ground, but the weight of the burden on my back held me down.

Tears welled up in my eyes, yet I dared not wipe them, not with my hands covered in disgusting slime and muck. So close to getting out, yet on my own, I had no chance.

"What are you doing?"

A voice! Clear as day, despite the thick, dark mist surrounding me.

I opened my eyes and looked up to see a man about my age, but with a larger build, a healthy look in his eye, and a kind smile on his face.

"Sir!" I spat out some of the mud that had gotten into my mouth. "I was told to go this way by a man named Evangelist. He sent me to the gate so I might escape judgement, but as I was going there, I fell in here!"

The man's smile grew, but there was no mocking in those eyes. "My name is Help."

"I am Christian," I replied.

"Tell me, Christian. Why didn't you look for the steps across the Slough of Despond?"

"I…" I shook my head. "Truthfully, I was so scared of the coming judgement that I ran so hard, I didn't even see what I was walking into until I fell in!"

"Then," Help replied, "give me your hand."

I reached out, and Help's strong hand gripped mine. I immediately felt my body lurch upwards and out of the mud as my new friend pulled me out. When he finally let go, I found myself on solid ground.

Turning to Help, I nearly hugged him, but held back so as not to cover him in what covered me. His warm smile filled me with gratitude as he pointed the way towards the gate.[23]

---

23 Ps. 40:2.

2. The Gate

Before I left Help's side,[1] I turned to him and asked, "Sir, if this is the way from the City of Destruction to the gate, why has no one fixed this mess? If someone would do this, travellers like me might make it through safely."

"I'm sorry, Christian," he began, shaking his head. "There is no way I know of to fix this muddy swamp. This is the very place where all the scum and filth that goes with the conviction of sin ends up. Because of this, it's called the Slough of Despond. Christian, when a sinner sees how lost they are, fears, doubts, and discouraging anxieties bubble up inside. It all has to go somewhere, and this swamp is where it ends up settling. This is why the land is so damaged."

He turned back to the Slough of Despond and crouched by the edge, staring into the bog. "The King doesn't want this land to remain like this, Christian.[2] In

---

[1] In the original, Christian has, by this point, moved on, and this entire conversation is actually held between the man named Help and the Dreamer, i.e. Bunyan. This section has been adjusted to be from Christian's perspective.

[2] Isa. 35:3, 4.

fact, for the last two thousand years,[3] his workers, through the direction of his surveyors, have concentrated on this patch of ground, trying to fix it. As far as I know, this swamp has swallowed at least twenty thousand loads dumped here—millions of good, wholesome teachings offered from all over the King's dominion. Everyone knows this instruction is the best material to fix this ground. If it was possible, all of that teaching would have levelled it out and made it safe, yet for all the effort, it remains the Slough of Despond and will remain that no matter what is done."

He stood again and turned back to me. "Now, there are solid steps placed in the swamp by direction of the Law-giver, but because of the filth continually spewed out of this swamp and because of the weather, pilgrims rarely see them. Sadly, even if a traveller sees the steps, once on them, in the mist and thick, stink of the air, their heads often grow dizzy and they miss their footing, falling in, even though the steps are right there!" With a kind look in his eye, he added, "But, Christian, don't worry. Once travellers reach the gate, the ground is solid."[4]

With that, we said our goodbyes, and I resumed my journey, heading towards the gate, leaving the Slough of Despond behind.

Now the dreamer, as he dreamed his dream, saw by that time that Pliable had reached his house, and his neighbours came to visit him. They all reacted differently to him, some telling him he was smart to return, while others called him a fool for risking his life with Christian, while still others called him a coward, saying, "If we set out on this journey, we

---

[3] The original refers to sixteen hundred years, but in this modern update, I've extended it to include up until now.
[4] 1 Sam. 12:23.

wouldn't have been so weak as to give up the moment
we faced a little trouble!"
Because of all this, Pliable withdrew and avoided
people at first, but when his confidence came back, he
joined his neighbours in mocking Christian.

Now, as I walked all alone, I came to an area with fields on either side, and in the distance, I saw someone coming across the field on my left to meet me. I kept on my way, determined to reach the gate, but by chance, we met just as we crossed paths.

I knew the man, although not well. His name was Mr. Worldly Wiseman, and he lived in the town of Carnal Policy. Carnal Policy was a large town, right next to my former city.

Mr. Worldly Wiseman smiled when he saw me, and it didn't take long to learn that he already knew a bit about me. It's no wonder… word travels fast in small towns, and people talk a lot, even from town to town. When he recognized me from the stories he'd heard, seeing a man facing an arduous journey, along with my groans, bearing under the weight of my burden, he stopped to speak with me.

"Hey there, my good man, where are you going with that terrible burden?"

"It certainly is a terrible burden!" I replied. "In fact, I think I'm about as burdened as anyone's ever been! As for where I'm going, I'm heading to the wicket-gate. I've been told that is the way to be rid of my heavy burden."

Mr. Worldly Wiseman didn't respond to any of that at first. Instead, he asked, "Are you married? Do you have any children?"

I nodded and dropped my eyes to the ground. "Yes, but this burden on my shoulder weighs so heavily that I can't enjoy them like I used to. It's like I no longer have a wife or children."[5]

Worldly Wiseman nodded slowly, not saying anything for the moment. Instead, he just stared at me, as if trying to figure out the best way to talk to me. Finally, he asked, "If I give you some advice, will you consider it?"

I laughed. "If it's good advice, absolutely! I could really use some right about now!"

"Then, my dear friend, let me suggest you get rid of that burden as quickly as possible, because you're never going to be at peace until you do. You won't even be able to enjoy the good things God has given you as long as that weight sits on your shoulders."

I tried to answer without letting my irritation show, but the stress of it all overflowed. "That's what I'm trying to do!" I shouted before I could stop myself. I took a deep breath, doing all I could to calm myself down. In a pleading tone, I continued. "I want to get rid of it, but I can't get it off myself, nor have I found anyone who can take it off for me. That's why I'm heading this way, hoping to get rid of the burden."

"Who told you to go this way?" Worldly Wiseman asked.

"A man who seemed to be a very good and honourable person. He's named Evangelist."

Worldly Wiseman growled and spit on the ground. "Curse that man for his advice to you!" He turned and looked in the direction Evangelist had sent me and said, "There's no path more dangerous and wicked than the one he put you on! And you'll figure that out for yourself, if you stay on it!" Turning back to me, he leaned forward and asked, "You've already run into trouble, haven't you? I see

[5] 1 Cor 7:29.

the mud from the Slough of Despond on your clothes. Christian… that swamp is only the beginning!" He stepped up really close and put his hand on my shoulder. "Listen to me. I'm older than you are—been around a bit longer than a young guy like you. If you keep going this way, you'll face exhaustion, pain, hunger, danger, nakedness, the sword, lions, dragons, darkness, and, to put it plainly, death! I know this is true because of how many people have told me about it." He shook his head and asked, "Why would you so carelessly throw away your life by listening to a stranger like Evangelist?"

"Because," I replied, "this burden I carry is worse than all those things you mentioned. I don't care what the path is like or what I have to face, just so long as I can get rid of this weight!"

"Well, how did you come by it in the first place?" Worldly Wiseman asked.

I raised the old, worn book in my hand. "By reading this."

The man's face twisted in what looked like disdain, and I thought he might have rolled his eyes just a little. "Thought so," Worldly Wiseman said with a shake of his head. "That's the way it happens with a lot of weak men. You see, people meddle in things they don't understand and get distracted from what's important. The distractions not only knock men down as it's done to you, but those who fall for these things go to great lengths to rid themselves of their burden, but… they don't even know what they're looking for!"

"I know what I'm after. I'm after freedom from my burden!"

"But why," Worldly Wiseman asked me, "would you go after it this way, knowing that it's so dangerous? Especially when you can find freedom another way, if you'll just hear me out. The way I suggest not only involves no danger whatsoever, but it's also close by. Besides, instead of danger, you'll find safety, friendship, and happiness."

Hearing this, my eyes opened wide, and I stepped forward, tears filling my eyes as hope flooded my heart. "Please, Sir, tell me how I can get rid of my burden!"

"Of course!" Worldly Wiseman replied with a laugh. "It's easy! In fact, you can get rid of it in the village just over there."

I turned to look in the direction he pointed. I saw little, other than rolling hills and open fields. But one thing was obvious: Worldly Wiseman's path was easier than the one I was on!

"The village," Worldly Wiseman continued, "is named Morality, and a man named Legality lives there. He's a very sensible man. Everyone likes him, and, most importantly, he knows how to help men get burdens off their shoulders. From what I know, he's done a lot of good for many people this way, and he can even help with the crazy thoughts people get when their burdens weigh them down. If you go to this guy, you can get the help you need right away. In fact, he's less than a mile from here, and if he's not at home, he has a son whose name is Civility, and he's just as good as his father. You can get that burden taken off your shoulders, and if you don't want to go back to your previous home, and I wouldn't want you to, you can send for your wife and children to come to you! There are a lot of affordable houses available in the village of Morality; it's a cheap place to live so you can buy all you want. Good neighbourhoods, too! The people are honest, good people who take care of themselves."

I hesitated for a moment, unsure what to do. I had the word of Evangelist of a way to get my burden removed, but everything I'd heard and experienced so far told me it was a hard road. But… the man in front of me had a way to do it all, a way that had proven successful for many people! I struggled with the choice for a moment longer, but thought, "If what this guy says is true, the best thing I can do is to take his advice!"

And with that, I asked, "Sir, how do I get there?"

"Do you see that hill?" Wiseman asked me, pointing off into the distance.

I stared off into the distance in the direction Worldly Wiseman pointed. I hadn't quite noticed it before, but rising above the fields and rolling hills stood a larger hill. "Oh yes, of course!"

"Head towards the hill, and the first house you reach is his!"

I smiled and thanked the man. Already this was easier! Turning out of my way, I took off toward Mr. Legality's house, hopeful that I might find freedom from my heavy burden!

I moved as fast as I could, although that wasn't all that quickly due to the weight on my shoulders, but the excitement of what I might find pushed me on. In less than half an hour, I reached the hill, ready to find my freedom, but instead I came to a grinding halt!

My heart beat fast, and I shook my head, not daring to walk any closer!

The hill itself was nothing like the gentle, rolling hills throughout the area. In fact, it stood far higher than I had realized from a distance! And not only that, but the side of the hill near me hung over the road so much, I dared not take another step! The rocks, the dirt, none of it looked solid, and I feared it could fall on me the moment I stepped beneath the overhang!

I remained in that spot, my feet rooted to the ground, unsure of what to do. As I waited, trying to figure out my next move, the weight on my shoulders, the burden itself, seemed to grow heavier than it had been while I travelled along the road to the gate.

A flash of fire shot out of the top of the hill, roaring across the sky like the fires of hell itself, and I jumped back, covering my head!

My heart raced, and my hands shook. What had I done? What had I gotten myself into? If I were to continue along that way, the mountain would crush me, or the fire would burn me to death!

So, there I stood, unable to move, shaking and sweating in my fear.[6]

When Christians unto carnal men give ear,
Out of their way they go, and pay for 't dear;
For Master Worldly Wiseman can but shew
A saint the way to bondage and to woe.[7]

My heart filled with grief and regret. I should never have taken Mr. Worldly Wiseman's advice. Hanging my head in shame, I wept there before the hill, lost and discouraged, for I had found no hope in that place.

After a time, I wiped the tears from my eyes. I didn't know where to go or what to do, but I couldn't weep for the rest of my life! Looking up, I caught sight of movement and focused on the man approaching my sorry

---

[6] Ex. 19:16, 18; Heb. 12:21.

[7] Due to the fact that I am far from a quality poet, I have decided not to change the poems at all for fear that I will not only make them terrible, but that I will, out of a desire to do good, destroy all that is good and holy in this world. Thus, the poems remain archaic.

state. As I began to make out who it was, I nearly cheered, but then shame overcame my excitement.

Evangelist had found me again.

Evangelist walked straight towards me, and when he reached me, he said nothing at first. Instead, he examined me, a disappointed look in his eye and his lips pursed. After a few minutes, he spoke in a quiet, slow voice and simply asked, "What are you doing here, Christian?"

I stood there, speechless, no idea what to say or how to respond.

Evangelist took a step closer and examined my face a little more. "Aren't you the man I found weeping outside the walls of the City of Destruction?"

I nodded. "Yes, Sir, that was me."

"Didn't I send you to the wicket-gate?"

I hung my head in shame, my arms hanging limply at my sides. "Yes, Sir, you did."

"How come you've turned aside from the path so quickly? You know you're off the path, don't you?"

I took a deep breath and closed my eyes for a moment, bowing my head to help me hide my shame. "I met someone." Shaking my head, I raised my eyes to explain it all to Evangelist. "As soon as I got through the Slough of Despond, a man approached me. He told me someone here in this village could take away my burden. And I... I believed him."

"Describe him to me!" Evangelist ordered.

"He seemed like a great guy, and we spoke for a while. Eventually, he convinced me I could find what I was looking for here, so I took his advice. When I arrived here, I saw the hill and how it hangs over the road, and I stopped right away, afraid if I walked under it, it would fall on my head."

"What did he say to you?"

"He asked me where I was going, and I told him."

"And then what did he say?" Evangelist asked.

"He asked if I had a family. I told him I do, but I also told him I'm so weighed down by my burden that I can't enjoy them like I used to."

"And then? What did he say next?"

"He told me to quickly get rid of my burden, and I said that's what I'm after, the ease of not carrying this anymore. I told him I was going to the gate to find out how I can get rid of the burden, but he said he could show me a better way. A way not filled with difficulties like the one you set me on. He pointed to this house, telling me this man has the skill to take off this kind of burden, and I believed him. So, I turned away from the path, hoping I could be lucky enough to find relief." I looked back at the hill once again, but quickly turned back to Evangelist. "When I came to this place and saw what's here, I stopped in my tracks. I was afraid of the danger. And now… now I don't know what to do."

Evangelist listened patiently through my entire story, but when I finished, he ordered me to stand still while he showed me the words of God. So, I stood, but trembled while he spoke.

"See that you do not refuse him who is speaking. For if they did not escape when they refused him who warned them on earth, much less will we escape if we reject him who warns from heaven."[8] He also said, "But my righteous one shall live by faith, and if he shrinks back, my

---

[8] Heb. 12:25.

soul has no pleasure in him."[9] He paused and seemed to realize that I needed it explained to me. "You, Christian, are the man who's running into this misery! You've rejected the counsel of the Most High and stepped away from the path of peace, almost to the point of risking hell itself!"

My mouth dropped open as the strength left my legs. I collapsed to the ground and lay before Evangelist, crying out, "I blew it! I ruined everything!"

When he saw me lying there, humbling myself, Evangelist reached down and took my hand. In a kind voice, he said, "Christian? Every sin and blasphemy will be forgiven people.[10] Don't disbelieve but believe."[11]

Upon hearing his kind words, I felt a little strength come back, and I climbed to my feet. However, despite the encouragement, I still shook as I stood before him.

He stepped in close and put his firm hand on my shoulder. "Christian, pay close attention to the things I'm about to tell you. I'm going to explain to you who deceived you, and to whom he sent you. Worldly Wiseman is the name of the man you met, and his name fits him well. Part of the reason his name fits is he only craves the beliefs of this world—that's why he always goes to the town of Morality to attend church. His name also fits him well because he loves that morality saves him from the cross. Finally, his name fits because of his wicked mindset. He always tries to twist my words, even though what I say is true.

"Now, Christian, there are three things this man has done, and you must absolutely hate all three! First, he turned you away from the path, and you agreed to it. To do such a thing is to reject God's counsel and to replace it with

---

[9] Heb. 10:38.
[10] Matt. 12:31; Mark 3:28.
[11] John 20:27.

Worldly Wiseman's advice. The Lord says, 'Strive to enter through the narrow door,'[12] the one to which I sent you, 'for the gate is narrow and the way is hard that leads to life, and those who find it are few.'[13] Worldly Wiseman turned you from this narrow wicket-gate and from the path leading there. Because of this, he has almost led you to your death! Hate, therefore, what he's done! Hate how he turned you away from the path! And be mad at yourself for listening to him![14]

"Second, you must hate that he turned your heart away from the cross, making the cross itself repulsive to you. For you should desire the cross more than all the pleasures and temptations around you.[15] Besides, the King of Glory has told us that 'whoever would save his life will lose it.'[16] And, 'if anyone comes to me and does not hate his own father and mother and wife and children and brothers and sisters, yes, and even his own life, he cannot be my disciple.'[17] So, I tell you, Christian, for someone to work hard to convince you of a path that leads to death, a path that, if you walk it, the truth tells us you cannot have eternal life… you have to hate that teaching! Despise it!

"And third, my friend, he put you on a different path, one which leads to death. And to understand this, you must know to whom he sent you and how incapable that man is of delivering you from your burden!" His eyes filled

---

[12] Luke 13:24.
[13] Matt. 7:14.
[14] NOTE: the original says here to *hate yourself* for listening to Worldly Wiseman. While I am doing my best to keep the flow of the original and would have kept that wording, to our 21st century ears, *hating yourself* is heard not in terms of hating your actions or your sinfulness, but of extreme depression, insecurity, and more. Such a view could lead to a misunderstanding of this section. As such, I have changed this so as not to cause misunderstandings of what Bunyan was seeking to express.
[15] Heb. 11:25-26.
[16] Mark 8:35; John 12:25; Matt. 10:39.
[17] Luke 14:26.

with compassion, and he stepped even closer. When he spoke, his voice came out quietly and filled with kindness. "The one he sent you to, Christian, the one who was supposed to give you relief from your burden, the one named Legality? He is the son of a slave-woman who is now in bondage with her children.[18] In a way, in a mystery, this woman is Mount Sinai, this mountain which you have feared will fall on your head. Now if she, with her children, is in bondage, how can you expect any of them to set you free? This man named Legality cannot give you relief from your burden. In fact, he's never set anyone free from their burden, nor will he ever! You cannot be made right by the works of the law, for by the works of the law, no one can be free of his burden!

"Christian, please understand, Mr. Worldly Wiseman is an alien,[19] and Mr. Legality is a cheat. His son, Civility, even with his pleasant looks and smiles, is a hypocrite, and even he can't help you! Believe me, there is nothing in all you've heard from these inebriated fools but a desire to deceive you out of your salvation by turning you away from the path I had set you on!"

When he finished explaining all this to me, Evangelist stepped back and, raising his hands to the heavens, called out for God to confirm what he had said. In response, words and fire came out of the mountain in front of me, and all the hairs on the back of my neck stood up. I even heard a loud, deep, booming voice declare, "Cursed be everyone who does not abide by all things written in the Book of the Law and do them!"[20]

---

[18] Gal 4:21-27.
[19] The word *alien* in this context would refer to someone who is not from around here. For more information, see *Answers and Extra Thoughts* at the end of the study guide.
[20] Gal. 3:10.

At hearing all this, my heart fell, certain that there was no chance of anything in my future but death. The tears streamed down my face as I cried out, cursing the time I spent listening to the deceit of Mr. Worldly Wiseman. I called myself a thousand fools for taking his advice, and I couldn't believe I'd fallen for his lies, seeing now that they flowed from his own desires. I had believed all his lies and left the true path!

Turning to Evangelist, I pleaded, "Sir? Is there still hope for me? Do I have a chance? Can I still go back to the wicket-gate? Will the gatekeeper reject me for this? Will he send me back, humiliated? I'm so sorry I took Worldly Wiseman's advice. I'm so, so sorry! Is it possible for my sin to be forgiven?"

"Your sin, Christian, is terrible," Evangelist said. "Through it, you have done two wicked things: first, you turned away from the path that is good, and second, you walked on a different path, one that is forbidden! Even so, the man at the gate will welcome you, for he loves all men. Only," Evangelist said, gripping my arm and holding tightly, "watch out that you don't turn away again! 'Lest he be angry, and you perish in the way, for his wrath is quickly kindled.'"[21]

I smiled, although I still felt disappointment in myself for what I'd done. Nodding my head, I determined I would return to the path no matter what! When I told Evangelist this, he gave me a kiss of blessing and bid me God-speed.

Without another word, I turned and ran!

On my way back, I passed many people, but I dared not speak to any of them. If anyone asked me a question, I refused to answer. I went on like this, knowing that I was treading on forbidden ground. All the while, with

[21] Ps. 2:12.

each step I took, I could not believe I was safe until I was once again on the path, the very one I'd left to follow Mr. Worldly Wiseman's advice.

On the path, I pushed on towards the gate. With my burden on my back, my journey proved difficult, but I refused to slow my pace until I finally reached the gate itself! When I did, I came to a halt.

There at the wicket-gate, I did my best to take it all in. The door stood before me, a simple door, made of wood, but with solid steel straps secured across the front. It was indeed a narrow gate, barely wide enough to get through, and overtop, the words clearly written read, "To the one who knocks it will be opened."[22]

He that will enter in must first without
Stand knocking at the Gate, nor need he doubt
That is A KNOCKER but to enter in;
For God can love him, and forgive his sin.

---

[22] Matt. 7:8.

3. The Interpreter

I banged my fist against the door, then banged again before anyone could have a chance to answer. I waited a few more seconds, then beat my fist against the door once again. My heart raced as I listened for the door to unlatch, for movement on the other side, for anything at all! I needed someone to come, to show me mercy, but no matter how hard I knocked, no answer came.

Finally, I cried out,

"May I now enter here?
Will he within open to sorry me,
though I have been an undeserving rebel?
Then shall I not fail to sing his lasting praise on
high."

Relief flooded my heart as I heard a noise from the other side of the door. Someone came to the gate and swung open a small opening in the door, about head height, just large enough for me to see a quiet, serious man staring intently at me. "My name is Good-will. Who are you? Where have you come from? And… what do you want?"

My mouth moved, but no sound came out at first. When I found my voice, I said, "I'm a poor, burdened sinner. I've come from the City of Destruction, but I'm going to Mount Zion, hoping to be delivered from the coming wrath. I've heard this is the gate through which I must enter to get there, so I wish to know if you will let me in."

Upon hearing my request, Good-will shouted, "I am willing with all my heart!" And with that, he opened the gate.

I stepped forward, excited about what I might find, but before I could get too far on my own, Good-will grabbed me by the arm and dragged me inside.

I stumbled forward and stepped back from Good-will as he slammed the door shut, bolting it securely from the inside.

"What was that all about?" I asked, doing my best to recover.

Good-will's expression remained serious as he explained, "If you are to enter this gate, you cannot delay. Near this gate, a strong castle sits. Beelzebub is the captain of that place, and he and those with him shoot arrows at those who come to this gate, hoping, by chance, to kill them before they can enter."

My mouth dropped open, and I trembled with fear. "I'm grateful you pulled me in so quickly!"

The man gave a quick nod and then asked, "Who sent you to me?"

"Evangelist told me to come here and knock, as I did. He said that you, Sir, would tell me what I must do."

Good-will nodded. "An open door is set before you, and no man can shut it."[1]

I smiled. "Now I can enjoy the benefits of enduring such difficulty."

Good-will didn't comment on my words, but instead asked, "Why did you come alone?"

I closed my eyes and shook my head. So many left behind… "None of my neighbours saw the danger. Only me."

"Did any know you were coming here?"

"Yes," I replied. "My wife and children saw me coming right away, but they tried to convince me not to come. Even some of my neighbours stood crying and calling out to me to return, but I covered my ears and continued on my way."

"No one followed you?" Good-will asked. "No one tried to talk you into going back?"

"Oh, yes, two men named Obstinate and Pliable. But when they saw they couldn't convince me, Obstinate went back complaining about me, but Pliable joined me for a little while."

"And why didn't he continue? Why did he only come a short distance?"

"We walked together until we reached the Slough of Despond, and we both fell in. It was horrible, and Pliable grew upset and discouraged. He didn't want to continue beyond that point. He got out on the side closest to his own house and told me I could have the brave country all to myself. So, he returned home, and I

_____

[1] Rev. 3:8.

continued on the path. He went after Obstinate, and I towards this gate."

Good-will's face filled with disappointment, and he slowly shook his head. "Alas, the poor man. Is the Celestial glory so small a thing to him it's not worth going through a few difficulties to gain it?"

At that, I felt my face burn, and shame filled my heart. "I've told you the truth about Pliable, but if I'm being totally honest, there's no difference between him and me. It's true, he went back home, but I also turned away; I turned to the way of death. A man named Worldly Wiseman talked me into leaving the path. I listened to his carnal arguments and fell for it all."

"Hmm," the man said with a slow nod. "Worldly Wiseman found you, did he? He would have sent you to Mr. Legality, correct? They are, the two of them, a couple of cheats. And you say you took his counsel?"

"I did, at least as far as I dared go. I tried to find Mr. Legality, but I was afraid when I saw the mountain, the one that stands by his house. I… I thought it was going to fall on me, and that forced me to stop."

"That mountain," Good-will said to me slowly, "has been the death of many. And it will be the death of many more! It's good you escaped, otherwise the mountain would have dashed you to pieces."

"If Evangelist hadn't found me there," I explained, "I don't know what would have happened! But by God's mercy, while I stood there, lost and unsure of what to do, he found me. Otherwise, I never would have made it! And here I am, a man more deserving of death by that mountain than to talk with you, my Lord. But… I can't express what a gift this is to be welcomed here!"

"We don't turn anyone away," Good-will said with a smile. "Doesn't matter what they've done before today;

no one is cast out![2] And because of this, good Christian, come with me and I'll teach you about the path ahead. The patriarchs, prophets, and Christ and his apostles set it up, and it's as straight as you can make it! This is the path you must follow."

I hesitated, confused by what I'd just heard. "Do you mean to tell me there are no turns at all? No way for anyone to lose their way?"

"Oh, there are many other paths that meet up with the path ahead, and they're all crooked and wide. That's how you can tell the difference between the right path and the wrong path. The right one is straight and narrow!"[3]

As he led me toward the path I would need to take, I asked him if he could help me with my burden. I still hadn't gotten rid of it, and there was no way to get it off my shoulders without help.

"As for your burden," Good-will replied, "you'll need to be content to carry it until you come to the place of deliverance. When you get there, the burden will fall from your back all on its own!"

I nodded, unsure of what lay ahead, but determined to follow this path. I turned to go, but Good-will grabbed my arm and gave me one last bit of direction. He told me that a little way down the path, I'd come to the house of the Interpreter. I should knock on his door, and in that place, the master of the house would show me amazing things.

With a big smile on my face, I left my new friend, and Good-will bid me God-speed.

I rushed along as fast as I could, keeping my feet on the straight and narrow path. It wasn't long, however,

[2] John 6:37.
[3] Matt. 7:14.

before I came to the house of the Interpreter. Filled with joy and curiosity, I knocked and knocked and knocked on the door until someone finally came.

The door opened, and a short, thin man peered out, examining me from top to bottom. "Who are you?"

"Sir," I began, "I'm a traveller sent by a friend of the owner of this house. I was told to stop here so I could see amazing things for my own good. I would like to speak to the owner of the house."

The man nodded at me and then turned, calling out for Interpreter. I stood outside, waiting, looking forward to what I might learn, but wondering what might cause the man to delay. Eventually, however, the master of the house came to the door and asked me what I wanted.

"Sir," I explained to Interpreter, "I've come from the City of Destruction, and I'm now going to Mount Zion. The man who stands at the gate, the one at the head of this path, told me that if I stopped in here, you would show me amazing things that would help me along my way."

A smile grew on the Interpreter's face, and then he laughed. Throwing the door open wide, he welcomed me in by saying, "Of course! Come in! I will certainly show you things that will help you!"

The First Excellent Thing[4]

Interpreter turned to the man I'd first met at the door and ordered, "Light a candle!" He then gestured for

---

[4] These titles were not in the original Pilgrim's Progress but have been added here in these editions based on Good-Will's description of what Interpreter had to tell Christian. I've added the titles in the hopes that they might help ease us through the challenge of keeping track of these signs and interpretations.

me to follow him. Leading me down a hallway, he stopped in front of a door, and then ordered his servant to open it before we stepped into a private room.

The room lay empty, the floors free of furniture, and vacant of anyone other than us. The only thing of interest was a painting hanging on the wall.

I examined the painting, sure that it was what Interpreter wished to show me. The image was one of a quiet and serious man, his eyes lifted to heaven. He held in his hands the best of books, the law of truth was written upon his lips, and the world lay behind his back. He stood as if he pleaded with men, and a crown of gold hung above his head.

Upon seeing the man, my curiosity grew. "What does this mean?"

Interpreter stepped forward and smiled. "The man in the picture is one of a thousand. He can birth children, endure the hardship of a difficult birth, and even nurse them once they are born. And as you see his eyes lifted to heaven, the best of books in his hand, and the law of truth written upon his lips, that is to teach you that his work is to know and reveal dark things to sinners. In fact, you can see how he stands pleading with men. And, my dear friend, do you notice the world tossed away behind him? And do you see the crown over his head? These images will help you understand the need to despise the things of this world, but to have a love for serving your Master. This man is guaranteed to have a reward of glory in the life to come.

"Now," Interpreter continued, "I have shown you this picture first because the man whose picture this is, he's the only man whom the Lord of the place you are going to has authorized to be your guide in all the difficulties you will face along the way. So, pay close attention to what I've shown you here and keep in mind what you've seen. If you do not pay attention, then while on your journey, you will meet those who pretend to lead you right but will instead lead you to death."[5]

The Second Excellent Thing

Then the Interpreter grabbed me by my hand and led me out of that room and down a hallway. At the end of the hallway, we turned left into a very large parlour.

I turned slowly around, taking in the room. While it was a beautiful room, comfortable, with plenty of soft chairs in which to sit and relax, to talk with friends and meet with those you love, it appeared no one had sat here for a long time. A thick layer of dust sat upon the floor, the chairs, the shelves, and more. I suspected no one had ever swept that room.

Once I'd had some time to take it all in, the Interpreter called for someone to come. A man entered, broom in hand, and swept. As he worked, since someone had never swept the room, the dust didn't collect on the floor, but flew into the air, filling the room, sending me into a coughing fit, and leaving me choking on the dust.

While I hacked and coughed, a young woman entered, and turning to her, the Interpreter ordered, "Bring in the water and sprinkle it in the room." She came in quickly and, much to my relief, once she had finished, she easily swept and cleaned the room.

"What does this mean?" I asked once my breathing had calmed.

The Interpreter turned to me, ready to explain this next mystery. "This parlour is the heart of a man, but it is the heart of a man never sanctified by the sweet grace of

---

[5] 1 Cor. 4:15; Gal. 4:19.

the gospel. The dust is his original sin and the corruption of his heart. These have defiled him entirely. The man who swept at the beginning, he's the Law. But the young woman who brought water and sprinkled it in the room, she's the Gospel.

"Now, my friend, you saw how as soon as the man swept, the dust flew around the room so much that he could not clean it—and you nearly choked on it. This is to show you that the Law, instead of cleansing the heart of sin by its work in you, actually revives the sin, puts strength into it, and even increases it in the soul! Though the Law reveals and forbids the sin, it can empower no one to conquer sin.[6]

"But then the young woman came in and sprinkled the room with water. Once this was done, the room was easily and happily cleaned! This is to show you that when the Gospel comes, sweetly and beautifully influencing your heart, then just as you saw the young woman settle the dust by sprinkling the water, so is sin conquered and subdued. And in this, the soul is made clean through faith and, as a result, made fit for the King of Glory to inhabit!"[7]

The Third Excellent Thing

While I was still trying to take it all in, the Interpreter once again took me by my hand, but this time, he led me to a small room. In the room sat two chairs, each one occupied by a child.

As I stared at the two young boys, I noticed they wore their names stitched onto their shirts. The name of

---

[6] Rom. 5:20; Rom. 7:6; 1 Cor. 15:56.
[7] John 15:3, 13; Acts 15:9; Rom. 16:25-26; Eph. 5:26.

the younger child was Patience. He sat comfortably in his chair, quiet and content.

The name of the older child was Passion. Passion did not sit comfortably. In fact, he fidgeted and struggled, upset and, overall, clearly discontent.

"Why is Passion so discontent?" I asked.

"Ah, now that is interesting!" the Interpreter said. "Their guardian desires that these two children wait till the beginning of next year to receive their presents. Passion is not pleased with this, as he demands them all now. Patience, however, will wait."

I stepped out of the way as a man brushed by me, moving toward Passion. The man held a bulging bag full of treasures, and when he reached Passion, he dumped it all on the floor at the young child's feet. Passion's face lit up, and he dropped off the chair into the pile of treasure, cheering that he had received what he wanted. After a few moments, he turned to Patience and laughed at him and mocked him until Patience felt worthless.

As I watched the young child play with his treasure, a strange thing happened. The treasure, though it was great, wore out, bit by bit, more and more until there remained nothing left, and the boy himself sat there in nothing but rags.

I turned to the Interpreter, shaking my head. "Please, explain this to me."

"These two lads are illustrations. Passion is a picture of the men of this world, while Patience is a picture of the men who are of that which is to come. Passion must have all things now, just as the men of this world must have all their good things now. They cannot wait until the next life for what God might offer. The proverb, 'A bird in the hand is worth two in the bush' means more to them than anything God might promise them in the world to come.

This young lad, he spent it all and was left with nothing but rags. So it will be with all men like Passion at the end of the world."

"Now I understand," I replied with a slow nod. "Patience has deep wisdom. First, he is wise because he waits for what is best. And second, he is wise because he has chosen a path that leads him to have the glory of his own treasure when the other child has nothing but rags."

"Oh, but there's more!" the Interpreter exclaimed with an enormous smile on his face. "The glory of the next world will never wear out, while the things of this world are quickly lost. Because of that, Passion had no reason to laugh at Patience, even though he had his good things first. In fact, Patience will soon laugh at Passion because he had his best things last. For first must give way to last, because last must have its time to come. Last, however, gives way to nothing, for there is nothing to come after last. The one who receives his treasure first will spend it, but the one who has it last will have it forever. Because of this, it was said to the rich man,[8] 'Remember that you in your lifetime received your good things, and Lazarus in like manner bad things; but now he is comforted here, and you are in anguish.'"[9]

"Then," I replied, "I see it is best not to covet things in this life, but to wait for things in the life to come."

"Exactly!" the Interpreter said with a smile. "'For the things that are seen are transient, but the things that are unseen are eternal.'[10] But since the things of this world and our own appetites are neighbours, and because the things to come and our own fleshly desires are strangers, the first

---

[8] The original uses the name *Dives* here which is an old word (from the Latin Vulgate) to refer to the rich man in the parable of Lazarus and the Rich Man, Luke 16:19-31.
[9] Luke 16:25.
[10] 2 Cor. 4:18.

of these become friends, and the second remains strangers."

The Fourth Excellent Thing

The Interpreter took me by my hand again and led me out of the small room to a place with a beautiful fireplace built into a wall. Next to the fire stood a man, and he continually threw water on the fire, doing all he could to quench the flames. Yet, even though he threw more and more water, the fire burned higher and hotter.

"What does this mean?" I asked.

"The fire, dear Christian, is the work of grace that is active in the heart. The one who casts water on it, hoping to extinguish the flames, is the Devil. But even so, the fire burns brighter and hotter. Let me show you why."

So, the Interpreter took me around behind the wall to the back of the fireplace. On that side, a man with a jar of oil in his hand secretly poured oil into the fire.

"What does this mean?"

"This, my friend, is Jesus. And he continually, with the oil of his grace, maintains the work already begun in the heart. Because of his work in us, no matter what the Devil can do, the souls of Christ's people remain filled with grace. And you see how Jesus stands behind the wall to maintain the fire? That is to teach you it is hard while enduring temptation to see how the work of grace is maintained in the soul."[11]

---

[11] 2 Cor. 12:9.

The Fifth Excellent Thing

Again, a fifth time, the Interpreter took me by my hand. This time, he led me out of the house and into a large garden. We walked along a path leading through the trees and shrubs to a pleasant place filled with flowers. Before us stood a palace, beautiful to behold. Upon seeing this palace, my heart filled with joy, and on the top of the wall, people walked, clothed in gold.

"May we go in?" I asked, hoping to see inside such a beautiful and grand place.

In response, the Interpreter took me by the hand again and led me up towards the door of the palace. When we came close, a large group of men stood waiting to go in, but they remained back, not daring to approach.

Near the crowd, another man sat at a table with a book and pen before him, ready to take the name of whoever was to enter within. When I looked ahead to see what might prevent the crowd from signing up and entering the palace, I caught sight of another crowd standing before the entrance to the magnificent palace. This other crowd stood armed, ready to attack anyone who dared try to get past them, determined to injure all those who tried to enter and prevent them from finding their way through.

I shook my head, amazed and confused, doing my best to take it all in.

Finally, when every man in the crowd had pulled back for fear of the armed men, a new man arrived. He stood tall, well built, and ready for battle. This new man approached the one at the table and ordered, "Write down my name, Sir!"

When the recorder had done so, the strong man drew his sword and put a helmet on his head. Without hesitation, he rushed forward, right at the armed men standing in the doorway. The men leapt into action, attacking him with deadly force, doing all they could to stop him, to hold him back from entering the palace, but as hard as they resisted him, the strong man would not pull back, but attacked even more fiercely!

And after he had not only received but also given many wounds to those who stood barring his way, he broke through their ranks and pushed forward into the palace.

As I watched and listened, a beautiful voice called out from within, "Come in! Come in! Eternal glory you shall win!"[12]

So, the man entered, and inside they clothed him with beautiful garments just like those inside already wore.

I smiled and turned to the Interpreter, gladness filling my heart. "I think I know the meaning of this!" With one more glance at the palace, I said, "Now, let me leave this place and continue my journey."

"Oh, no!" the Interpreter said, shaking his head. "Please, stay until I have shown you a little more. After that, you may go on your way."

The Sixth Excellent Thing

Again, the Interpreter took me by my hand, leading me back to the house. Once there, he led me into a dark, gloomy room. I strained in the darkness to see, but at first, I couldn't make out anything until my eyes gradually adjusted. In the dim light, I made out a cage sitting before me, an iron cage, and inside a man sat.

---

[12] Acts 14:22.

Now, the man, I could see he was quite sad. He sat with his eyes on the ground, and his hands folded together. As I watched him, he let out a sigh so filled with pain that I thought his heart must be about to break.

"What does this mean?" I asked.

The Interpreter didn't answer me. Instead, he just pointed at the man.

"What… what are you?" I asked the man in the cage.

"I am what I was once not."

Confused, I asked, "What were you once?"

With his eyes still downcast, he explained, "I was once a good and growing follower of Christ, professing his name. Not only did I think this about myself, but others did as well. I once was, as I thought, a perfect fit for the Celestial City." He paused for just a moment, shaking his head, and then slumped forward even more. "I… longed for that eternal home, my heart filling with joy whenever I thought about reaching that place."[13]

I stepped forward and crouched down in front of him, peering at him through the bars. "But… what are you now?"

"I'm now a man of despair, locked up in my despair in the same way that I'm locked within this iron cage. I can't get out." He ground his teeth, shook his head, and groaned, "Oh, how I can't get out!"

"But how did this happen? How did you get stuck in despair?"

The man frowned an even deeper frown and said, "I no longer remained sober and watched. Instead, I gave

---

[13] Luke 8:13.

47

control of my life to my lusts. I sinned against the light of the Word and the goodness of God. I grieved the Spirit, and he's gone. I called to the devil, and he came to me.[14] I incited God to anger, and he left me. I hardened my heart so much that I can't repent."

At first, I couldn't think of anything to say, nor could I truly understand everything the man said. But as his words sunk into my heart, my hands shook, and my eyes filled with tears. Turning quickly to the Interpreter, I asked, "Is there no hope for such a man as this?"

"Ask him," the Interpreter ordered.

"No," I replied, unable to bring myself to do it. "Please, Sir, you ask him."

Leaning towards the man in the cage, the Interpreter asked, "Do you really need to be kept in the iron cage of despair? Is there no hope for you?"

The man shook his head. "No. None at all."

"Why not?" the Interpreter asked. "The Son of the Blessed is very merciful."[15]

The man didn't move at all as he explained, "I have crucified Christ yet again. I despised who he is and his righteousness. I treated his blood as unholy, and I've shown contempt to the Spirit of grace. Therefore, I've shut myself out of all the promises, and there now remains for me nothing but threats, dreadful threats, fearful threats of certain judgement and fiery wrath which will devour me as an enemy."[16]

---

[14] The original for this sentence is, "I tempted the devil, and he is come to me."
[15] The original calls him *pitiful* which is harder to work with in the 21st century and so close to sounding like something Mr. T would say.
[16] Luke 19:14; Heb. 6:6; Heb. 10:28-29.

The Interpreter frowned. "And what were you after? What did you seek that brought you into this state?"

"I was after satisfying my lusts and pleasures, seeking the profits of this world. I was sure that by enjoying these things, I would find much delight. But now, every one of those things bite and gnaws at me like a burning worm."

"But can you not," the Interpreter asked, "even now turn and repent?"

He shook his head vehemently. "God has denied me repentance," the man said with a groan. "His Word gives me no encouragement to believe. In fact, he himself shut me up in this cage, and there's not a man on earth who can set me free." Crying aloud, the man called, "Oh, eternity! Eternity! How shall I face the misery that I must meet with in eternity?"

Turning back to me, the Interpreter warned, "Remember this man's misery, Christian. Let it be an everlasting warning for you."

My hands continued to shake, and my forehead broke out in sweat. "This… this is terrifying! May God help me watch and be sober! And to pray that I may turn from the things which caused this man's misery!" To the Interpreter, I asked, "Sir, is it now time for me to go on my way?"

"Not yet, Christian. Remain here until I show you one more thing. Then you shall go."

The Seventh Excellent Thing

Interpreter took my hand and led me into yet another room. In this one, a bed sat on the floor, and in the bed, a man who had just slept. When we entered, he was climbing out of bed and putting on his clothes, but as he dressed, he shook and trembled.

"Why is this man trembling?" I asked the Interpreter.

The Interpreter spoke to the man and asked him to tell me the reason for his fear.

The man turned to me, his face filled with sadness. "While I slept, I had a dream. And in my dream, the sky grew extremely dark, and it thundered, and lightning flashed across the sky in such a terrifying way that it left me in agony! And then the clouds came crashing together and upon the clouds sat a man, surrounded by thousands of other men and women from heaven. All those with him wore flaming fire, and the heavens also burned in flame.

"And then I heard a voice call out, 'Arise all you dead and come to judgement!' With that command, the rocks tore apart, the graves opened, and the dead who were in them came out. Some of the dead were happy and looked upwards, while others sought to hide themselves under the mountains. Then the man on the cloud opened a book and called the world to draw near, yet there was, because of the flame which came out from before him, a distance between Him and them as between a judge and prisoners in court.[17]

"I then heard it proclaimed to those who surrounded the Man on the cloud, 'Gather the tares, the chaff, and the stubble. Cast them all into the burning lake of fire.' And with that, the bottomless pit opened just where I stood! And out of the mouth of the pit poured smoke and coals of fire, along with hideous noises.

---

[17] 1 Cor. 15:52; 1 Thess. 4:16; Jude 14; John 5:28-29; 2 Thess. 1:7-8; Rev. 20:11-14; Isa. 26:21; Micah 7:16-17; Ps. 95:1-3; Dan. 7:10; Mal. 3:2-3; Dan. 7:9-10.

"Then those who surrounded the Man on the cloud were ordered, 'Gather my wheat into the storehouse!' So those around him gathered up and carried away into the clouds many of those who had just risen from the grave, but…" Tears streamed down the man's face, and he looked intently at me as he shouted, "He left me behind!" He shook his head and wept as he continued. "So, I tried to hide myself, but I couldn't because the Man who sat on the cloud kept his eye on me. And then I remembered all my sins, and my conscience accused me in every way! And that's when I awoke."[18]

I stared at the man for a moment. It was quite a dream, but it was still only a dream! "What is it that made you so afraid of all this?"

"I thought," the man with the dream explained, "that the day of judgement had come, and that I was not ready. But what terrified me the most was that the angels gathered up many people for glory[19] but left me behind. And, of course, the pit of hell opened her mouth right at my feet! And… my conscience, for it convicted me, and I thought the Judge had his eye on me, watching me with an angry look."

Then the Interpreter asked me, "Have you considered everything you've seen?"

"Yes," I replied as I thought through all I had learned. "But it puts me in both hope and fear!"

---

[18] Matt. 3:12; 13:30; Mal. 4:1; Luke 3:17; 1 Thes. 4:16-17; Rom. 3:14-15.
[19] "for glory" has been added here since it helped to distinguish the gathering of the saints from the gathering of the sinners.

"Keep it all in mind, Christian. Let it be a constant reminder to you to push you forward in the way you need to go!"[20]

Then I prepared myself to leave on my journey, and the Interpreter said to me, "May the Comforter always be with you, good Christian, to guide you in the way that leads to the City."

With that, I thanked the man and left his house, grateful for all I had learned.

So I went on my way saying,

Here I have seen things rare and profitable; Things pleasant, dreadful, things to make me stable in what I have begun to take in hand; Then let me think on them, and understand wherefore they showed me were, and let me be thankful, O good Interpreter, to thee.[21]

---

[20] The original phrase here is, "keep all things so in thy mind that they may be as a goad in thy sides, to prick thee forward in the way thou must go."

[21] Since this had the feel of a verse or poetry, I did not change it into modern language. Poetry is my nemesis.

4. A Hill Called Difficulty

I raced down the road, running as hard as I could. I was finally on the path I needed to be on, and nothing was going to stop me!

On either side of the path, a wall stood, fencing my way in. The One who had built the wall, built it with large stones, held together with well-maintained mortar, and the wall itself stood far too high to climb. I found comfort in the barrier at this point in my journey.

The name of the wall was Salvation.

I ran between the walls on the straight and narrow path, pushing on as hard as I could. The burden itself still weighed me down, and every step took such great effort, but I had finally reached the path![1]

I ran in this way until I reached an incline, at which point I came to a halt. The incline led up for a short distance, and at the top of the hill stood a cross, old and

---

[1] Isa. 26:1.

fashioned out of wood. From the marks and stains on the cross, I knew it was more than decoration, but had been a tool of such cruelty as I had read about in the book.

A little below this cross, someone had dug a grave[2] into the rock. The entrance, a large, oval hole, led only to darkness.

I started forward again and pushed on up the hill. The weight of my burden, which had been so heavy along the level ground, now weighed me down even more! Each step took all my effort as if the burden itself feared what lay ahead. I groaned under the weight but forced myself to push forward. The cross itself was proof of my Lord's love for me, and I would not shy away.

As I drew near the cross, I heard a quiet snap and nearly shouted with joy as my burden, all of it, the weight, the struggle, the agony, the fear… it all… it fell from my shoulders! Spinning around, I watched with tears in my eyes as it tumbled back down the hill the way I had come. It bounced and rolled until it came to the mouth of the grave, and, rolling inside, it disappeared into the darkness. From that moment on, for the rest of my life, I never saw that burden again!

I stared in wonder for a moment, but then stood straight, stretching my back. No longer held down by the weight of that burden, my heart filled with joy, and I could not help but shout! With a cheerful heart, I cried out, "He has given me rest by his sorrow, and life by his death!"

Turning back around again, I stared at the cross in wonder, considering in awe how an object of such cruelty had been turned into an object of freedom by my Lord! It surprised me that the sight of the cross should ease me of my burden, but it had! Why would such a thing happen?

---

[2] The original used the word *sepulchre*.

As I remained there before the cross, staring, wondering, the tears flowed down my cheeks like springs of water. I didn't bother to wipe them away. Instead, I stood there for a long time weeping, until three Shining Ones came near and greeted me. "Peace be with you!"

I smiled, for I had nothing else I could say after receiving such a gift of freedom.

The first Shining One said to me, "Your sins are forgiven." The second one came close and stripped me of my rags, replacing them with a new outfit. The third came and stood right before me. He reached out and put a mark on my forehead, then gave me a scroll with a seal on it. "Christian," he ordered, "Read this as you run, and then give it in at the Celestial Gate when you reach that place."

And with that, without another word, they left me standing there before the cross.[3]

Who's this? the Pilgrim. How! 'tis very true,
Old things are past away, all's become new.
Strange! He's another man, upon my word,
They be fine feathers that make a fine bird.

I then jumped three times for joy and sang:
Thus far I did come laden with my sin;
Nor could aught ease the grief that I was in
Till I came hither: What a place is this!
Must here be the beginning of my bliss?
Must here the burden fall from off my back?
Must here the strings that bound it to me crack?
Blest cross! blest sepulchre! blest rather be
The Man that there was put to shame for me!

---

3 Zech. 12:10; Mark 2:5; Zech. 3:4; Eph. 1:13.

With an enormous smile on my face, I moved on from there, continuing down the hill until the path levelled out. I had nothing but joy in my heart and excitement for what lay ahead!

At the bottom of the hill, however, I saw something I did not expect. Just off the path, a little out of the way, three men lay fast asleep. All three had unkempt beards growing every which way, clothes that hung on them like rags, and they all smelled like they had lain out in the rain and sun for a long time. But what caught my eye first off were the old, solid steel shackles secured to their ankles.

My heart went out to them, bound as they were, unable to continue their journey. Running to their side, hoping to wake them, I called out, "You are like those who sleep on the top of a mast! The Dead Sea is under you, a gulf that has no bottom! Wake up and get away from this place! If you're willing to leave these chains behind, I'll help you get them off!" Looking all around, fearing for the safety of these poor men, I pleaded with them, "If he that goes about like a roaring lion comes by, he'll certainly devour you!"

The men stirred, and I moved to the side of the one closest to me. As he tried to blink himself awake, I asked him his name. "My name's Simple!" he told me. Looking around, he frowned and grumbled, "I don't see any danger!"

I stared back at him in shock! How could he not know what danger lies all around? The next man groaned and barely opened his eyes to look at me. I asked him who he was, and he told me his name was Sloth. He then rolled back over, mumbling, "Just a little more sleep."

The last man sat right up, unlike his companions. He frowned at me, and before I could ask him anything, growled, "My name's Presumption![4] Now you go away! Leave us alone! You take care of yourself![5] I've nothing else to say to you!"

And with that, Presumption rolled back over, and all three immediately fell asleep. I sat back on the ground, my mind spinning with the shock of what I had just witnessed. How could anyone be so foolish? I considered trying to wake them once again, but then I remembered why I was on this path. Nothing could be done about these men; I could only continue on my way. Climbing to my feet, I left them to their slumber as I returned to the path.[6]

With each step, the sight of those three men continued to trouble my heart. I couldn't imagine men in such danger could have such a low view of help offered freely to them. I not only awakened them and offered them advice, but I offered to free them from their chains!

As I continued to wrestle with my troubled feelings, something off to the left, just at the top of the wall, caught my eye. At first, I couldn't make sense of what it was. Stepping a little closer, then coming to a stop, I watched cautiously, curious about what might happen.

Right at the top of the wall, I saw movement. It wasn't a bird, but something small slid along the edge. I heard a grunt, followed by another, then I saw what it was

---

[4] *Presumption* refers to believing something unproven.
[5] The original says here, "Every fat must stand upon its own bottom." It not only appears to be an unusual phrase, but the meaning is also not entirely known. The way it's written above is likely a decent understanding. Now, I wish to leave you with a piece of advice. I encourage you to remember this phrase. The next time you want to tell someone to leave you alone, holler out, "Every fat must stand upon its own bottom!" I have my doubts anyone will have a decent comeback, and... you might find they'll simply turn and walk away. Win-win!!
[6] Prov. 23:34; 1 Pet. 5:8.

as it slipped up a little further, and fingers wrapped around the edge.

Someone was climbing up from the other side!

I stood there and waited while whoever it was climbed a little higher, and after a few more seconds, I saw it was not just one man, but two! With a little more struggle, both men tumbled over the wall.

The men landed at the base of the wall with a loud thud, right on the path, and brushed the dust off their shirt and pants. When they appeared satisfied that they were sufficiently clean, they looked up at me and smiled before standing up.

"Hello, gentlemen," I said slowly, beginning the conversation. "My name is Christian."

"Ah! What a wonderful name!" the taller of the two men replied with an enormous smile and in a strong, clear, and precise tone of voice. "My name, good sir, is Formalist! And this here, my good companion, is Hypocrisy!"

Hypocrisy gave a deep bow to me, smiling as well, but his smile didn't reach his eyes. In a casual tone, he said, "G'day."

"Thank you!" I replied. "Where are you from, and where are you going?"

Formalist gave me another bow and smiled yet again. "We were, dear Christian, born in the land of Vainglory and are going for praise to Mount Zion. Are you going there as well?"[7]

---

[7] In the original, Formalist and Hypocrisy both reply together—at the same time. It's like they're speaking in unison. I didn't feel it was necessary to the flow of the book to have such a borg-like

"I am," I replied.

"Then let us walk together, shall we?" Formalist said, still with his enormous smile.

The two men turned and walked down the path, and I came quickly up beside them. "Why didn't you enter through the gate at the beginning of the way?" I asked. "Don't you know that it's written that the one who doesn't come in by the door 'but climbs in by another way, that man is a thief and a robber'?"[8]

Hypocrisy laughed and shook his head. "All our buddies think the long way aroun', goin' through the gate, is far too long of a journey. The best way is to take the shortcut. Climb over the wall as we just did!"

"But…" I began, but found myself unable to come up with any words as my heart filled with concern. I looked back and forth from one to the other, their smiles at odds with the absurdity of what Hypocrisy had just said! When I finally found my voice, I asked, "Won't it be considered a sin against the Lord of the city where we're heading? I mean… you're violating what he's revealed to us!"

"Oh, as for that," Hypocrisy replied with another laugh, "don't you worry now! Don't trouble your head about it! What we did was okay because it's our custom! If needed, we can show that all our buddies have been doing this for a long time—that'll be our witness that it's okay. I mean… come on! Our people have done it this way for over a thousand years!"

I shook my head slowly back and forth, still struggling to believe they could approach the path in such

---

response and, as such, split the dialogue up between Formalist and Hypocrisy, giving Formalist an overly formal form of speech, and Hypocrisy a more relaxed form.
[8] John 10:1.

a manner! "Will that hold up in court? I mean… your custom?"

"Since our people," Formalist explained in his proper tone, "have followed this custom for so long, my dear Christian, even more than a thousand years, any impartial judge will undoubtedly recognize it as legal. Besides," he added with a shrug, "if we have reached the path, what does it matter how we came in? If we are in, we are in! You came in, we understand, by the gate, and we are also on the same path, but we came over the wall. How is your situation any better than ours?"

I frowned as irritation built inside. "I follow the path of my Master! You walk by the ignorant fickleness of your own opinions. You're already considered thieves by the Lord of the way; therefore, I doubt he'll find you true at the end of this journey! If you come in by yourselves without his direction, you'll end up going out by yourselves without his mercy!"

They came to a halt right there, staring at me with their mouths hanging open. I waited, but at first, they said nothing, until finally Formalist shook his head slowly and snapped, "You worry about yourself, Christian!" He turned to walk away from me, and Hypocrisy followed close behind. After a few steps, he stopped again and turned back. "As to laws and commands, I figure we will follow them just as well as you. Therefore, we doubt there is much difference between you and us, other than the coat you wear on your back, which, we suspect, some of your neighbours likely gave you to keep you from walking around naked!"

At that, I shook my head. "You won't be saved by following rules and commands, Formalist! Especially since you didn't come through the gate. As for this coat, the Lord of the place to which I'm heading gave it to me, but yes, you are right in one thing: he gave it to me to cover my nakedness. And I think of the coat as proof of his kindness because I had nothing to wear before, other than rags. And besides, that's comforting to me as I believe that when I reach the gate of the city, the Lord of the place will know me since I have this coat on my back—a coat he himself gave me freely on the day that he took away my rags!"

I took a step forward, the confidence building in me. "I also have a mark on my forehead, Formalist, but perhaps you haven't noticed that. One of my Lord's close friends fixed it there on the day my burden fell off my shoulders. And to tell you even more, they also gave me a sealed scroll to comfort me by reading as I travel the path. I'm to give it in at the Celestial Gate as my ticket into that place." I paused for a moment and examined the men before adding, "I think you're missing all these things because you didn't come in at the gate."[9]

Formalist didn't answer, nor did Hypocrisy. Instead, they looked at each other, rolled their eyes, laughed, and then walked on without me. From that point on, we didn't travel together again, but it wasn't long before I overtook them and moved ahead with them falling behind.

As I travelled, I walked alone. Sometimes I enjoyed the quiet, the peace of journeying along the path by myself. At other times, I longed for a companion. I did, however, have the scroll, the one given to me by the Shining Ones, and I often read from it along the path, finding refreshment on my journey.

The path continued as it had for quite some time, but eventually, I saw ahead that the path rose steeply, and an hour later, I reached the foot of a hill named Difficulty.

Right there at the base of the hill, a spring flowed out of the rocks, and just after the spring, two other roads

[9] Gal. 2:16.

left the main one at this point. One path turned to the left, and a sign nearby declared it to be the way of Danger. The other road turned to the right, a similar sign naming it Destruction. The narrow, straight path, however, continued straight up the hill named Difficulty.

I dropped to my knees next to the spring and drank freely from it, its cool, clean water refreshing my soul. Once I felt satisfied, I went straight up the hill singing,[10]

> *The hill, though high, I covet to ascend,*
> *The difficulty will not me offend;*
> *For I perceive the way to life lies here.*
> *Come, pluck up heart, let's neither faint nor fear;*
> *Better, though difficult, the right way to go,*
> *Than wrong, though easy, where the end is woe.*

I climbed for some time until I reached a bit of an open area, high on the side of the hill. Stopping to look around, I saw far below me, Formalist and Hypocrisy, approach this hill called Difficulty. Curious about what they might do, I watched for a time.

I couldn't hear their voices from that distance, of course, but the two men gestured back and forth, pointing at the roads leading to the right and left and also the path leading up the hill. After a few minutes, one man moved off to the left, while the other took the road to the right.

My heart raced as I saw them go, afraid for them and their wicked decision to leave the path. Simply to avoid difficulty! From the way they gestured to each other, I suspected they thought they would meet up again on the other side, but as I watched each of them go, able to see them clearly from my perch up on that hill, I saw one man, I couldn't distinguish which one, the one who took the road to Danger, followed the path into a great forest. I

---

[10] Isa. 49:10.

watched for some time, but he never came out again. The other man, the one who took the road to Destruction, found himself in a wide field full of dark mountains. He managed just fine for a time, but eventually he stumbled along the way and, sadly, never rose again.

Shall they who wrong begin yet rightly end?
Shall they at all have safety for their friend?
No, no; in headstrong manner they set out,
And headlong will they fall at last no doubt.

I turned from that sight, more determined than ever to stay on the path! I raced up the hill as fast as I could, but even without my burden, it didn't take long before my strength failed. The hill only grew steeper, slowing my climb in such a way that I went from running, to walking, then from walking to crawling on my hands and knees. Every bit of ground gained was a struggle.

Finally, I reached what appeared to be the halfway point up the hill and spotted a shelter, a beautiful arbour made by the Lord of the hill to refresh travellers such as myself. I cried out with joy and made my way to the side of the path where the arbour sat and collapsed there on the bench, grateful for a chance to rest.

Stretching out my legs, I smiled to myself, enjoying the moment of peace, of rest amid an arduous climb. I felt my body relax as I pulled out my scroll to read, to comfort myself with the words written for me. I also took some time to examine the coat and garments given to me while I stood by the cross, something I had not done until that moment. The coat and garments were of the most beautiful style and quality workmanship. With an outfit such as that, I would never need another outfit. Those clothes would last me my entire journey.

After a few minutes, perhaps longer, maybe an hour, I felt my eyes droop, but rather than get up and back on the path, I remained there until I dozed off, falling into a deep sleep for many hours, wasting the light until the day was nearly gone.

To my shame, while I slept, my scroll slipped from my fingers.

"Wake up!"

My eyes shot open, and I looked around, trying to make sense of where I was and what was going on. A man stood before me, a cross expression on his face as he scolded me, saying, "Go to the ant, O sluggard; consider her ways, and be wise."[11]

I jumped to my feet, stumbling a little until I got my balance. Once I felt steady, I ran up the hill without another word to the man who had shaken me awake, pushing on in the fading hours of the day as hard as I could until I came to the top of the hill.

Clambering over the crest of the hill and coming to a large, relatively flat area, I entered a forest that covered the top of the hill. The path continued straight as always, and I rushed forward, but ahead, I saw two men. As fast as I was running, they ran faster towards me, and when we reached each other, we all stopped, although they edged bit by bit past me, clearly wanting nothing more than to run on back the way I just came.

---

[11] Prov. 6:6.

"Sirs," I began, "What's wrong? You're running the wrong way!"

"Uh…" the one man began, "Uh… um…" Every few seconds, he looked back over his shoulder, while the other man barely stopped scanning the trees and the path. Something had these men terrified.

"What is your name?" I asked, trying to calm them down.

"I'm, uh, um… Timorous…" the one man began. "And this is…"

"I'm Mistrust!" the other man interrupted, not taking his eyes off the trees or path, scanning everything, and jumping at every movement, every snap of a twig or movement of a squirrel.

"What's scared you?" I asked. "You know you're running the wrong way, right?"

"We… uh…" Timorous began, then stopped to wipe his brow before saying, "We were going to the City of Zion, and we got up the Hill called Difficulty, but… but… with every step, this journey gets more dangerous! More and more dangerous—always more dangerous! We're, uh… uh…" Looking back and forth and even over his shoulders as if he feared what might come up behind him, he whispered, "We've had enough. We're not doing this anymore. We're turning back!"

"I agree!" Mistrust added. "It just gets worse all the time. Just a little farther down the path, two lions lie in the road." He stopped, pointed his finger at me, and growled, "Did you know about this? DID YOU?"

"No, of course not," I replied.

He looked at me for a few seconds, his eyes full of suspicion, before he finally said, "We don't know if the lions are awake or asleep, but we're sure if we get too close, they'll attack and rip us to shreds!"

My mouth dropped open, and my heart raced. "That's terrifying! But… where can I go to be safe?" I looked from one to the next, then said, "If I go back home, that place is going to be destroyed with fire and brimstone—I'll die there! If I can get to the Celestial City, I'll be safe. I…" I shook my head, resolve flooding my heart. "I have to go on. I *must* go on! To go back is death for me, but to go forward is fear of death and everlasting life on the other side of it." With that, despite the fear that these men had put in my heart, I knew what to do. "I'm still going on!"

Neither man said anything else to me. Instead, they just ran past me, back down the hill I'd just climbed. But for me, there was only one direction, forward, so I continued on the path.

Still, the fear continued in my heart. I needed some comfort, and for that, I needed my scroll. I reached into my cloak, hoping to read from it… but I couldn't find it. Feeling around here and there, I thought for sure it would be there somewhere. My heart turned to ice, and my hands shook.

It wasn't there!

Spinning around, I searched the ground by my feet, checking my other pockets while I scanned the path, desperately hoping to find it somewhere on me… or perhaps I just dropped it a moment ago! I had to have it! Without it, I didn't know what to do! I not only needed the comfort and relief the scroll could provide along the way, but it was my ticket into the Celestial City!

I felt at a loss for how to move forward, desperately working through my memories of everything I'd done since I last saw the scroll. I couldn't imagine it fell out during my conversation with Timorous and Mistrust, and the climb up the hill… sure I'd moved fast, but my pockets were secure!

It was then I remembered that I'd slept in the arbour on the side of the hill. Falling to my knees, I humbly asked God to forgive me for such a foolish act, then climbed to my feet and rushed back to look for my scroll.

All the way back down that hill, grief overwhelmed my heart. At times, I couldn't stop myself from sighing out loud, while at other times I wept, and then at other times I scolded myself for being so foolish to fall asleep in the arbour.

The arbour was there for refreshment, not sleep!

With every step down the hill, I searched the sides of the path—if, by chance, I might find my scroll, the very thing that had offered me so much comfort along the way.

When I finally caught sight of the arbour, my head drooped forward as the grief of what I'd done came crashing back down on me. And so, the last few steps to the arbour, I cried out, "Oh, I'm such a terrible man! I slept during the day! How could I sleep during difficult times? How could I feed my flesh, using the rest offered by the Lord of the hill for relief of pilgrims for my own fleshly desires?"[12]

The grief in my heart overwhelmed me, and I couldn't hold it in. "I've wasted so many steps! Just as Israel, because of their sin, had to go back by way of the Red Sea, now, I've had to walk these steps with sadness, the very steps I might have been able to walk with joy, had I not fallen into a wicked sleep. I would have been so much farther along the path by now! Now I have to walk these same steps three times… a part of the path I would only

[12] Rev. 2:5; 1 Thess. 5:6-8.

67

have had to walk once. And to make it worse, the sun has almost set, and I'm about to have to walk in darkness! Oh, I wish I'd never slept!"

When I reached the arbour, I was so overcome with my grief that I dropped onto the bench and wept. After a little while, I looked down in my sadness, and under the bench, I saw my scroll! I lunged for it, my hands shaking, and grabbed hold of it, pulling it close and tucking it away in my cloak.

When I stood, all my grief from a moment before faded away in the joy I felt at finding my scroll! The scroll, that very thing which was my assurance of life and acceptance at the haven I pursued, I had it back! Because of this, I placed it close to my heart and gave thanks to God for directing my eye to the place where the scroll had fallen. With both joy in my heart and tears in my eyes, I set out again on my journey, but despite the steepness of the hill, it was nothing to me now that I had found my scroll!

Yet, as I reached the top of the hill,[13] the sun dropped below the horizon, plunging me into darkness. The change in light brought back the memory of my foolishness, sleeping in the arbour, and once again, I poured out my grief. "O wicked sleep! Because of you, I will have to walk in darkness! I now have to walk without the sun's light, and darkness will cover the path before my feet. To add to it, I'll have to listen to the sounds of sad creatures in the dark, all because of my wicked sleep!"[14]

As I travelled along the path, I also remembered what I'd heard from Timorous and Mistrust, of how scared they were by the sight of lions. "Those beasts," I thought

---

[13] The original says here that he was left in darkness before he stood up from the bench, but that doesn't fit with the previous paragraph. As such, I've made this adjustment to help the story flow better.

[14] 1 Thess. 5:6-8.

to myself, "hunt at night for their food. If they find me in the dark, how will I slip away from them? How will I escape being torn to shreds?"

With this thought plaguing my mind, I continued on my way, but as I wallowed in my regret, I looked ahead and saw a glorious palace before me, a palace named Beautiful, built just by the side of the path.

Upon seeing such a beautiful palace, I rushed forward in my excitement, hoping I might stay there for the night. But before I'd gone too far, I entered a narrow passage on the path, about a furlong[15] away from the porter's lodge.

I came to a sudden stop and sweat broke out on my forehead. There, one on each side of the path itself, lay two lions. "Oh no! Now I see the danger that drove Timorous and Mistrust to turn around!"[16]

---

[15] A furlong is 660 feet.
[16] The original includes the phrase here, "The lions were chained, but he did not see the chains." Well... isn't that lovely? Who doesn't want a spoiler to ruin a wonderful end-of-chapter cliffhanger? I left it out so only the footnote readers might have it spoiled for them. Now you know not to read the footnotes!

5. The House Beautiful

Fear overtook me, and, for just a moment, I considered turning around and going back after Timorous and Mistrust. If nothing but death lay ahead of me, why continue on?

But as I stood there on the path, trying to decide what to do, the porter, a man named Watchful, at his lodge outside the palace, saw me through his window standing there on the path in the dark. Coming outside, he figured I was about to turn around. Out of compassion, he called out, "Are you so weak?[1] Don't be afraid of the lions. They're chained and are placed there to test your faith and to discover those who have none!" In a kind voice, he added, "Stay in the middle of the path, and they won't hurt you."

---

[1] Mar. 8:34-37.

Difficulty is behind, Fear is before,
Though he's got on the hill, the lions roar;
A Christian man is never long at ease,
When one fright's gone, another doth him seize.

The man stood just at the gates to the palace, a lantern held high in his hands. He didn't appear to be trying to fool me, and I had nothing behind me but death. Taking his advice, I took a step forward, then another, then another, keeping to the centre of the path. My entire body trembled, but as I walked forward, I kept the porter's directions in mind.

A moment later, the lions awoke with a snarl and lunged at me! I cried out, but the snap of the chains around their necks held them back! I forced myself to continue my walk as the lions roared, snapped their teeth, and slashed at me with their claws, but the chains held fast, and they could not harm me.

Two steps to go, one… I reached the other side and cheered, relief flooding my heart! As I ran to the gate, I laughed and then came to a halt where the porter waited patiently for me.

"Sir," I asked, "what house is this? And may I lodge here tonight?"

The porter answered me, "The Lord of the hill built this house, and he built it here for the safety and relief of pilgrims. Where did you come from, and where are you going?"

"I'm from the City of Destruction," I replied. "I'm heading to Mount Zion, but the sun has set, and I hoped to lodge here tonight."

"What's your name?" he asked.

"My name is now Christian, but my name used to be Graceless.[2] I came from the family of Japheth, a people whom God will lead to dwell in the tents of Shem."[3]

"Welcome, Christian. My name is Watchful. But how is it you are arriving so late?"

I hung my head and closed my eyes. "I would have been here sooner, but wretched man that I am, I fell asleep in the arbour, the one that sits on the way up the hill. But that's not the worst of it. While I slept, I lost my evidence, my scroll, but because I didn't know I had dropped it while sleeping, I came up the hill without it. Once I reached the top, I looked for it, but couldn't find it, so I had to, with great sadness in my heart, go back to where I fell asleep. When I found it, I climbed back up the hill and now I'm here."

The Porter gave me a nod. "I will call one of the young women[4] of the house. If she accepts what you say, she'll take you to see the rest of the family, according to the rule of the house."

So Watchful, the Porter, rang a bell, and in very little time, the door to the house opened. A beautiful young woman named Discretion stepped out. With a solemn expression on her face, she examined me from head to toe before asking the porter why she had been summoned.

"This man is on a journey from the City of Destruction to Mount Zion," the Porter explained. "He arrived exhausted after dark and asked if he could stay here tonight. I told him I would call for you, who, after speaking

---

[2] Isn't this interesting? We learn our pilgrim had a different name prior to faith in Christ! He went from Graceless to Christian!

[3] Gen. 9:27.

[4] In the original, the women are called the *virgins*, but it's not a typical manner of describing women today, so I adjusted it.

with him, might do as you see fit, according to the rule of the house."

Turning to me, she asked me from where I'd come and to where I was travelling, and I answered her. She then asked me how I got onto the path, and I told her that as well. She also asked me what I'd seen and met with along the way, and I told her.

Finally, she asked my name, and I said, "It's Christian. And the longer I wait, the more I want to stay here tonight because the Lord of the hill has built this house for pilgrims like me, for our safety and rest!"

When I finished, she smiled at me, but I noticed tears had formed in her eyes. She remained silent for a few moments, as if considering all I had said before responding. "I will call two or three of my sisters." Stepping back through the door, she called out for Prudence, Piety, and Charity, who came and spoke with me before opening the door to welcome me in. As the door opened wide, I saw many sisters waiting there for me, welcoming me and saying, "Come in, O blessed of the Lord. The Lord of the hill built this house to show hospitality to pilgrims."

I gratefully bowed my head before stepping forward. Once inside, my mouth dropped open. I'd never seen such beauty portrayed in such a simple manner. The walls, the curtains, the furnishings, all of it added to the comfort and encouragement of the house. They led me down a hallway and into a large sitting room where we gathered around, and they offered me a place to sit and something to drink.

Together, we spoke of many things while we waited for dinner, using the time well. But as we spoke, the sisters decided that Piety, Prudence, and Charity should be the ones to lead the conversation while the others listened in.

"Christian," Piety began, taking the lead right away, "since we've been so loving in welcoming you into our house tonight, let's talk so we can grow together. Please, tell us everything you've faced so far since you set out."

I leaned forward, my face stretching into an enormous smile. "I'd love to! I'm glad you want to hear of it!"

"What brought you to set out as a pilgrim?" Piety asked.

"It was the sound of death and destruction in my ears," I confessed. "That's what drove me from my home country. I wanted to escape the destruction that I knew was coming if I remained where I was."

"But," Piety continued, "what brought you along this path?"

"God brought it about!" I said with a smile. "I was so afraid of the coming destruction, and I didn't know which way I should go, but by chance a man came by, right to me, as I wept and trembled. His name is Evangelist, and he pointed me towards the wicket-gate—I'd never have found it on my own—and he set me on the path to this house."

"Did you stop in at the house of the Interpreter?"

"Oh, absolutely!" I replied. "And I saw so many things there which have stuck with me and will until the day I die! But… three things stand out to me more than any others. The first, that Jesus, despite Satan's efforts, continues his work of grace in the heart. Second, how the man had sinned himself out of the hope of God's mercy, and third, the dream of the man who thought the day of judgement had come."

"Did he tell you his dream?" Piety asked me.

"He did! And it was terrible. My heart ached as he told it, but I'm still glad I heard it."

"Was that everything you saw there?"

"No, he also showed me a beautiful palace and how the people inside wore gold. I saw a brave man fight his way past those who stood guard into the palace, and I saw him welcomed in to win eternal glory. Those things captured my heart, and I would have stayed there a year, but I knew I had far to travel yet."

"What else did you see along the way?" she asked.

"What else?" My heart filled with joy as I explained what happened next. "I went a little farther along the path, and I saw the cross! I imagined seeing Christ hang on it, bleeding on that tree![5] The very sight of him made my burden fall off my back, for I had suffered under a very heavy weight. It was so strange to me since I'd seen nothing like it before. And while I stared up at the cross—I found I couldn't look anywhere else—three Shining Ones came to me. One told me my sins were forgiven; another stripped me of my rages and gave me this broidered coat; and the third gave me this mark on my forehead. And..." I said, pulling out my scroll, "he also gave me this sealed roll!"

"But," Piety asked, "you saw more than that, didn't you?"

"Well, I did," I replied with a laugh, "but those are the best things. The others weren't as wonderful. I saw three men named Simple, Sloth, and Presumption, shackled and sleeping a little off the path. When I tried to wake them, they wouldn't get up! I also saw two men named Formality and Hypocrisy tumble over the wall onto

---

[5] The original says, "and I saw one, as I thought in my mind, hang bleeding upon the tree."

the path, making a show[6] of going to Zion, but they were lost soon after. I warned them, but they wouldn't believe me. But above all, out of those things I've faced since taking the path, I found it very hard to get up this hill, and then to face lions… Honestly, if it hadn't been for the porter, I might have turned around. But, I thank God that I am here, and I thank you for welcoming me."

Piety leaned back in her chair, satisfied with my answers. Next, Prudence leaned forward to ask me some questions. "Do you sometimes think back to the country you came from?"

"I do," I confessed, "but I feel a lot of shame. I not only detest my former life, but truthfully, if I thought of it more, I might have returned. But now I desire a better country… a heavenly one."[7]

"Do you still struggle with the patterns of your old life?" Prudence asked me.

"Yes, but not willingly. I fight it all as hard as I can, especially my deep, sinful thoughts. Those are things that I and all the people from back home enjoyed a lot, but now those things cause me grief. If I could choose, I'd never think those things ever again." I took a deep breath and shook my head. "When I want to be doing good things, the worst things are still with me."[8]

"Do you find, sometimes, that those evil ways are like they're conquered and defeated in your life, those very things which, at other times, have entangled you?"

I nodded. "Yes, but that's rare. When those times do come, those are good days."

---

[6] The original word was *pretending* but that carries a different connotation in 21st century English than I believe was intended.
[7] Heb. 11:15-16.
[8] Rom. 7:16-19.

"Do you remember what you do to live in victory at those times?"

"Yes, I remember. When I think about what I saw at the cross, that does it! And when I look upon my righteous coat, that does it! Of course, when I read the scroll that I carry next to my heart, that does it, too! And when I think affectionately about where I'm going, that does it!"

"What makes you desire Mount Zion so much?" Prudence asked.

At that, I couldn't help but break out in a grin. "I hope to see him alive, the One who hung dead on the cross! And when I get there, I hope to be free of all these things that hurt me here. They say there is no death in that place, and that I'll live with the people I love most."[9] My smile grew, and I leaned forward. "To tell the truth, I love him because he's the One who freed me from my burden! And... I'm just so tired of my inward sickness! I would gladly be in a place where I will no longer die and with people who will continually cry out, 'Holy, Holy, Holy!'"

Prudence smiled and sat back, and then Charity leaned forward to ask me some questions. "Do you have a family? Are you married?"

"I have a wife and four small children."

"Why didn't you bring them with you on the path?" she asked.

At that question, my face fell, and I broke down and cried. "Oh Charity," I began, but had to stop as I tried to compose myself. "I... honestly, I would have brought them along if I could! But they all stood against my coming!"

9 Isa. 25:8; Rev. 21:4.

"But you should have talked to them!" she exclaimed. "You should have tried hard to show them the danger they faced staying behind."

Hanging my head, I wiped a few tears away. "I did. I tried over and over! I told them what God had shown me about the destruction of our city, but they thought I was joking[10] and didn't believe me."

"Did you ask God to bless your words to them?" she asked me.

"Yes, and I prayed with a great deal of affection!" I lowered my head and closed my eyes. In a quiet voice, I added, "Please know that I love my wife and children!"

"But did you tell them," Charity asked intently, "how heavy this was on your heart and how much you feared the destruction? I assume you could see the destruction!"

"Repeatedly!" I cried, meeting Charity's eyes again. "They could even see the fear written across my face, in my tears, in my trembling! All this because of the dread I felt for the coming judgement, hanging over our heads. But none of it got through to them." I took a deep breath to keep my voice steady. "Nothing I said, nothing I did, nothing at all was enough to convince them to come with me!"

Charity reached over and put a hand on my arm, her kind smile bringing me comfort. "Did they explain why they wouldn't come?"

"My wife feared losing this world, and my children just loved the foolish things of youth. But regardless of their reasons, they left me to take this journey alone."

---

[10] Gen. 19:14.

She nodded, and then asked, "Christian, did you hurt your witness with them through sin? Did it hinder your ability to convince them?"

My shoulders slumped. "My life's not perfect," I admitted. "I know the way I live can destroy the message I share with others to follow Christ, so I was very careful not to give them any reason, any foolish choice on my part to make them turn away from joining me on this journey. And because of that, they told me I was too perfect, denying myself things that they thought were good." A sigh escaped my lips, and I explained, "No, I think if anything about the way I lived pushed them away from following this path, it was how careful I was to not sin against God or my neighbours."

"Yes," Charity said with a nod. "Cain hated his brother 'because his own deeds were evil and his brother's righteous.' If your wife and children were upset with you for doing good, it shows you couldn't persuade them by doing good, and you 'have delivered your soul.'"[11]

Although I felt grateful that I had honoured Christ in my actions and witness, the weight on my heart for my wife and children, the longing that they could join me on my journey, remained. Sadly, unless the Lord changed their hearts, I would have to continue to walk alone.

We carried on our conversation until dinner was ready and then sat down to eat. The smell was enough to make my mouth water, and on the table sat good food and excellent wine for us to enjoy. We thanked the Lord for our meal, praying a blessing over the food, and then as we ate, all our conversation over dinner was about the Lord of the hill, speaking about what he'd done, where he had done it all, and why he built the house. From what I heard from my hostesses, he had been a great warrior and had fought

---

[11] 1 John 3:12; Ezek. 3:19.

and killed "the one who has the power of death."[12] But he did not do this without great risk to himself, and when I learned this, my love for him grew even stronger.

They explained he defeated the one who has the power of death at the price of his own blood, but what put glory into it was that he did it out of love for his country. Some of those in that household had even spoken with him and seen him since he had died on the cross. They heard from his own mouth that he loved poor pilgrims, more than anyone else.

They even gave me an example of how one time he had humbled himself by leaving his glory behind so that he might save the poor, and those I ate with once heard him say that he was not willing to live on Mount Zion alone. He had even made many Pilgrims into princes, even though they'd been born as beggars and come from the dunghill.[13]

We talked late into the evening, enjoying one another's company and growing in the Lord. When it came time to turn in for the night, we committed ourselves to the Lord's protection and went each to our own beds.

I stepped into my bedroom and closed the door behind me. The room had been aptly named Peace, and I smiled at the chance to stay there. In the dim light cast by the lantern in my hand, I wandered around the large room assigned to me on the upper floor. A bed, a wardrobe, a small writing desk, everything I needed for my time here. I threw open the window and breathed in the fresh night air. Facing east, I looked forward to watching the sunrise from my room.

I moved the chair by the window to the writing desk and sat down. The sun had long since set, and I

---

[12] Heb. 2:14-15.
[13] 1 Sam. 2:8; Ps. 113:7.

listened to the peaceful sounds of crickets, the occasional hoot of an owl, and bullfrogs from a small pond on the property. I couldn't help but smile, being at such peace in this wonderful house.

As I sat there, in the light of a lamp, I made a decision. I would take paper and a pen and ink, and along my journey, I would record what the Lord did for me on the path.[14] I began immediately, recording much of what had happened to me so far, writing long into the night, but even so, there was more to write. When my eyelids grew heavy, I set aside the pen and ink, put out the lantern, and crawled into the warm blankets, covering myself and feeling my body sink into a deep sleep.

I slept soundly until first light and then awoke with a song on my lips.

> *Where am I now? Is this the love and care*
> *Of Jesus for the men that pilgrims are?*
> *Thus to provide! that I should be forgiven!*
> *And dwell already the next door to heaven!*

I crawled out of bed and dressed immediately, excited about what the new day would hold. Leaving my room and heading downstairs to the parlour, I found the others, and we spent some time sitting, enjoying one another's company as we had the night before, talking and growing in the Lord. When I felt it was time to get back on my journey, they told me I shouldn't leave right away. Instead, they encouraged me to take the time to see some of the unique collections in the house.

---

[14] This matter of the journal, as explained in *Shawn P. B. Robinson's Apology* for this book, is not in the original. I've added the journal to help with the flow of the story near the end of the book. For more information, read the *Apology*.

I agreed, and they took me into the study, where they showed me some extremely old records. First, they showed me the honourable ancestry of the Lord of the hill, that he was the Son of the Ancient of Days, eternally generated by the Father.[15]

In this room were also records, more fully detailed, of the things the Lord of the hill had accomplished along with the names of hundreds of men and women he had taken into his service. The records showed how the Lord of the hill had given them such homes that neither time nor decay could ever ruin!

They also read to me some of the wonderful things his servants had done, how they had "conquered kingdoms, enforced justice, obtained promises, stopped the mouths of lions, quenched the power of fire, escaped the edge of the sword, were made strong out of weakness, became mighty in war, and put foreign armies to flight."[16]

Then they led me to another room with more records. In reading some of them, I learned how willing our[17] Lord was to graciously welcome anyone—even if they had offended him or his works terribly in the past. In that room were histories of many famous events, all of which I already knew about, both ancient and modern, along with prophecies and predictions of things that will one day come about. Those things, I understood, would continue to both amaze and horrify the enemies of the Lord, but would comfort and console his pilgrims.

---

[15] The original phrase here is, "and came by that eternal generation." This appears to be a clear reference to an old theological description of how Christ is related to the Father in his Sonship—that Christ is eternally generated of the Father. That is why I have phrased the rewalked version this way.
[16] Heb. 11:33-34.
[17] The original uses the word *their*, but I felt it fit better to use *our*. There is another instance of this two paragraphs later.

I stayed there all that day, considering those things. At night, I continued in my journal, recording all that had happened to me, until I fell asleep.

The next day, they took me to the armoury. In that room, they showed me armour which their Lord had provided for pilgrims. I saw swords, shields, helmets, breastplates, All-Prayer, and shoes that would never wear out. As I took it all in, I perceived there was enough armour there to equip as many pilgrims for the service of our Lord as there were stars in the heavens!

My hosts also showed me artifacts from significant events in the past such as Moses's rod, the hammer and nail which slew Sisera, and the pitchers, trumpets and lamps which Gideon used when he fought the armies of Midian. They showed me the ox goad with which Shamgar killed six hundred men and the jawbone Samson used to fight against the Philistines.

They even showed me David's sling and stone, which he used to kill Goliath of Gath, and the sword the Lord will use to kill the Man of Sin on the day he will meet his end. So much more they showed me, and I found myself thrilled to see it all!

When we were done, we all settled in for another night, and yet again, I wrote of my journey. Though I had to write late into the night, I finished my story until that day, which meant all I had to write from that point on was what I might face in the days, weeks, and years to come.

The next day, I rose to set out on the path, but the sisters urged me to stay one more day, promising me that if the skies proved clear, they would show me the Delectable Mountains. Such a sight, they told me, would add to my comfort as the mountains were closer to my desired haven than where we were at that moment.

So, I agreed to stay, enjoying their company for a little longer and they took me to the roof of the house. Once there, they had me look south. I stared off in that direction and in the distance saw a glorious mountainous country, covered with beautiful forests, vineyards, fruits of all kinds, flowers and springs and fountains—all pleasing to look at.[18]

Such a sight left me in awe, and I could not help but grin like a fool. "What's the name of that country?"

"It is Immanuel's Land," they told me. "It's a place that is common for all pilgrims—just as common as this place here. When you reach it, Christian, you may see the gate of the Celestial City from there as the shepherds who live there will show it to you."

With my heart filled with hope and a large smile on my face, I told them I wanted to set out again on my journey. The women of the house agreed with me, but before I could go, one of the young women said, "First, before you go, let's return to the armoury."

We entered through the door in the roof, and climbed down the stairs, reaching the armoury on the main level. Inside, they had me stand in the centre of the room while they equipped me from head to foot with strong armour out of concern that I might meet with danger on the way.

When finished, suited in solid armour, I left the house and moved through the gate with my friends by my side.

I smiled when I saw the Porter, and he greeted me. "Sir," I asked, "while I have been in the house, have any pilgrims passed by this way?"

---

[18] Isa. 33:16-17.

He gave a quick bow and replied, "Yes, there was a man who walked along the path."

"Did you know him?" I asked.

"I asked him his name," the Porter replied, "and he told me it was Faithful."

My heart filled with joy, and I laughed in my excitement. "I know him! He's from my town, a close neighbour of mine! He comes from the same place where I was born. How far ahead do you think he is?"

"I'd say by this point he's at the bottom of the hill."

"Well, good Porter," I said with a smile, "the Lord be with you and bless you greatly for all the kindness you've shown me."

So I set out on the path, but my friends, Discretion, Piety, Charity, and Prudence wanted to walk with me to the bottom of the hill. So, for the first leg of the journey after leaving the house, we went on together, talking once again of the same things we'd already spoken of, till we reached the point where the path took us down the hill.

Standing at the top of the hill, I grimaced. "Just as it was difficult coming up, it looks like it's dangerous going down."

"Yes," said Prudence, "it is." She paused, and her voice grew serious. "It's difficult for a man to go down into the Valley of Humiliation as you are now and not to slip. Because of this, we're going to walk you down there."

So, I went down the path, but carefully. But try as I might to watch my step, I still slipped more than once.

When we reached the bottom of the hill, my good friends gave me a loaf of bread, a bottle of wine, and a cluster of raisins. And with that, I went on my way.

6. The Valleys

I stood at the bottom of the hill, my eyes focused on the path ahead. The path itself led straight, as always, without a single twist or turn, but that wasn't the problem. Before me lay rocks, gravel, potholes.

Looking back, I caught sight of my friends from the palace called Beautiful as they climbed the hill. They moved with purpose, eyes focused on their climb, and I watched until I could no longer see them, then turned back to the path.

Almost immediately as I set out, my feet ached, and I struggled with every step as I pushed on into the Valley of Humiliation. The many rocks and uneven ground threatened to turn my ankle at any moment.

Looking up for a moment from the path, I caught sight of someone… or something… approaching from the left, coming across a rocky field towards me.

My heart filled with dread, and my breath caught in my throat. I recognized the monster… the creature… the demon who approached. His name was Apollyon, and the sight of him made me shake.

I briefly considered turning and running in the opposite direction, back the way I'd come. Perhaps my friends could protect me, or I could find some place to hide! I had no desire to face this master of cruelty, but then I remember the gift of armour I wore. Although the breastplate, the shield, all of it, was made of the best material, solid and just right for my protection, the blacksmith who'd created this armour crafted it for the wearer to take a stand, not retreat. My back lay exposed, not a bit of armour. If I turned and ran, I would bare my most vulnerable area to Apollyon, and he would quickly drive one of his wicked darts into my flesh.

I gritted my teeth and committed myself to face the beast, resolving to take my stand. The only way to save my life, the only way to live through the next few minutes, was to stand firm!

Apollyon reached the path not far ahead of me, and I moved forward to stand before him, face to face.

The creature stood tall, well above my head, large enough that his legs could straddle the entire path, one foot on each side. His appearance was hideous. His clothing, crafted of scales like a fish, hung on his body as if the very clothes he wore were his pride. Sticking out his back, huge wings like that of a dragon spread out to either side. His feet were like that of a bear's, and his mouth, the teeth, it all was like a lion's. Out of his stomach came fire and smoke, and he looked at me with disdain, eyeing me up and down.

With his gaze firmly fixed on me, disgust in his eyes, he snarled before he began his interrogation. "Where do you come from and where are you going?"

Forcing my voice to remain steady, I held his gaze with as much confidence as I could muster, trusting the Lord of the way for strength. "I come from the City of

Destruction, the place of all evil, but I am going to the City of Zion."

"Ah, I see," Apollyon said with a growl as he slowly clenched his fists, his eyes flashing with fire. "You're one of mine! That entire country belongs to me, and I am the prince and god of it. So, tell me, traveller, why have you run away from your king?" His eyes filled with hate, and he leaned forward a little as he growled, "If it weren't for the fact that I thought you might be of service to me, I'd kill you now, driving you to the ground with one blow!"

I took a deep breath and composed myself, doing all I could to force down the fear that threatened to overcome me. "I was born in your land, that's true," I replied, "but your service was hard, and I couldn't live on your wages, 'for the wages of sin is death.'[1] So, when I grew up, I did what other thinking people do. I did all I could to clean myself up!"

Apollyon leaned forward even more, the rage flashing in his eyes for just a moment, but then his expression softened, his voice filling with compassion. "Traveller, there is no prince anywhere who will just give up his subjects; and… I don't want to lose you either. But since you're complaining about your work and pay, I'll make you a deal." He smiled and inclined his head slightly towards me. "Be willing to go back, dear traveller, and what our country can afford, I will give you. I promise."

I shook my head. "But I've promised myself to another—to the King of princes! How can I possibly, in fairness, go back with you?"

Apollyon shrugged. "You've done according to the proverb, 'changed a bad for a worse!' But don't worry. It's common for those who have declared themselves his

---

[1] Rom. 6:23.

servants to, after a little while, slip away and return to me. If you do the same, it'll all be well."

Again, I shook my head. "I have turned to the Lord and sworn allegiance to him! How can I turn back and not be hanged as a traitor?"

"You did the same to me," Apollyon answered kindly, "yet I'll overlook it, if only you'll turn around and go back."

"What I promised you," I replied, "was in my youth, and I know the Prince under whose banner I now stand will absolve me of my guilt. In fact, he's even able to pardon me for what I did while I lived in your wicked kingdom! To add to this, O you, destroying Apollyon,[2] truthfully, I like his service and servants, his wages, his government, his company, and his country—I like it all better than yours! So, forget trying to convince me to turn back! I'm his servant, and I'll follow him!"

Apollyon's face softened even more, his entire demeanour appearing quite relaxed and unoffended. "Consider this when you have a cool head... consider what you're likely to meet on this path. You know, most of his servants come to an awful end because they've sinned against me. How many are put to death? And... in shameful ways? And besides, you say you like his service better than mine? You're not considering the fact that he's never left his city to rescue any of those who served him out of the hands of those who wanted to kill them. But for me, how many times, as everyone knows, have I delivered those who faithfully serve me from his servants? Sometimes I use my power and sometimes I use fraud, but I rescue them! And I'll do the same for you."

---

[2] This is awkward wording, but the original says, "O thou destroying Apollyon!" and I didn't want to lose that language.

I stood my ground and shook my head. "When he holds back from delivering them for the time being, it is to test their love. Their stand shows if they will hold to him until the very end! But as for the terrible end you say they come to, they actually see their deaths as a wonderful thing! They don't expect deliverance, for they hold on for glory, and they'll receive it when their Prince comes in glory and in the glory of the angels!"

A cruel smile crept up on Apollyon's face, and his eyes bored into mine. In a quiet voice filled with venom, he laid out his accusation. "You have already been unfaithful to him, traveller! How do you think you'll receive wages?"

"In what, O Apollyon, have I been unfaithful?"

"You grew weak when you first set out and almost choked in the Slough of Despond.[3] You attempted to get rid of your burden in wicked ways rather than wait until your Prince took it off you. You sinfully fell asleep and lost your choice item. You were also nearly persuaded to turn around at the sight of the lions. And, when you talk of your journey, of what you've seen and heard, you inwardly desire to glorify yourself in all that you say and do."

"It is all true," I admitted, but my confidence remained strong. "Not only that, but there's much more which you've left out. But the Prince whom I serve and honour is merciful, ready to forgive. Besides, these weaknesses controlled me while living in your country. There, I welcomed them, but I have groaned under their weight, been sorry for them, and my Prince has pardoned me."

Apollyon snarled, his face filling with terrible rage. With a loud roar, he cried out, "I am an enemy to this

---

[3] In the original, it calls the Slough of Despond the *Gulf* of Despond in this section.

Prince! I hate him! I hate his laws! I hate his people! And I've come here to stand against you!"

"Careful, Apollyon!" I shouted back in warning. "Beware what you do. I'm on the King's highway, the path of holiness! Pay attention to yourself!"

Apollyon, his face still filled with rage, set himself right across the path, one foot on each side. In a shout filled with his terrible wrath, he called out, "I feel no fear! Prepare to die! I SWEAR BY HELL ITSELF THAT YOU WILL GO NO FURTHER! I WILL SPILL YOUR SOUL IN THIS PLACE!"

With threats still on his tongue, Apollyon launched a flaming dart directly at my chest! I quickly threw up my shield, and the dart slammed against it, the force nearly knocking me over onto my back!

The time for talk had ended; the time of battle had begun. I drew my sword, ready to stand and fight!

Apollyon charged, throwing darts as he ran. They fell on me as thick as hail, and I held fast to my shield to avoid injury. When he reached me, more flaming darts appeared in his hand, and he slammed them against my shield. I fought hard to avoid injury, but despite my shield and my return attacks with my sword, the beast wounded me in my head, my hand, my foot.

Still, I fought on, minutes, hours… time dragged on, second by second! My arms, my legs, my back, my neck, everything began to tire, and with the injuries I'd sustained, I stumbled back a little. Seeing my weakness, Apollyon drove forward with all his strength, attacking, slashing, throwing darts. Even in my exhaustion, I gathered up my courage and fought hard, doing whatever I could to stand.

In those moments, receiving blow after blow, there was not much else I could do but stand.

The battle wore on for hours, lasting more than half the day, wearing me out, the exhaustion building to where tears streamed down my cheeks. I gasped for air, fighting with all I had to stand strong, but with my wounds, I grew weaker and weaker.

In my weakened state, Apollyon saw his opportunity. He rushed forward and grabbed me with his enormous fist. Before I could react, he threw me to the ground! I slammed against the hard dirt of the path, the impact knocking the sword from my grip, leaving me without my only weapon.

Laying there on the ground, I stared up at my abuser, unsure if any fight remained in me. "I have you now!" Apollyon shouted with a laugh.

He came at me again, and I held up my shield. The beast slammed his immense weight against it, against me, pushing down with all his strength. As hard as I resisted, Apollyon pressed even harder, nearly to the point of killing me! In that moment, as I lay on my back, tired, injured, and bleeding, a new feeling crept in, one I despised, yet welcomed.

In my heart, I found I hated my life.

Apollyon laughed again, a look of triumph filling his eyes. He raised his hand, one of his fiery darts gripped in his fist, preparing to strike the final blow and end my life.

But... as God had planned in his mercy, I quickly stretched out my hand for my sword.

My fingers felt the hilt of my blade, and I wrapped my hand firmly around the grip. Crying out, I shouted,

"Rejoice not over me, O my enemy; when I fall, I shall rise!"[4]

I drove my sword up and into my enemy's chest. He reeled back as though receiving a mortal wound, and when I saw him stumble, I scrambled to my feet again, attacking with all my strength. In faith, I called out, "No, in all these things we are more than conquerors through him who loved us."[5]

The great demon, the attacker, my enemy, stumbled back even more, pulling away from me as I renewed the fight. The Lord's strength coursed through me, filling me, making me ready for battle, able to stand firm! I charged forward, and fear filled my enemy's eyes. He took three more large steps back and snarled before he pulled away, spreading his dragon wings, and taking flight, flying off and away from me.

I dropped to my knees in my exhaustion, but rather than rest, I took my chance to thank the Lord. The battle had raged for what felt like an eternity, and I knew that only those who had heard such a battle would understand what kind of yelling and hideous roaring came from that wicked creature, Apollyon, throughout the fight. His voice sounded like a dragon, terrifying and unnatural.

And while as Apollyon had sounded like a dragon, I had spent the entire battle crying out with groans of anguish, pouring from deep in my heart! Throughout the fight with the demon, I could manage nothing but sounds of agony until I saw I had wounded Apollyon with my two-edged sword.

---

[4] Mic. 7:8.
[5] Rom. 8:37.

At that moment, I smiled and looked upward to heaven, despite that the battle had been the worst I could have imagined.

> *A more unequal match can hardly be,*
> *Christian must fight an Angel; but you see,*
> *The valiant man by handling Sword and Shield,*
> *Doth make him, tho' a Dragon, quit the field.*

With Apollyon gone and the battle at an end, I took my opportunity to turn my heart upwards. I shouted, "I will give thanks to him who delivered me out of the mouth of the lion, to him who helped me against Apollyon." So, I declared,

> *Great Beelzebub, the captain of this fiend,*
> *Design'd my ruin; therefore to this end*
> *He sent him harness'd out: and he with rage*
> *That hellish was, did fiercely me engage.*
> *But blessed Michael helped me, and I,*
> *By dint[6] of sword, did quickly make him fly.*
> *Therefore to him let me give lasting praise,*
> *And thank and bless his holy name always.*

And for a time, I did not see Apollyon again,[7] for which I am grateful.

I forced myself back to my feet, having to fight hard just to keep my balance and catch my breath! But as hard as I tried, I no longer had the strength to walk because of my injuries.

---

[6] *Dint* means *a blow or strike from a weapon.*

[7] Jam. 4:7. This phrase, in the original, appears immediately after Apollyon leaves, but I felt it flowed better in this place.

I stood there, wobbling on my weak and injured legs, in desperate need of help. In my strength, I had no hope of carrying on, but by God's mercy, a hand appeared before me, holding out as a gift the leaves of the tree of life! I took the leaves, gratitude filling my heart, and laid them over my wounds. Despite the severity of my injuries, relief washed over me, and when I pulled back the leaves, my wounds were completely healed!

In that place, the very place of my battle with Apollyon, I sat down to eat the bread and drink the wine the young women from the House Beautiful had given me. Once refreshed, I also took the time to record the battle in my journal, careful to give glory to God for a victory won!

When finished, I stood to continue my journey, but I moved forward with my sword in my hand, thinking, "I don't know if there are more enemies ahead." By the grace of the Lord, as I continued through the valley, Apollyon made no more attacks.

When I reached the end of that valley, I immediately came upon another, the next aptly named the Valley of the Shadow of Death. My path to the Celestial City, sadly, lay through the midst of it, so I pushed on.

As I descended into this new valley, I quickly found it was a lonely place, described well by Jeremiah the prophet. "A wilderness, in a land of deserts and pits, in a land of drought and deep darkness, in a land that none," but a Christian, "passes through, where no man dwells."[8]

This valley, the Valley of the Shadow of Death, differed from the previous valley. In all honesty, it was far worse. Even worse than my fight with Apollyon.

As soon as I reached the border of the Shadow of Death, I met two men, children of those who had brought

---

[8] Jer. 2:6.

back an evil report of the good land.[9] The two men ran towards me, fleeing from something ahead of me on the path.

"Where are you going?" I called out as they approached.

"Back, back!" they replied as they quickly grew closer. "If you care about your life or about peace, you'd run back too!"

"Why? What's wrong?"

"What's wrong?" they asked, coming to a halt as they reached me. "We were going the same way you are and went as far as we dared. In fact, we were so far along this path, if we'd kept going, we'd never have survived, and then we wouldn't be here to warn you."

I looked from one to the other, unsure of what this all meant. "What's ahead? What have you met?"

"We'd almost reached the Valley of the Shadow of Death, but by chance, we looked ahead and saw the danger before we came to it."[10]

"What have you seen?" I pleaded. The men, despite their panic, couldn't seem to give me a straightforward answer.

"Seen?" one of the men shouted. The other kept looking back over his shoulder as if something might come after him. "Seen? We've seen the valley itself! It's pitch black down there! And we saw hobgoblins, satyrs, and dragons of the pit. Out of the valley comes continual howling and yelling—it sounds like people in unspeakable misery, bound in suffering and chains. Over the entire valley hangs discouraging clouds of confusion, and death

---

[9] Num. 13.
[10] Ps. 44:19; 107:10.

97

always has its wings spread over it." Leaning in close and with desperation in his eyes, he wailed, "Everything about it, down to the smallest detail, is terrible. It's all… it's all chaos!"[11]

I paused, not because I considered turning back, but just to collect my thoughts and my words. After a moment, I said confidently, "This is my way. This is the way to my haven."[12]

The man laughed at me as if he thought I was insane. "Have it your way! We're not travelling this path!"

They pushed past me without another word and resumed their run, terror driving their steps. But as for me, I had no other path, no other direction, no other hope! I moved forward, still with sword in hand, for fear that I might come under attack.

The valley itself spread out before me, but not as an open plain or fields for planting. On the right-hand side of the path, as far as the valley reached, the ground dropped away into a deep ditch. It was into such a ditch that I know the blind have led the blind throughout all history. And in that place, both have perished.[13]

On the left hand of the path, a bog spread out into the distance, filled with rotting plants. I could see that even if a righteous man fell into it, he would find no bottom. I remembered it was into that very bog that King David fell. Shaking my head in horror, I knew he'd never have made it out if the One who is able had not pulled him to safety.

The path before me grew extremely narrow. One false step to the left or the right, and I'd be gone. And with

---

[11] Job 3:5; 10:22.
[12] Jer. 2:6.
[13] Ps. 69:14-15.

each move forward, the light grew less, and darkness settled in around me.

In the growing darkness, I struggled to keep my footing. I tried to avoid the ditch on the one side, but while I avoided the ditch, I'd nearly slip into the bog. And when I tried to avoid the bog, if I was not careful, I would nearly fall into the ditch.

Walking along at a crawl, I let out a loud, bitter sigh. Not only did I face the constant threat of falling one way or the other, but the path here was so dark, I often couldn't even see where my foot might land when I set it down with each step!

Poor man! where art thou now? thy day is night.
Good man, be not cast down, thou yet art right,
Thy way to heaven lies by the gates of Hell;
Cheer up, hold out, with thee it shall go well.

Step by step, I moved through the valley, careful not to slide one way or fall to the other. Ahead, despite my inability to see through the thick darkness, I knew I approached something horrible. The fear and terror grew inside, and I couldn't help but shake as my heart beat rapidly inside my chest, screaming as though it were about to burst! Off to the one side, near to where I stood, I finally, through the dark gloom, made out what my heart dreaded. I had hoped I was wrong, but the sight of what I feared drove me to scream, "WHAT DO I DO?" and I froze there in that spot.

There, before me, rose the mouth of hell itself, and it was far worse than I could have imagined!

Flame and smoke poured out of that vile place, shooting up into the sky in spurts. Sparks flew every direction, and hideous, terrifying noises echoed up towards me. Somehow, I knew the noises came from creatures which would not fear my sword as Apollyon had, so I sheathed my blade and committed myself to another weapon, one called All-Prayer.[14]

And with that weapon, I cried out, "O Lord! I beg you, save my soul!"[15]

I pushed on, trusting the Lord to care for me, to rescue me even at such a time. The mouth of hell stretched out for a long time, and with each step, the flames reached for me. While I travelled, voices cried out, voices filled with overwhelming sadness and grief, and I could hear things rush back and forth. In the darkness, I couldn't see anything, but I feared that whatever it was might find me and tear me to pieces, or at the very least, trample over me like mud in the streets.

Even though I couldn't see much of anything on the path, the one thing that remained clear before my eyes was the sight of hell, made worse by the dreadful noises echoing throughout the valley.

I came to a halt. Something approached!

I cried out in fear. I could hear them. Not just one thing, many things. Demons… an entire swarm of them… I heard them running… rushing… charging towards me, the relentless beat of their footsteps and their feet scraping along the rough ground growing louder by the second!

What could I possibly do?

I thought perhaps I should go back, but then I also thought I might be at least half-way through the valley by that point. I remembered as well that I'd already faced and

---

14 Eph. 6:18.
15 Ps. 116:4.

conquered many dangers, and the danger of going back might be much worse than what I faced ahead.

With that in mind, I resolved to move forward.

But despite my resolve, the demons... they continued to approach. I heard their footsteps, stomping, scraping, sliding along the ground, their growls from deep in their throats, muffled in the thick, heavy air of the valley, filling me with dread.

But this was my only path, my only direction, my only hope! And so I pushed on. As the sound of their approach grew louder, and they were nearly upon me, I cried out with passion, clinging desperately to faith in the One who is above, "I will walk in the strength of the Lord God!"

Immediately, the footsteps, the growls, the approaching horde itself came to a halt at my declaration of my faith in God, and I heard them turn around, scrambling away from me.

But despite the relief from that danger, I spun around, unsure of so many things. I looked up, then down, then right, then left, backwards, forwards, unsure of which way to go or how to move on. In my confusion, I even struggled to recognize my own voice!

Moving along past the mouth of hell, unknown to me, one of the wicked ones climbed up onto the path behind me, creeping along, quietly approaching as I struggled to keep my footing. It did not attack, at least not directly. Instead, it whispered into my ear wicked blasphemies. With each new word spoken in my ear, I thought the words were not from some wicked creature behind me, but I believed they were my own words from my own mind.

The words floating around my thoughts tore through my soul, causing more painful hardship than anything I'd faced until that day. To think I was now blaspheming the One I'd loved so much! If I could have helped it, I'd never have done such a thing! Sadly, I didn't have the wisdom to know I should cover my ears, nor did I know from whom the blasphemies truly came!

Each step added to my pain, to the agony I felt in my heart and mind and soul, yet still I pushed on, suffering with the endless thoughts and struggles.

But then, amid the darkness and loneliness, I heard a new sound, the voice of a man, one going before me. He called out, "Even though I walk through the valley of the shadow of death, I will fear no evil, for you are with me."[16]

With those words, gladness filled my heart. They left me with joy for these reasons.

First, I figured from what I heard that there were others in this valley who feared and trusted God. I was not alone.

Second, I understood God was with whoever walked before me, though they were also in such a dark and depressing place. I thought, "If God is with them, why wouldn't he be with me? Even though I can't see it because of the effect[17] of this place!"[18]

And third, I hoped in that moment that I could catch up to the man ahead and we could walk together.

So, I pushed on and called out to whomever walked before me, but the man didn't reply because, as I learned later, he thought he was alone. Forcing my way

---

[16] Ps. 23:4.
[17] The original speaks of the *impediment that attends this place.* This is perhaps an important point to remember. When you are in the Valley of the Shadow of Death, it is difficult to see and understand God's presence. Can I give some advice? When you are in that place, remember the truth that God is with you!
[18] Job. 9:11.

forward, I put my trust in the Lord, and in time, day broke through the gloom, the darkness lifted, and I cried out in my joy, "He has turned 'deep darkness into the morning!'"[19]

In the light of the early dawn, I looked back, not out of a desire to return, but to see in the light of day what dangers I had faced in the dark. In looking back, I saw the ditch on the one side clearly along with the bog on the other. I examined from afar the narrow path, straight and true, running between the ditch and the bog and how narrow it truly had become. And I also saw the hobgoblins, the satyrs, and the dragons of the pit, but they were all far away because once the sun rose, they didn't come close. But they were, in the light, uncovered for me as it is written, "He uncovers the deeps out of darkness, and brings deep darkness to light."[20]

Upon seeing what lay behind, a flood of emotion rushed over me as I began to truly understand how the Lord of the way had delivered me from such a lonely place. The dangers and threats, though I had feared them so much, were now visible to me in the day's light as the sun shone upon them and revealed them for what they truly were.

The sun's rising, giving me warmth, and shedding light on the path was also another great mercy for me. I could not only see how dangerous that path had been, but I saw what lay ahead was even worse, if possible. From my position now having left that first half, I saw ahead that snares, traps, gins,[21] and nets filled the path ahead. It was

---

[19] Amos 5:8.
[20] Job 12:22.
[21] Perhaps everyone already knows this word, but I did not. However, I thought it was fantastic enough to leave in, despite how unknown it was to me until I searched it out. A gin is a kind of trap. So... snares, traps, gins, and nets means "traps, traps, traps, and traps".

so full of pits, pitfalls, deep holes, and more that if it had still been dark as it had been when I came through the first half of this valley, I would never make it through, even if I had a thousand lives in which to attempt the journey. But with the rising of the sun, I cried out, "His lamp shone upon my head, and by his light I walked through darkness."[22]

In the clear light of day, I made my way past all the traps and snares until I reached the end of the valley, stepping out past the dangers of such a horrible place.

But as I left the valley, I came to a halt. Before me lay fresh horrors. On the ground at my feet, spread across the path, along the ditch on the side of the road, and in the fields close by, lay bones, ashes, mangled bodies of men, and blood... so much blood. These were the remains of pilgrims who had travelled this path before me!

While I stared at this sight, trying to understand it, I saw a cave not far away. In that cave, two giants had lived in times past. Their names had been Pope and Pagan, and by their power, the men whose bones, blood, and ashes lay all around were cruelly put to death.

As I passed by, I saw, sitting in the cave's mouth, an old man named Pope. He sat, shrivelled and weak, frowning at me. I didn't know what to think of him, especially when he spoke. Although he could not come after me, he called out, "You will never repent until more of you are burned!"

I hesitated for a moment, yet he sat there, unable to come after me. After a few minutes of watching him, I understood the times of threat had passed, and I moved on, unharmed. Since that day, I have learned that Pagan has been dead for many years, and as for the other, though he still lives, he is, by reason of age and of so many wicked

---

[22] Job 29:3.

actions in his younger days, grown insane in his mind and stiff in his joints. Now, he can't do much more than sit in the mouth of his cave, grinning at pilgrims as they go by, biting his nails because he cannot harm them.

So, I walked on, holding my tongue and with a smile on my lips, moving along without injury.

Then I sang,

> *O world of wonders! (I can say no less),*
> *That I should be preserved in that distress*
> *That I have met with here! O blessed be*
> *That hand that from it hath deliver'd me!*
> *Dangers in darkness, devils, hell, and sin*
> *Did compass me, while I this vale was in:*
> *Yea, snares, and pits, and traps, and nets, did lie*
> *My path about, that worthless, silly I*
> *Might have been catch'd, entangled, and cast down;*
> *But since I live, let JESUS wear the crown.*

7. A Faithful Companion

I trudged along the narrow, straight path, always moving towards my goal, seeking the eternal city. The land in this area lay somewhat flat, although the occasional rolling hill added a little variety to the scenery.

After the events of the last day or so, I appreciated the simple view. I walked peacefully and easily for a time until I came to a small hill.

At the bottom of the hill, I came to a stop. On the side of the path, someone had driven a thick stake with a small plaque attached to it into the ground. Crouching down, I leaned in to read the engraved words. The message spoke of the hill itself, and it turned out the Lord of the way had placed that hill in that spot simply to give Pilgrims a look ahead.

I stood back up with a smile on my face, grateful to the Lord for such care. The hill was not steep, and I easily reached the top. Taking a deep breath of the fresh, clean air, I looked out over the plains ahead of me.

A second later, my heart leapt in my chest, and I couldn't help but laugh. Not far ahead, just past the bottom of the small hill, another pilgrim moved quickly along the path. Even before I saw his face, I knew who it was.

Faithful, my countryman, a little further along on his journey.

"Hey!" I called out. "Hey! Wait up! I'll join you!" Coming to a halt, Faithful turned around at the sound of my voice, but did not stop. I called out again, "Wait! Wait until I reach you!"

"No way!" Faithful replied with a big shake of his head, walking backwards with his eyes on me. "I'm running for my life, and the avenger of blood is after me!"

Hope and excitement flooded my heart, and I took off running down the hill, my feet moving as fast as I could move them. In less than a minute, I caught up to Faithful, but when I reached him, instead of coming to a halt, I kept running and even outran him, despite the fact that he fled from the avenger of blood!

In doing this, I made the last into first.

I finally stopped and spun around, facing back towards Faithful, a smile breaking out on my face at the thought that I'd outrun him. But in my heart, something else grew. Something dark, wicked... evil. Pride and arrogance crept up in me as I considered how I had outrun my brother.

I took a few steps, walking backwards with an arrogant grin on my face, keeping my eyes on Faithful. But in my pride, I didn't watch my steps! I stumbled, falling to the ground, and hit hard. Pain shot up through my back and down my one leg. I tried to roll over and get myself back onto my feet, but with each attempt, the pain increased. In the end, I had to give up and just lay there, unable to help myself.

A shadow fell across the path as Faithful came up beside me. Crouching down, he smiled at me, but not unkindly. I saw no mocking in his eyes. "Do you need a hand, Christian?"

I felt my face turn red, but I nodded and accepted my humiliation. "Thank you, Faithful. I seem to have fallen, and I can't get up."

He stretched out his hand, and I took it. Pulling with all his might, he got me back onto my feet, and from there, I could take a few tentative steps, then some more. With each step, I felt the pain from my back and leg ease as the movement worked it out.

But as for Faithful and me, we immediately became fast friends, both on the same journey to the same place.

We walked on for hours, enjoying each other's company, feeling refreshed simply by conversation, but also by good fellowship from another who longed to see the Lord of the way. As we travelled, we told each other our stories, sharing all that had happened along the way.

"My honoured and well-loved brother Faithful," I said with a huge grin. "I'm glad I've finally caught up to you. I think God has made us a good fit to walk together along the path."

Faithful smiled back at me, but I could see sadness in his eyes as well. "I had hoped to join you from the start, right from our city, but you left before I was ready, and I've had to come all this way alone."

That surprised me, and I asked, "How long after I left did you leave the City of Destruction?"

Frowning, he shook his head. "I stayed until I couldn't stand it any longer. After you left, the entire city kept talking about how fire would come down from heaven and burn us to the ground!"

"People were really saying that? Our neighbours?"

Faithful nodded slowly. "Everyone was talking about it... at least for a while."

"Really?" I struggled to imagine how that could be. "And no one else fled the danger?"

"Well," Faithful explained with a joyless laugh, "there was a lot of talk, but I don't think anyone really believed it. In all they said, I heard some making fun of you and of your desperate journey, as they called it. But..." He stopped, turned to me, and grabbed my arm. "I believed, Christian! And I still do! I know the end of that city will be fire and brimstone from above. Because of that, I made my escape!"

I patted his hand on my arm, and we resumed our journey. "And what about Pliable? Did you hear anything about him?"

"I did! I heard he followed you until you reached the Slough of Despond. Some say he fell in, but he wouldn't admit it. From the sludge I saw all over him, I'm confident he fell right in!"

"And what did everyone say to him?"

"Since he returned, many people have mocked and hated him. In fact, he's having trouble finding work because most people won't even hire him anymore. His situation's now seven times worse than it was before."

I frowned, unsure what to make of it all. "But... why? Why are they so upset with him for leaving the path? They hate the path!"

"Oh," Faithful replied, "they talk about hanging him as a traitor! They actually criticize him for not being true to his profession of faith. I think, to be honest, God has stirred up Pliable's enemies to despise and hate him because he turned away from the path."[1]

"Did you talk with him at all before you left?"

Faithful grimaced and glanced over at me while we walked side-by-side. "Well," he explained, "I bumped into him once, but he turned quickly and crossed to the other side of the street like he was ashamed of what he'd done. So… I didn't pursue him."

I hung my head in disappointment. "When I first set out, I hoped for his salvation, but now I'm afraid he'll die when the city is destroyed. It's happened to him just like in the proverb, 'The dog returns to its own vomit, and the sow, after washing herself, returns to wallow in the mire.'"[2]

"That's what I'm afraid of as well," Faithful added, "but you can't change what's going to be."

"Well, neighbour," I said, trying to lighten the conversation, "let's change the subject and talk about things that have to do with us here and now. Tell me your story. What's happened to you along the path? I'm sure you've faced a lot. If not, that's a miracle in and of itself!"

Faithful smiled and laughed. "Well, I escaped the Slough of Despond, which I suspect you fell into, and reached the gate without difficulty, although I met someone along the way named Wanton. She tried to cause me trouble."

"It was good you didn't get caught in her net," I interjected. "Joseph had a hard time with her, and he escaped her as you did, but if he hadn't, it might have cost him his life![3] What did she do to you?"

---

[1] Jer. 29:18-19.
[2] 2 Pet. 2:22.
[3] Gen. 39:11-13.

"Oh," explained Faithful, "you can't imagine what kind of flattering tongue she had! She pushed me hard to go with her, promising me many things."

"I bet she couldn't promise you a good conscience!"

"You know what I mean," he said with a chuckle. "She offered me… evil, worldly things."

"I'm glad you escaped!" I replied. "The mouth of the forbidden woman is a deep pit; he with whom the LORD is angry will fall into it."[4]

"Yes, but I don't really know if I did fully escape her."

"What?" I asked. "I didn't think you'd give in to her desires!"

"No," he said with a slow shake of his head, "I didn't defile myself. I remembered an old writing that I'd read. 'Her steps follow the path to Sheol.' So, I closed my eyes so her looks wouldn't tempt me and went on my way while she complained and yelled after me."[5]

"Did you meet with no more assaults along the way?"

"Well," Faithful continued, "when I reached the foot of the hill called Difficulty, I met an ancient man. He asked me who I was and where I was going. I told him I'm a pilgrim on my way to the Celestial City. He then said to me, 'You look like an honest man. What do you think about coming to work for me?' Then I asked him his name and where he lived. He told me his name was Adam the First and that he lived in the town of Deceit. So, I asked him what kind of job and how much he'd pay me, and he

---

4 Prov. 22:14
5 Prov. 5:5; Job 31:1.

112

told me his work was all fun, and for pay, he'd make me the heir to his estate since he has no one else to leave it to. So, I asked him about the house he lived in, his estate, and about his other servants. He told me he kept his house with all the best things in the world, and his servants were those he had collected. Then I asked if he had any children, and he told me he had only three daughters, The Lust of the Flesh, The Lust of the Eyes, and The Pride of Life. He even told me I could marry all three, if I wanted to.[6] Finally, I asked him how long he wanted me to live with him, and he told me he'd like me to stay there as long as he lived."

"Hmm… what did you and that old man decide?"

"At first," Faithful explained, "I wanted to take the job. What he offered sounded good to me, but then I looked at his forehead and read the words, 'Put off the old man and his deeds.'"[7]

"So, what happened?" I asked.

"Then it all made sense! I knew that no matter what he promised me and however he flattered me, when we reached his house, he would sell me as a slave! So I told him to stop talking and that I'd never go to his house, but he grew angry and insulted me, and threatened that he was going to send someone after me who would make my life horrible! When I turned to go on my way, he grabbed hold of my flesh and wrenched me so hard I thought he had ripped a part of me clean off! It hurt so bad that I cried out, 'Wretched man that I am!'[8] And when I finally got away from him, I pushed on up the hill."

Faithful paused for just a moment as he shook his head before continuing his story. "When I reached what appeared to be about the halfway point up the side of the

---

[6] 1 John 2:16.
[7] Eph. 4:22.
[8] Rom. 7:24.

hill, I looked back and saw someone coming after me. He moved like the wind and caught up to me about the place where the shelter sits!"

"I sat down there to rest," I confessed, "then fell asleep and lost my scroll."

"Let me finish, brother," Faithful said. "When the man caught up to me, he hit me so hard it knocked me to the ground, and I couldn't get up! He could have killed me! When I came to a few minutes later, I climbed back to my feet and asked him why he'd attacked me. He told me it was because I secretly wanted to go with Adam the First. And with that, he hit me again in the chest, nearly killing me yet again, and beat me down to the ground! So, I lay there, like a dead man! When I came around yet again, I managed to get back on my feet and begged him for mercy, but he said, 'I don't know how to show mercy!' and knocked me down yet again! If someone else hadn't come along and stopped him, no doubt he would have killed me!"

"Who was it?" I asked.

"Well, at first, I didn't know who he was, but then as he turned to leave, I saw the holes in his hands and side. From that, I figured he was our Lord!"

"Oh, I see," I replied, grateful to know Faithful was not only rescued, but by our Master himself! "That man… the one who attacked you. I know who he was. That was Moses. He spares no one, and he doesn't know how to show mercy to anyone who breaks his law!"

"Oh Christian, I know that was him!" Faithful glanced over at me and added, "That wasn't the first time I've met him. He came to me while I still lived safely at home and threatened to burn my house down if I didn't leave."

That didn't surprise me, but then I wondered about something else. "The house, the one that stood on top of the hill after Moses attacked you. Didn't you see it?"

"I did, and I saw the lions too, but I think they were asleep as it was sometime around noon. I didn't end up stopping in at the house, though, because I had so much sun left in the day. Instead, I passed by the porter and came down the hill."

"He mentioned he saw you, but I really wish you'd stopped in. They would have shown you some amazing things—things you'd never forget! But, after the hill, in the Valley of Humility, did you meet anyone?"

"I met a man named Discontent who tried hard to convince me to go back with him. He told me the valley was entirely without honour. He even told me that if I continued along the path, I'd be disobeying all my friends such as Pride, Arrogance, Self-conceit, Worldly-glory, and all the others." Faithful laughed and shook his head. "He told me I'd offend them if I was so foolish as to wade through the valley."

"What did you say to him?"

"I told him that even though the people he mentioned claimed I was their relative, and… to be honest, I really am related to them, at least according to my old life, but now that I'm a pilgrim, they've all disowned me. Besides, I've rejected them, too, and now it's like they were never related to me at all." Faithful smiled and added, "And I told him he was wrong about the valley. If honour comes, humility must come first. An arrogant spirit comes before a fall. Because of that, I told him I'd rather go through the Valley of Humiliation to find the honour that the wisest among us see as truly good than choose what he thought I'd want."

I returned the smile. Faithful certainly was true to his name. "Did you meet anyone else in the valley?"

"I sure did! I met with Shame, but… of everyone I've met so far on the path, I think Shame has the wrong name. All the others can be argued with and overcome, but not Shame. Nothing would make him back off."

"Why?" I asked. "What did he say?"

"He objected to religion[9] itself!" Faithful replied. "He said holding to a faith was a pathetic, low, sneaky business and that having a tender conscience is unmanly. Shame argued that to not enjoy the overwhelming freedom that brave men and women today enjoy makes you a laughingstock. He pointed out that few strong, rich, or wise people ever held such a faith,[10] and he told me that those of the strong and wise who bought into religion were convinced to be fools, to love the chance to risk losing everything for who knows what! He pointed out that most pilgrims throughout the ages were poor, low-living people, ignorant of the natural sciences."

Faithful frowned and shook his head. "That man pushed me hard on all this and about a lot more. He even argued that it was shameful to groan under a sermon and a shame to moan and groan on your way home after church. He said it was a shame to ask my neighbour for forgiveness for small things and to make restitution if I've stolen from anyone. Shame said that religion made a man awkward around popular people because you don't hold all the same

[9] Throughout this conversation (and much of the book), the Christian faith is referred to as religion. That's proper and normal (and Scriptural), but since it's common today to make a distinction between religion and faith (a distinction which is at times helpful, and at other times, merely splitting hairs), I've sometimes rephrased "religion" as "faith" or "the Christian faith," but at other times, when I felt the reading flows better, left the word as it is.

[10] 1 Cor. 1:26, 3:18; Phil. 3:7-8; John 7:48.

vices—which he called by different names than we use, names that made the vices sound like good things. And he said that religion makes us own and respect the low things of the world because of the kind of people who also hold to the faith. And then he asked me if that was not all an absolute shame!"

"Wow!" I replied. "And what did you say to him?"

Faithful shook his head again. "I didn't know what to say! In fact, he pushed me so hard on it all that my face grew all hot and red with embarrassment. When Shame saw it, he pushed me harder because of it! But then... at last... I considered that 'what is exalted among men is an abomination in the sight of God.'[11] Not only that, I also realized that Shame was only telling me what men are, but he told me nothing of what God or the Word of God is! And I thought about how at the end, at the judgement, the day of doom, we won't be doomed by those who bully us in the world, but according to the wisdom and law of the Highest—God himself! Because of that, I knew that what God says is best—even if every man and woman on earth is against it! So, since God wants this faith from us and he desires a tender conscience in us, and seeing that those who make themselves fools for the kingdom of heaven are truly the wisest among us, and since the poor man who loves Jesus is richer than the greatest man in a world who hates him, I said, 'Shame! Go away! You're an enemy of my salvation! Do you really think I'm going to listen to you over my sovereign Lord? If I did that, how would I look him in the face when he returns? If I'm ashamed of his ways and his followers, how could I expect him to bless me?'"[12]

"Did that end it? Did it drive him away?"

---

[11] Lk. 16:15.
[12] Mark 8:38.

Faithful frowned. "No, not at all! He's bold. A truly daring villain! I couldn't get rid of him. He'd probably still be haunting me, whispering in my ear, something or other about some difficulty of believing in God, but I told him it was a waste of time to keep going at me about it all. I told him that the things that he hated, those were the things in which I saw the most glory. So, finally, I got rid of him who had so harassed me. And once he was gone, I sang:

> *"The trials that those men do meet withal,*
> *That are obedient to the heavenly call,*
> *Are manifold, and suited to the flesh,*
> *And come, and come, and come again afresh;*
> *That now, or sometime else, we by them may*
> *Be taken, overcome, and cast away.*
> *Oh, let the pilgrims, let the pilgrims, then*
> *Be vigilant, and quit themselves like men."*

"I'm so glad you stood strong, brother," I said with an enormous smile. "I'm also glad that you kept your courage and held off such a dangerous man. I think I agree with you that he has the wrong name! He's so bold to follow us in the streets and to put us to shame in the eyes of other people, trying to make us ashamed of what's good. If he weren't so bold, he'd never try to do that kind of thing! But, even so… we still have to resist him. Aside from his bravado, the only ones he fools are the fools themselves. Solomon once said, 'the wise will inherit honour, but fools get disgrace.'"[13]

"I think we have to cry out to Jesus for help against Shame," Faithful added. "He's the one who wants us to be courageous for truth on this earth."

---

[13] Prov. 3:35.

"You're right!" I replied. "Did you meet anyone else in the valley?"

"No, no one else. I had sunshine all the way through and even through the Valley of the Shadow of Death."

"That's good!" I replied, happy to hear he didn't struggle as I did. "It was much harder for me through that area. For a long time, I had to face off against an evil demon named Apollyon. In fact, I thought he was going to kill me, especially when he knocked me down and put his weight on me, nearly crushing me." I shook my head and shivered at the memory. "At one point, he threw me, and I lost my sword—right out of my hand! He even told me he'd won against me, but I cried to God, and he heard me, delivering me out of all my troubles. Then, when I entered the Valley of the Shadow of Death, it was so dark I could barely see for about half the way through it. I thought I was going to be killed there, many times, but then at last the sun rose on a new day, and the rest of the way was much easier."

I grinned like a fool. To have a companion on the way was a gift from God himself! It would be a lot easier to face what lay before us, walking side by side.

8. A Talkative Companion

The path grew wider in the next stage of the journey, enough that we could walk side-by-side comfortably. As we walked, the path widened more and more to the left and the right. We felt we could relax as we enjoyed the smooth path, the gentle breeze, and the sun, warm on our faces.

After a few hours, by chance, Faithful happened to look to one side and saw a man walking beside us, not far away.

I recognized the man right away. His name was Talkative, although Faithful didn't know him. He was a tall man, someone who looked more handsome at a distance than up close.

"Friend!" Faithful called out to the man. "Where are you going? Are you heading to the heavenly country?"

Talkative turned his head enough to look at us. "I sure am! I'm heading to the same place as you!"

"Great!" Faithful replied. "Would you like to walk with us?"

"Absolutely! I'd be happy to join you," he said, and without missing a step, he veered towards us.

As he reached us, Faithful said, "Let's walk together, and we can talk about things that are good for us."

"Ah, that sounds great!" Talkative replied. Although I knew his name, he still hadn't told Faithful who he was. "I love chatting about good things with anyone and everyone! I just love to talk! I'm glad I've met some people who love to do what's good—to discuss the truth." We all shook hands and then continued on our journey while Talkative added, "Few people these days will spend their time while travelling talking about good things—instead they like to talk about things of no profit to anyone. It's been so frustrating!"

"That's too bad," Faithful said with a shake of his head. "There's nothing better to talk about than the things of the God of heaven."

Talkative laughed, and I could see how thrilled he was. He glanced at Faithful and said, "I think I'm going to enjoy spending time with you! You speak with conviction, and I'll add that there's nothing so wonderful and profitable but to speak of the things of God! What things are so good, if anyone cares what's good? For example, if someone likes to talk about history, or mysteries, or miracles, wonders, or signs, where will he find it so beautifully written if not the Holy Scriptures?"

"True!" Faithful replied. "But… if we're going to gain anything from it, we have to be intentional to keep our focus on what's profitable."

"That's what I said," Talkative agreed. "To speak of these things is definitely profitable. As we talk, we gain knowledge and learn so much. We can learn of how vain and empty the things of this world are, and how beneficial the things of above are. In general, but specifically in this discussion, one can learn of things such as the new birth, the insufficiency of our works, the need of Christ's righteousness, and more! Besides, by conversation, we can learn what it is to repent, to believe, to pray, to suffer, and more. We may even learn about the great promises and the comfort of the gospel. To add to this, we can even learn to refute false ideas, to stand firmly for the truth, and to instruct the ignorant."

"That's so true!" Faithful replied with a huge smile. "I'm glad to hear you say this!"

Talkative gave a quick nod, but his face filled with grief. "I think it's because we don't talk about these things enough that so many don't understand the need for faith and how necessary it is for us to have a work of grace in our soul if we're to receive eternal life. Instead, people live ignorantly in the works of the law." He ground his teeth and shook his head. "No one by the law can obtain the kingdom of heaven!"

"But," Faithful interjected, "if I can add one thing, spiritual knowledge of these things is a gift of God. No one can gain this by any human effort, not even by talking about them."

"Oh, that I know so well!" Talkative replied. "No one can receive anything except what's given from Heaven. Everything is of grace, not of works. I could point to a hundred Scriptures that speak of this."

Faithful's smile had grown to fill his face, and he asked, "What's something that we can talk about then?"

"Whatever you want!" Talkative replied. "I'll gladly chat about heavenly things, earthly things, morality, or evangelism. I'll talk about sacred or secular things, historical or future matters, things close to home or things foreign to us, things necessary or things we need only now and then. I'll chat about anything at all, as long as it's profitable."

I watched as Faithful took it all in, the admiration growing on his face along with gratefulness to have someone like this man to join us. He still didn't know who Talkative was, however. Turning back to me, he stepped in close. "Wow, Christian! This guy's great! I think this is the perfect companion to have on our journey!"

I gave Faithful a small smile. "This man you're quite impressed with is quite the charmer! He'll fool you with his words. In fact, he'll fool twenty men if they don't know who he really is!"

Faithful's brows came close together as he stared at me in shock. "You know him?"

"Know him?" I laughed. "I know him better than he knows himself."

Faithful's eyebrows shot up. "Who is he?"

"His name is Talkative," I explained. "He lives in our town, actually. I'm surprised you've never met him, but then again, many people live in our town."

"Who's he related to, and where does he live?"

"He's Say-well's son, and they lived in Prating Row.[1] Everyone who knows him in Prating Row calls him Talkative. Aside from his smooth tongue, he's a worthless man!"

Faithful glanced back at our new companion for a moment, then said, "He seems decent enough."

_____

[1] To *prate* is *to speak not only foolishly, but also in a long-winded manner.*

"Absolutely," I replied. "If you don't actually know him, he seems great! He's the kind of person who's great if you don't get too close; he's better when he stands far away. Up close, he's ugly. Your comment about how he seems decent makes me think of a painter whose pictures show best at a distance, but up close, they're terrible."

"Ah, you're joking, right?" Faithful said with a laugh. "I saw you grin."

"God forbid I joke about this kind of thing or accuse anyone falsely! I did smile, but what I say is sincere. I'll tell you a little more. This man will hang out with anyone and talk about anything! The way he speaks with you now is the way he'll speak at the bar, and the more he drinks, the more things he has to say. Religion and faith have no place in his heart or house or conversation. Everything he has is all talk, and his religion is simply to make noise with that tongue of his."

"Wow!" Faithful said. We walked for a few steps with no conversation, but then he finally added in a quiet voice, "He really fooled me."

"Fooled?" I replied. "He sure did! Remember the proverb, 'For they preach, but do not practice.' 'For the kingdom of God does not consist in talk but in power.' He talks of prayer, repentance, faith, and of the new birth, but he only knows of these things through talking about them. I've been to his home, and I've seen him at home and abroad. I know what I'm talking about! His home is as empty of religion as the white of an egg is of flavour. There's neither prayer nor repentance in that place. In fact, a brute of a man serves God better than Talkative! He's a stain, a reproach, and shame for religion to all who know him. His actions and behaviours make everyone think poorly of the faith! Those who know him say he's a saint abroad, but a devil at home, and his poor family has to endure it all. He's rude and cruel. In fact, he's so unreasonable with his servants that they don't know what to do or how to speak around him. Anyone who deals with him says you'd get along better with a violent man than with him. This Talkative, if it's possible, will go beyond anyone in theft, deceit, and more. He's even trained his sons to live the same way. If he finds any of them foolishly fearful, for that's what he thinks of someone with a tender conscience, he calls them fools and blockheads and won't give them work or speak well of them to others. He has, by his wicked life, caused many to stumble and fall, and if God doesn't stop him, he'll cause many more to fall in the years to come."[2]

"Well, my brother," Faithful replied quietly, glancing back at Talkative, "I'm inclined to trust you on this matter, not only because you know him, but also because you evaluate others as a Christian should. I know you well enough to know that you wouldn't say these things out of a desire to hurt this man, but as one who's simply telling me the way it is."

I could hear the disappointment in Faithful's voice, and I replied in a gentle voice, "If I'd just met him, Faithful, I'd have thought the same of him as you did. If I'd heard all this about him from those who hate the faith, I'd have just assumed it was slander. A lot of lies, slander, and gossip come from those who want to tear down the name and work of those who follow Christ! But all that I've told you and much more is all true—I've seen it all myself. Besides, Faithful, good men are ashamed of Talkative. They won't call him a brother, or even call him a friend. Anyone who knows him is ashamed to even mention his name."

"I understand. Saying and doing are two very different things. I'm going to have to keep a better eye out to discern between the two."

---

[2] Matt. 23:3; 1 Cor 4:20; Rom. 2:24-25.

I smiled at Faithful. "They are definitely two different things, and they're as different as the soul and the body. The body without the soul is just a corpse. The soul of religion is the practical part. 'Religion that is pure and undefiled before God, the Father, is this: to visit orphans and widows in their affliction, and to keep oneself unstained from the world.' Talkative doesn't understand this. He thinks hearing what's good and then speaking about it will make him a good Christian. He's deceived his own soul. Hearing is just like sowing a seed, and talking is not enough to prove that there's fruit of that seed in the heart and life. Let's always remember that on the day of doom, God will judge people according to their fruit. It won't be asked, 'Did you believe?' but, 'Were you doers or only talkers?' That's how they'll be judged! The end of the world is like a harvest, and you know that at harvest time, the only thing that matters is fruit! Although… not that anything will be accepted if it's not from faith." I took a deep breath and shook my head. "Faithful, I say this to show you how worthless Talkative's profession will be on that day.[3]

"That reminds me of when Moses described the clean animals,"[4] Faithful said with a slow nod, glancing quickly at our new companion. Talkative, despite his name, continued to walk silently along the path with us, but just out of earshot. "The clean animals," Faithful continued, "are those which part the hoof and chew the cud. Not those that part the hoof only, or those that chew the cud only. A hare chews the cud but is unclean because it doesn't part the hoof. That's like Talkative. He chews the cud, seeking knowledge, chewing on the Word, but he doesn't part the hoof—doesn't leave behind the ways of sinners.

---

3 James 1:22-27; Matt. 13, 25.
4 Lev. 11:3-7; Deut. 14:6-8.

Just like the hare, he holds onto the foot of a dog or a bear and is unclean."

I smiled. "From what I know, you've interpreted those passages well, Faithful, pulling the true gospel sense from those texts. Let me add one more thing, though. Paul calls some people, those who are also great talkers, a noisy gong or a clanging cymbal. In another place, he speaks of things without life giving sound.[5] Those things without life are those who have no true faith and have not received the grace of the gospel. Because of this, they'll never stand in the kingdom of heaven next to those who are the children of life." I took a deep breath and added, "Even if the sounds they make, the words they speak, are like the tongues and voices of angels!"

"Well," Faithful replied, "I wasn't that fond of his company at first, but I'm sick of it now! How do we get rid of him?"

A small laugh escaped my lips. As we'd been talking, a plan had formed in my mind, and I shared it with my friend. "Here's my advice, Faithful. Do this and you'll find that he'll quickly be sick of your company—unless God touches his heart and changes it."

"What do you suggest?"

"Go talk with him again but, this time, have a deep discussion about the power of religion. Once he's agreed to talk about that—and he definitely will—ask him whether the power of religion should live in his heart, his house, or the way he lives from day to day."[6]

---

[5] 1 Cor. 13:1-3, 14:7.
[6] In the original, the word *conversation* is used here, however, in older English, *conversation* often refers to the way you live among others, not necessarily what you talk about with others. As such, I've *translated* it in this place as well as others as referring to lifestyle.

Faithful nodded and gave me a grateful smile before rejoining Talkative. In a friendly voice, he asked, "How are things?"

"Great!" Talkative replied. "Thanks for asking. But… to be honest… I thought by this time we'd have talked a lot more."

"Well," Faithful said, "if you're up for it, we could chat now. Since you left it up to me to come up with the topic, let me pose this question: How does the saving grace of God show itself when it is in the heart?"

"Oh, wow!" Talkative replied with a laugh. "That's a brilliant question! I see you want to talk about spiritual power, and I'd love to chat about that! Okay, so let me start with a short answer. First, when the grace of God is in the heart, it causes a great outcry against sin. Second…"

"Whoa, whoa, whoa! Hold on!" Faithful interrupted. "Let's talk about one thing at a time. I suggest, perhaps, you should have said that when the grace of God is in the heart, it shows itself by making the soul hate its sin."

"What's the difference between crying out against and hating sin?" Talkative asked.

"Oh, there's a huge difference!" Faithful declared. "Someone can cry out against sinful actions, but he can't hate the sin unless there is a deep, godly hatred in his heart against it. I've heard some people cry out against sin from the pulpit, but they seem fine with it in their heart, their house, and even in their day-to-day lives. The wife of Joseph's master cried out with a loud voice as if she'd been holy in her actions, but she was quite happy to commit an unclean act with him. Some cry out against sin even as a mother cries out against her child on her lap for their inappropriate behaviour, but then hugs and kisses the child after."

"You set a trap for me, Faithful," Talkative said with a frown.

"Oh, no... I didn't," Faithful replied. "I'm merely correcting an error. But what's the second proof you have for how the saving grace of God shows itself in the heart?"

"It shows itself through expert knowledge of gospel mysteries," Talkative said hesitantly.

"Ah," Faithful replied, "this should have been first! But first or last, it's also wrong. Someone can find knowledge in the mysteries of the gospel without a work of grace in their heart! If that person has all knowledge, they may still have nothing and, as a result, not be a child of God. When Christ asked, 'Do you know all these things?' and the disciples said that they did, he added, 'Blessed are you if you do them.' He doesn't say you're blessed for knowing them, but for doing them! There is knowledge that doesn't go hand in hand with doing. Some can know their master's will and not do it. A man may know like an angel, but not be a Christian, so, because of that, your sign is not true. To know something is a thing that pleases talkers and boasters, but to do it is to please God." Faithful stopped for a moment and turned to Talkative, looking intently at him while he said, "It's not that the heart can be good without knowledge, for without knowledge, the heart is nothing. But there's knowledge... and there's *knowledge*! Knowledge can be merely about speculation, and knowledge can come with the grace of faith and love—and the second kind is the kind that sets someone on the path of doing God's will from the heart. The first kind of knowledge only fits with those who are all talk, but without the knowledge that drives us to serve God... well... no true Christian will be content with that.

'Give me understanding, that I may keep your law and observe it with my whole heart.'"[7]

Talkative balled his fists, and his cheeks flushed red. "You set another trap for me!" he shouted. "This kind of conversation doesn't build anyone up!"

"Okay, okay," Faithful replied peacefully. He put his hands up as if to calm Talkative down a little. "If you're willing, give me another sign of how saving grace shows itself when it's in the heart."

"Nope, not me," Talkative replied, eyeing Faithful suspiciously. "We won't agree."

"Well, if you won't come up with another one," Faithful said with a smile, "am I free to offer one?"

"Do what you want," Talkative growled.

"A work of grace in the soul," Faithful began, "shows itself both to the one who has it in their heart and to others who can see it in him."

Faithful walked on, and Talkative, a curious expression on his face, followed. Continuing with an explanation, Faithful said, "To the one who has it in his soul, it gives him a conviction of sin, especially of those sins which defile his nature along with the sin of unbelief. Of course, the sin of unbelief will lead him to hell, if he doesn't find mercy from God's hand by faith in Jesus Christ. So, for the conviction of sin, the sight and feel of this conviction working in him brings sorrow and shame for sin, and he'll then find the Saviour of the world revealed in his heart and see how necessary it is to settle with the Saviour for eternal life. He's then filled with a hunger and thirst for Jesus, driving him to turn his life over to the one who can satisfy. So, now that he has this grace in him, he'll experience joy and peace according the strength or

7 John 13:17; 1 Cor. 13; Ps. 119:34.

131

weakness of his faith in his Saviour. And not only that, but also his love of holiness, his desire to know Christ more, and his desire to serve him in this world... these things will also be experienced according to his faith in his Saviour! But, even though I say that this saving grace shows itself to him, yet it's rare that he'll be able to understand that this is a work of grace because his corruption and his perverted reason make him unable to understand the matter. Therefore, before anyone can conclude for himself that this is truly a work of grace in him, he must have a very sound judgement.[8]

"Now, to others," Faithful continued, "saving grace shows itself through two things. First, through the experience of witnessing the person's confession of faith in Christ.[9]

"Second, it shows itself by a life that responds to that confession—a life that lives in line with the confession made. By that I mean it shows itself in a life of holiness—holiness of the heart, holiness in the family if he has one, and by holiness in how he lives in the world. This kind of holiness teaches him in his heart to hate his sin and even himself for his sin, to seek to keep his family from falling into sin, and to promote holiness in the world. Of course, as he promotes holiness, that's not through just words as a hypocrite or talkative person might, but through a real, practical submission to the power of the Word in faith and love.[10]

"And now, Sir," Faithful said, coming to a stop again and turning to Talkative, "as for my brief description of the work of grace and how it shows itself, if you have

---

[8] John 16:8; Rom. 7:24; John 16:9; Mark 16:16; Ps. 38:18; Jer. 31:19; Gal. 2:16; Acts 4:12; Matt. 5:6; Rev. 21:6.
[9] Rom. 10:10; Phil. 1:27; Matt. 5:19.
[10] John 14:15; Ps. 50:23; Job 42:5-6; Eze. 20:43.

something you want to disagree with, go ahead. If not, then let me ask you a second question."

"No, it's not my job to object right now, but to listen," Talkative replied. "Let me have your second question."

Faithful nodded and walked on again. "Well, it's this. Do you experience this first part of what I've described? I mean, the conviction of sin, the hunger and thirst for Jesus, and so on? And, to add to that, does your life and the way you live among others testify that this is true in you? Or does your religion live only in words and in your tongue, not your actions and in truth?" He paused for a moment before adding, "Please, if you're up for answering, please do, but… say nothing unless you know God will respond to it with a loud 'Amen!'—say nothing that your conscience can't justify. For, as we know, 'it's not the one who commends himself who is approved, but the one whom the Lord commends.'[11] Besides, if I claim to be a certain way with my words when the way I live among others proves me a liar and even my neighbours tell me I'm lying… well… that's really wicked!"

Talkative's mouth dropped open, and his face turned a deep shade of red before he could recover his composure. Once he did, he replied, "You've now brought the entire conversation around to experience, to conscience, and to God, and to an appeal to God for him to justify what is spoken. I didn't enter this conversation for this kind of talk, and I'm not about to answer those kinds of questions. You're not above me, unless you consider yourself a teacher,[12] but even if you do, I won't let you judge me! Tell me why you're asking these questions!"

---

[11] 2 Cor. 10:18.
[12] The original word here was *catechiser*.

"Because!" Faithful responded confidently, once again coming to a stop and staring Talkative right in the eyes. "I saw you were quite willing to talk, but I wasn't sure your desire went anywhere past ideas and thoughts in your head. Besides, I've heard of you. They say that with religion, you're all talk, but the way you live among people proves the profession of your mouth is nothing but a lie. They say you are a stain among Christians, and that you bring the name of Christ to shame because of the wicked way you live, and because of the way you live, more people are in danger of being left to a fate of destruction. Your form of faith goes hand in hand with taverns, coveting, uncleanness, swearing, lying, hanging around evil company. The proverb that says a prostitute is a shame to all women is true of you! You are a shame to all those who profess the name of Christ!"

Talkative stomped his foot on the path and clenched his fists. Staring Faithful right in the eye, he spat, "Since you're so ready to listen to gossip and rumour and to judge so harshly, you're obviously either easily irritated or just a negative person![13] You're not the kind of person I want to talk with so… GOODBYE!" With that, Talkative turned and stormed away, leaving us by ourselves.

Stepping up next to Faithful, I said, "It looks like it happened just as I said. Your words and his lusts will never agree—he'd rather walk away than change his behaviour. But… he's gone now, as I suspected. Let him go; it's his loss. He's actually saved us the trouble of walking away from him because if he'd stayed and continued on in his lifestyle, he'd just have brought shame

---

[13] The original used the word *melancholy* which is often thought of today as a deep sadness or depression, but *a negative person* seemed to fit the context here a little better.

to us. Besides, the apostle says, 'Purge the evil person from among you!'"[14]

Faithful smiled, and we continued on our journey together. "You know," Faithful replied, "I'm glad we met up with him. Maybe one day he'll think about what I said. But either way, I was clear, and I won't bear any guilt for his blood if he dies in his sins."

"You did well, Faithful, to speak so plainly to him," I said with a smile. "Few people will be so blunt these days, and that makes our faith repulsive to so many. There are many today who are all talk in the faith. They're immoral and worthless in their lifestyle, so when they continue in the church, they confuse the world, bring shame to Christianity, and grieve those who are sincere. I wish all Christians would speak as plainly with this kind of person as you have. If they did, these men who are all talk would either learn to be truer to their faith or the company of the saints would be too hot for them to continue among us."

Faithful nodded and said,

How Talkative at first lifts up his plumes!
How bravely doth he speak! How he presumes
To drive down all before him! But so soon
As Faithful talks of heart-work, like the moon
That's past the full, into the wane he goes.
And so will all, but he that HEART-WORK
knows.

---

[14] 1 Cor. 5:13. The original points to 1Tim. 6:5 in the KJV which reads, "From such withdraw thyself."

9. Vanity Fair

Over the following days, we pushed on down the path, talking of those things we had seen along the way. In time, we came to a rough area where the dirt crunched below our feet and the plants along the sides of the path grew sparsely. It appeared as though rain came rarely in that area, and the dry heat made the wilderness difficult to traverse. We found comfort, however, in our conversation and time together. Our friendship and the encouragement we found in one another made our travels that much easier.

After nearly three days in the wilderness, I saw something ahead that caught my attention. We pushed on, excited to see what lay before us and came to an area much different from what we had just endured. The grass before us grew thick and green, and the soil of the path looked softer than what we had endured on for so long.

A gentle breeze reached us, and we smiled for no other reason than to know the path would soon be easier to walk. As we chatted, Faithful turned around, looking back behind us, as we often did, just to see where we'd come from.

Walking backwards, he slowed just a little and pointed. An enormous grin broke out, and he said, "Christian! I see someone I know. Do you know who that is?"

I turned around and found a similar smile break out on my face. "That's my good friend Evangelist!"

"Mine too," Faithful said to me. "He's the one who told me how to get to the gate!"

Evangelist approached quickly, coming to a halt only when he'd caught up. Without saying a word, he examined both of us, each in turn, while we remained silent. Finally, with a serious look in his eye, he said, "Peace be with you, my brothers! And peace to those who have helped you!"

I laughed, despite Evangelist's stern tone. "It's great to see you, Evangelist! You've been so good to me, working so hard for my eternal good."

"And a thousand welcomes to you!" Faithful added. "Seeing you is just what two tired pilgrims need."

Evangelist nodded slowly as he examined us each again, two men he'd poured himself into in times past. While his expression remained serious, it was also kind and friendly. "How has it been, friends, since we last saw each other? What have you met along the way, and how have you walked?"

The two of us took some time to share with Evangelist all we'd gone through. We spoke of the good, but also the bad, and even of our difficulties along the way.

When we had finished, Evangelist nodded. "I am glad," he said with a great deal of affection, "not that you have faced so many trials, but that you have risen above them. And I am so glad that you have, despite your weakness, continued on the path until today. I am glad not only for your sake, but also for my own, since I have sowed, and you have reaped." Stepping close, he placed a firm hand on each of our shoulders and encouraged us, saying, "A day is coming, friends, when those who sow and those who reap will rejoice together—that is, if you hold on. The Scriptures promise, 'in due season we will reap, if we do not give up.' There is a crown before you, and it's not one that will ever rust or break down, so run! Run so you may win it! But know that there are some who set out after the crown, and after they've fought so hard for it, another comes and takes it away. Hold tight to what you have and don't let anyone take your crown! You are not yet out of range of the devil's attacks, and you haven't yet resisted to the point of blood in your striving against sin. Keep your eyes on the kingdom at all times, and don't let your belief in the invisible things be shaken. Don't let the things of this world, of this life, take root in you, and above all, be careful in your heart and be careful of your own lust. Remember, 'the heart is deceitful above all things, and desperately sick.' Grit your teeth and push forward, for you have all power in heaven and earth on your side!"[1]

We stood there in silence for a few minutes, trying to take in everything he had said. I felt his words had both encouraged and terrified me. As long as we walked the path, we could never let down our guard.

Finally, I took a deep breath and said, "Thank you, Evangelist. Your encouragement is so needed! Will you stay with us for a while? We'd like your help for the rest of the journey. We know you're a prophet, so please tell us what might happen to us in the days to come. Tell us how we can resist and overcome what we'll soon face."

Evangelist gave one of his rare smiles and nodded to me, filling my heart with hope. "My sons," he began,

---

[1] John 4:36; Gal. 6:9; 1 Cor. 9:24-27; Heb. 12:4; Jer. 17:9; Rev. 3:11.

"you've heard through the gospel that you must go through many tribulations before you enter the kingdom of heaven. You've also heard that in every city, you face arrest and affliction. Because of this, you can't expect to go long on your journey without facing this kind of thing, at least in some manner or another. You've already experienced this somewhat already, and more is about to come. You're almost out of this wilderness and soon you'll come to a new town. In that place, you will find many enemies who will stand strong against you. They will do all they can to kill you, and at least one of you, if not both, will seal the testimony you hold with your own blood." His eyes filled with compassion, and he added, "But friends, be faithful right to death, and the King will give you a crown of glory."[2]

Evangelist paused and examined each of us yet again before he continued. "The one who will die, even though his death will not be natural, and he may suffer greatly, he will ultimately have it better than the one who survives. Not only will the one who dies arrive in the Celestial City first, but he will also escape many miseries which the survivor will still need to face along the path. When you reach the town and things turn out as I have told you, then remember each other and stand strong.[3] Trust the Lord to keep your soul as you serve him, your faithful Creator!"

Evangelist, having finished his prophecies, bid us farewell, and we thanked him for giving us some insight into what lay ahead, although it was not the news we had hoped for. He then turned away from us, leaving us behind, knowing we would face great loss in the days to come.

---

[2] Acts 14:22; 20:23; Rev. 2:10.

[3] 1 Cor. 16:13. The original here says, *quit yourselves like men* which essentially means to be courageous and to stand strong.

We stood there for a moment in silence, the difficult message and abrupt exit leaving us speechless. But there was no benefit to remain where we were. I patted Faithful on the back, and we turned back to the path.

The wilderness before us slowly faded away, and when we reached the end, we soon saw a town laid out before us.

The town, called Vanity,[4] stood right on the path to the Celestial City, and to follow the straight and narrow road meant we would need to travel right through its midst. It lay before us, stretched out with its tall buildings, countless stands, and captivating entertainments. Even from a distance, the sound of cheers and celebrations and more echoed across the plains.

Although I had never seen the town before, I knew much of its history. Vanity is a town best known for its fair which runs all year round. The fair itself is called Vanity Fair because the town in which it resides is less than worthless, and because everything sold in that place and everything which comes to it is vanity. It reminded me of the wise saying, "All that comes is vanity."[5]

The fair, however, is not new, not by any means! It has stood in that place for thousands of years.

In fact, almost five thousand years ago, as pilgrims walked this path to the Celestial City, Beelzebub, Apollyon, and Legion, along with their many companions, noticed that the path itself led right through the town of Vanity. They took advantage of the situation and set up a fair in that place, a fair which would sell all sorts of worthless, vain things. A fair which could also run all year round.

---

[4] The word *vanity* here ultimately means *worthless, meaningless, and empty.*
[5] Eccl. 1, 2:11 & 17, 11:8; Isa. 11:17.

Because of this, the fair sells nearly everything, such as houses, lands, trades, places, honours, promotions, titles, countries, kingdoms, lusts, and pleasures. It also sells delights of the flesh such as prostitutes, women who run brothels, wives, husbands, children, masters, servants, lives, blood, bodies, souls, silver, gold, pearls, precious stones, and more.

At any moment in this fair, a visitor can witness juggling, cheats, games, plays, fools, apes, and every kind of dishonest person.[6]

There are even found in this place, and this is thought of as nothing by the people of the town, thefts, murders, adulteries, those who swear falsely, and all that of a blood-red colour.[7]

As in other, lesser fairs, everything is found on the various rows and streets throughout the area. These rows and streets are named after their countries and kingdoms. There is, of course, the Britain Row, the French Row, the Italian Row, the Spanish Row, the German Row; all these places are where vanities are to be sold. But, as in other fairs, the things of Rome and all her merchandise are heavily promoted. Only the English nation, along with some others, has taken a dislike to the things of Rome.

But sadly, since the path to the Celestial City ran directly through the town where this fast-paced fair sat, if we wanted to get to the Celestial City without going through the town of Vanity, we would have to leave the world.

I remembered learning that the Prince of princes himself went through the town of Vanity on his way to his

---

[6] In the original, Bunyan uses the terms *knaves* and *rogues* which seems to be a lot the same thing—dishonest people.
[7] The reference to a blood-red colour seems to imply that much in the fair is the result of violence, leaving all a blood-red colour.

own country, and the fair was running on that day as well. I think it was Beelzebub himself, the greatest lord of the fair, who led our Master through. Beelzebub invited him to buy of his vanities and even offered to make him lord of the fair, if our Master would only offer Beelzebub worship as he walked through the town.[8]

And because our Master was such a man of honour, Beelzebub took him from street to street and showed him all the kingdoms of the world in only a few moments, hoping that he might tempt the Blessed One to cheapen himself and buy some of the vain things. But our Master had no desire for the merchandise sold and therefore left the town without having spent a penny on anything!

The fair, Vanity Fair, that lay ahead of us… it was an ancient thing, held there for many thousands of years, and it was indeed very great.[9]

So, since we had no other choice but to go through the fair, we pressed on.

I stepped across the boundaries of Vanity and immediately wanted to turn around. Every which way I looked, people danced and yelled and called out, offering their merchandise. I found it overwhelming, as everything surrounding me was nothing more than the empty things of the world.

"Let's just try to make our way through quietly and peacefully," Faithful whispered, just loud enough for me to hear about the raucous noise.

I nodded. Passing right through unnoticed seemed like the perfect option.

---

[8] Matt. 4:1-11.
[9] 1 Cor. 5:10; Matt. 4:8, Luke 4:5-7.

But before we could take more than around five or six steps past the boundaries of the town, people turned their heads, staring, scowling, and even grumbling about us.

"Look at what that guy is wearing! You won't find anything like that sold anywhere!" one man shouted out.

Someone else shouted, "It's nothing like his partner. They dress like they don't know what's in style! No one's worn that kind of clothing in ages!"

The crowds laughed but didn't return to what they were doing before. Instead, they gathered around us, shouting, insulting us, and threatening us. Some stared at us as if they couldn't comprehend what had just walked into their fair. Others called us fools. Some thought we were insane, and others figured we were foreigners, unfamiliar with the local customs.[10]

As the attention focused on us, it wasn't long before the entire town was in an uproar! It wasn't just our clothing, however, that caused a stir. People also reacted to the way we spoke. Very few who walked the streets of Vanity Fair could understand what we said. They all spoke the language of Canaan, and those who ran the fair were not of the Celestial City but were of the world. Because of this, from street to street, from one end of the fair to the other, we and the people of the fair seemed like savages to each other.

And to add to our clothing and speech, which were strange to the people of the fair, the people reacted to one more thing, and this perhaps upset them most. We showed no interest in the items they sold. In fact, we were so committed to avoiding such things that we would not even look at the merchandise, and when someone would invite us to buy from them, we'd cover our ears and cry out,

---

[10] 1 Cor. 2:7-8.

"Turn my eyes from looking at worthless things!" and then we'd look up to show that our treasure was in heaven.[11]

The crowd pressed in and jostled us around as they pushed us back and forth, nevertheless, we pressed on, determined to make our way past all the temptation. The people, however, would not stand for it! Their anger at us for being so different from themselves grew with every moment until one particular confrontation which pushed them over the edge.

Struggling forward through the angry crowd, a voice called out above the noise. "What will you buy?"

To that, Faithful turned to him and said with a confident and serious look in his eye, "We buy the truth!"[12]

At this answer, the people reacted even more, and their hatred for us grew. Some mocked, some insulted, some rebuked, and some even called others to attack. The rage continued to build until a riot broke out, causing upheaval among the people to where there was no longer any order.

Amid the disturbance, unknown to us, word reached the Great One of the Fair of all that had happened. In response, he rushed to the scene of the commotion. Once he had fully taken it all in, he appointed some of his friends to arrest us for questioning, since we were thought to be the ones causing the riot.

A dozen men rushed in and grabbed my arms, throwing me to the ground. I hit hard, my face slamming against the hard packed dirt of the street, and I heard Faithful's grunt as he slammed down next to me. Someone wrenched my arms back, and I felt the rough edges of rope

---

[11] Ps. 119:37; Phil. 3:19-20.
[12] Prov. 23:23.

dig into my wrists as they tied my hands securely behind my back.

The people continued to yell and scream, insulting us with every false accusation they could as the men yanked us to our feet, and pushed us through the crowd, not seeming to care if anyone struck us on our way through.

Once out of the crowd, they took us down street after street, deeper into the town, until we reached a place far from the riots, a place where they could question us directly. Neither Faithful nor I had anything to hide, nor had we done anything wrong according to the way of our Master, but they interrogated us like criminals.

They asked us where we had come from and where we were going. They even demanded that we tell them why we wore such unusual clothing—or at least unusual to their eyes and ways of thinking.

We answered them honestly, telling them we were pilgrims, strangers in the world, and that we were travelling to our own country, the heavenly Jerusalem.[13] We told them we had given no reason to the men of the town or to the sellers to abuse us in this way and that they should allow us to resume our journey. The only thing we could admit to doing was when one man asked what we would buy, we told him we buy the truth.

They questioned us for hours on end, refusing to accept anything we said. In the end, they seemed to think we must have been insane—or else we had come for the purpose of causing such a riot.

Once they reached that conclusion, they pulled us to our feet and drove us out into a small courtyard. I felt the bonds holding my hands cut loose, and I hoped to be

---

[13] Heb. 11:13-16.

released from their custody. Instead, a sharp pain on the side of my head drove me to my knees.

A moment later, Faithful hit the ground beside me, and the men set about to beat us severely. I don't know how long the beating lasted, but every second was agony until they finally grew tired, then smeared dirt all over us. Once we were left bloody and covered in mud, they picked us up and threw our limp bodies into a cage.

Landing hard, I laid there for a moment, trying to gather my wits. I took a few shallow, ragged breaths and tried to open my eyes. They only opened just barely beyond slits, but I could see enough. Managing to get up on one elbow, I turned my head slowly towards my friend, hoping to check on Faithful. The slow rise and fall of his chest filled me with relief, but then my attention was drawn to something else. The cage itself, barely big enough for the two of us, had been placed upon large wheels. The men who had arrested, then questioned, then beaten us pushed the cage, and we rolled out into the middle of the street, surrounded by the people who hated us, leaving us as a spectacle to the men and women of the fair.

> *Behold Vanity Fair! the Pilgrims there*
> *Are chain'd and stand beside:*
> *Even so it was our Lord pass'd here,*
> *And on Mount Calvary died.*

My eyes jerked open as something hard hit my back, followed by familiar laughter. Pushing myself up to a seated position, I checked on Faithful. He had regained consciousness sometime yesterday afternoon, and we found encouragement from one another, but the constant mocking, insults, laughter, and thrown objects—some soft, some not so soft—wore away at us.

Someone threw something else—it might have been an apple—but that one missed us, thank the Lord.

As we sat there in our cage, we had no peace, no relief, and no justice. We slept when we could, but the crowd never let us sleep for long. The only good thing I found was the chance to write a bit in my journal. I hunched over, now and then, and got a few lines written.

Men and women passed by continually, hurling all manner of abuse at us, pouring out malice and revenge. Unable to do anything to protect ourselves or even to run or hide because of the bars surrounding us, we simply had to take it. And to make it all worse, the Great One of the fair, rather than come to our aid and protect us, showed up occasionally just to laugh at us, mocking us in our suffering.

But, by the grace of the Lord, the Spirit gave us patience, and we endured. We found in our suffering, though our old selves would have wished to insult our attackers back, instead we blessed the people. Every evil word given, we returned with good words. When they hurt us physically, we responded with kindness.

As the days wore on, we were grateful that not all the men of the fair were quite so cruel. In fact, in time, some who weren't filled with as much hatred began to call those who hurled abuse at us on their cruelty. They even blamed the others for the abuse. Sadly, the wicked men of the fair didn't listen, but they instead turned on their own people, declaring them to be as bad as we had been made out to be, accusing them of being allies with us, and suggesting they should suffer alongside us.

But the Lord was good and testified to our righteousness through those men who held back their cruelty. They replied to the abusers that we were quiet men, sensible even, and that we intended no harm to anyone. They even went so far as to point out that there were many who traded in the fair who should be put in the cage, or even stocks, before us.

Unsurprisingly, those who acted with sensible wisdom in defending us, those who stood strong, eventually found themselves face to face with our abusers, and a fight broke out, our defenders on one side, and our abusers on the other. We sat there, powerless to do anything about it as they injured one another. All we could do is pray, and pray we did!

Soldiers rushed into the street, roughly pushing people aside, forcing their way through the riot. When they reached those who fought in the street, however, they pushed on past them until they reached our cage.

Throwing open the door, they grabbed me by my arm and dragged me out, pushing me to the ground. A moment later, Faithful landed next to me, then they forced us back to our feet, and the soldiers shoved us through the crowd.

We reached the courtyard, the very one where they had beaten us before, and they took us back into the room where we had been questioned. The same men sat in there, the examiners, and they accused us of causing the riot, though we had nothing to do with it.

This went on for hours, accusations, insults, and more, and finally the examiners declared us guilty of the riot and then took us back out to the courtyard where they beat us terribly. When they had enough, they bound us in heavy chains, weighing us down, and led us up and down the streets of the fair. Humiliated, we walked before the people as an example to them and to cause fear among them, proving that no one should speak on our behalf or join with us.

But we, Faithful and I, still took care to act with wisdom. We received the disgrace and shame hurled at us with patience and meekness. In doing so, the Lord won over to us a few people, not many, but still several men of the fair turned to our side.

And this enraged the people of the fair even more!

Upon seeing their countrymen come to our side, the men of the fair called for our deaths, declaring that the cage and the chains were not enough. They thought we should be executed because of the abuse we had doled out and for deceiving the people of the fair. So, those in authority sent us back to our cage until a decision be made as to what should be done with us.

The soldiers dragged us back and threw us roughly into our cage. In my exhaustion, I laid where I landed, sprawled on the floor of our prison as they secured my feet in the stocks. When I managed to sit up again, my friend and companion, Faithful, sat next to me, his feet also held fast.

Even in our suffering, I managed a smile, and Faithful returned one of his own. We reminded one another of the words of our friend Evangelist, and as we did, our spirits were lifted knowing that we were exactly where God wanted us to be, despite our terrible suffering. We even comforted one another in what we had heard, that the one who would have to die would have the easier path. Oddly enough, each of us secretly wished that we might be the one who was to suffer death, but we committed ourselves to the eternally wise control of the One who rules all things, and in doing so, we were content to continue in that place until we were dealt with.

So, we remained in our cage for another two days while those in authority made their decision. The time moved slowly, yet still we found comfort in one another and in knowing that God remained in control.

Early one morning, just as the sun peaked above the horizon, I jolted awake at the sound of a rough voice bellowing, "Get up!"

Rolling over, I tugged on Faithful's arm, and he shook himself awake.

The man hollered again, then threw open the door. He grabbed me roughly by the ankle, and pulled me close enough to unlock the stocks, then wrenched my whole body out of the cage. I landed hard on the ground between a half dozen soldiers with Faithful landing next to me a few seconds later.

Strong hands pulled us to our feet and then shoved us back towards the same building we'd been in twice before. I feared another beating, but prayed silently, trusting myself to the Lord's care, once again hoping that if one of us was to find the easier route, to stand before our Lord today, I longed for it to be me.

The men pushed us along, and we stumbled through the courtyard, my legs only just starting to get some of the feeling back. On the far side of the courtyard, we entered the doors, held open by another two men, scowling at us.

Once through the door, before my eyes could fully adjust to the darkness of the corridor, a man shoved me, and I landed hard on the tiled floor. I knew enough by this point to scramble quickly back to my feet before more abuse came.

The men led us into an unfamiliar room this time, larger than the interrogation room we'd been in before, but it only took a moment to understand.

A convenient time for the people of the fair to put us on trial must have arrived.

They led us into the centre of the courtroom and had us stand on a small platform. I knew from the moment I walked in that we were not there for justice, but for condemnation.

Men filed into the room, all of them enemies of Faithful and me, to call us to answer to the charges laid on us. When they had all found their spots, a large man by the name of Lord Hate-good entered, taking his seat raised high above all others.

Laying out their indictment against us, we saw it was all the same at heart, although the specifics varied somewhat.

INDICTMENT AGAINST THE PRISONERS NAMED FAITHFUL AND CHRISTIAN:

These men are enemies to and disturbers of their trade; they had made commotions and divisions in the town and had won a party to their own most dangerous opinions in contempt of the law of their prince.[14]

---

[14] NOTE: this indictment has been left in the original wording, for the most part, as I felt it flowed better than a modern rewording.

Now, FAITHFUL, play the man, speak for thy God:
Fear not the wicked's malice; nor their rod:
Speak boldly, man, the truth is on thy side:
Die for it, and to life in triumph ride.

All eyes on us, the courtroom grew quiet as everyone waited for us to respond. With boldness, Faithful stepped forward, ready to give an answer to the accusation.

He cleared his throat, stared directly at the judge, Lord Hate-good, and declared, "I have only set myself against those things which themselves stand against him who is higher than the highest! As for the disturbance you speak of, I have made no disturbance. I am a man of peace and have acted as such. Those won to our side were not won by manipulation, but through seeing our truth and innocence, and in this, they turned from worse to better. But as for the king you speak of, since your king is Beelzebub, the enemy of our Lord, I defy him and all his angels!"

Lord Hate-good's eyes filled with rage and hatred as he bared his teeth at Faithful, then slowly shook his head. Turning to a small man by his side, he growled, "Send out word for anyone who has anything at all to say on behalf of their king against the prisoner at the bar. If anyone is found, they are to come immediately and share their evidence."

The man hurried out a side door near the judge, and then immediately led three men back inside. Obviously, they had been waiting outside for such a moment. He then introduced the three new arrivals as Envy, Superstition, and Pickthank, then asked each if they knew Faithful. When they had all affirmed they did, the Judge asked them what they had to say for their lord, the king, against him.

153

The first of the witnesses, Envy, stepped forward and gave a respectful bow to Lord Hate-good. He was a small man, standing no more than shoulder height to either myself or Faithful, and yet moved and acted as though he were as tall as the largest man in the room.[15] "My Lord," he began, "I have known this man for many years, and I can attest upon my oath before this honourable bench that he is…"

"Hold!" the Judge, Lord Hate-good, ordered. "Make him take his oath!"

Two men came forward and took Envy's oath, after which Envy declared, "My Lord, this man, despite his good name, is one of the most wicked men in our country. He cares nothing for the prince, the people, the laws, or our customs. He also does everything he can to convince others to hold to his disloyal and unacceptable ideas, those things he calls principles of faith and holiness. In fact, I once even heard him say that Christianity and the customs of our town of Vanity were completely opposite and there was no way they could fit together. By saying this, my Lord, he not only condemns our good ways, but also us since we follow them."

The Judge frowned again at Faithful but turned back to Envy. "Anything else to add?"

"My Lord," Envy replied, "I could say so much more, but I don't want to bore the court. Perhaps once the others have given their testimony, if there is need for more to convict them, I will add to my testimony against him."

The Judge accepted this and asked Envy to stand by while the next witness, Superstition, was called forward and ordered to look at the prisoner. He was asked what he

---

[15] The descriptions of Envy, Superstition, and Pickthank are not from the originals, but have been added here to give a bit more depth to their characters.

could say against Faithful for their lord, the king, and then they swore him in.

Superstition smiled hesitantly at the crowd. He stood taller than anyone in the room, yet his build was slight enough that I suspected a gentle breeze might blow him over.

"My Lord," Superstition began in a piercing, yet shaky voice, "I don't really know this man all that well, nor do I desire to get to know him. However, I know this: he is a harmful man, dangerous to those around him. The other day I spoke with him in town, and he said our religion was nothing, and that by it no one could please God. Saying this, my Lord, your Lordship well knows what this really means. It means, of course, that our worship is worthless, and we remain in our sins. It also means that we will be damned." Looking around at the crowd as if to see if everyone had accepted his words, he nodded and said, "That is all I have to say."

Superstition nodded one more time, then returned to his seat as Pickthank[16] came forward. He was a tall man, well built, with a pleasant bearing about him. I could see he was not only someone easily liked, but there was something about him that left me wondering as to the genuineness of his character. When he reached his place, they swore him in and asked him what he had to say on behalf of their lord the king against the prisoner at the bar.

"My Lord," Pickthank began with a large, friendly smile, "and all the gentlemen of the court, I have known this man for a long time and heard him say things no one should ever say! He has complained against our noble prince Beelzebub and has spoken with contempt towards his honourable friends, the Lord Old Man, the Lord Carnal

---

[16] A *pickthank* is someone who meddles in other's affairs or tells people what they want to hear in order to gain favour.

Delight, the Lord Luxurious, the Lord Desire of Vain Glory, my old Lord Lechery,[17] Sir Having Greedy, along with all the rest of our nobility. This prisoner even said that if everyone thought as he thought, not one of these nobles would remain in this town. He hasn't even been afraid to complain against you, my Lord, the very one appointed as his judge! He's called you an ungodly villain, and he's thrown many demeaning and cruel insults at the other good men of our town, slandering them without restraint." With another large, friendly smile at everyone in the room, Pickthank said, "That is all I have to say to my friends in this court."

Once Pickthank had finished and returned to his seat, Lord Hate-good turned to Faithful and growled, "You fugitive! You heretic and traitor! Have you heard what these honest gentlemen have witnessed against you?"

With a great deal of respect and meekness, Faithful stepped forward once again. Maintaining a calm composure, he asked, "May I speak a few words in my defence?"

"Oh, your Majesty!"[18] the Judge shouted out, adding a mocking bow. "You deserve to die, to be killed immediately! But to show how gentle and kind we are towards you, let us hear what you have to say, you wicked apostate!"

Faithful stood confidently and prepared himself to give an answer for the hope within.[19] Addressing the judge, he began. "To begin, Lord Hate-good, I wish to respond

---

[17] *Lechery* is extreme sexual desire or lust.
[18] The original used the phrase, "Sirrah! Sirrah!" Sirrah is a term kind of like "Sir" but for those of lower status than you. It is used here as a term of disrespect. I think in our context, it would flow better to mock the person by disrespectfully and mockingly giving them a higher status as is in the rewrite above.
[19] 1 Pet. 3:15.

to Mr. Envy's word. I declare I said nothing but this: all rules, laws, customs, or people who stand against the Word of God are diametrically opposed to Christianity. If this is wrong, please convince me of my error, and if you do, I am ready at this moment to recant.

"As to a response to the second witness, Mr. Superstition, and his charge against me, I said only this: in true worship of God, there must be a true faith from God—a divine faith—but there can be no divine faith without a divine revelation of the will of God. Because of this, whatever is added into the worship of God that does not agree with divine revelation cannot be from divine faith, but must come from human faith. And human faith can never lead to eternal life.

"Finally, as to the testimony of Mr. Pickthank, I will not respond to his comments about how I am said to complain against people, but I will address another matter. Regarding the prince of this town and the rioters, and the prince's nobles named by Mr. Pickthank, they are more fit for hell than for this town and country." Squaring his shoulders and standing true to his faith in our Lord, Faithful concluded his defence by confidently declaring, "The Lord have mercy upon me!"

The Judge glared at Faithful for a long time, grinding his teeth and wringing his hands. The longer he stared, the more his eyes filled with hate, as if he wanted nothing more than to send Faithful to the gallows. But even so, Faithful remained unmoved. I watched my friend stand confidently in the grace of the Lord, ready for what was about to come.

Lord Hate-good turned angrily toward the jury who, all that time, had stood by, listening and observing. "Gentlemen of the jury!" the Judge began. "You see this man, and you see the uproar in our town because of him. You have also heard what these worthy men have witnessed against him, and you have heard his reply and his confession. It now falls to you to save his life or send him to the gallows, but before I leave it with you, let me remind you of our ancient laws."

Lord Hate-good pulled out a few papers, rustling through them until he found what he was looking for. He lifted a small sheet and read a little before a look of satisfaction washed over his face and a sinister smile crossed his lips. He cleared his throat and read, "There was an Act made in the days of Pharaoh the Great, servant of our prince, regarding men such as this. A threat arose among those of a contrary religion in that their numbers increased to where they could soon turn on the established rule. So that their numbers could not give them such strength, it was decreed that their young males be thrown into the river.

"Again, there was also an Act made in the days of Nebuchadnezzar the Great, another of our prince's servants, that whoever would not fall down and worship his golden image should be thrown into a fiery furnace.

"Finally," Lord Hate-good continued, "there was also an Act made in the days of Darius. This Act prevented anyone, for a time, to call on any god but him. If they disobeyed, they were to be cast into the lions' den.

"Now, the substance of these laws has been broken by this rebellious man, not only in his heart but also in word and deed. This is, of course, quite intolerable.[20]

"As for Pharaoh, his law was made upon the understanding that a threat may come, since no crime had yet been committed, but in our case, the crime is very real. For the second and third examples I have given, you see

---

[20] Exo. 1:22; Dan. 3:6; Dan. 6.

158

this rebellious man stands against our religion. For the treason he has confessed, he deserves to die!"

Upon the conclusion of Lord Hate-good's summary, the jury rose and left the room to deliberate. Their names were as follows: Mr. Blind-man, Mr. No-good, Mr. Malice, Mr. Love-lust, Mr. Live-loose, Mr. Heady, Mr. High-mind, Mr. Enmity, Mr. Liar, Mr. Cruelty, Mr. Hate-light, and Mr. Implacable.

We were not, of course, privileged to hear anything of their conversation, but later on, I learned they all decided against Faithful among themselves and then unanimously concluded to declare him guilty before the Judge.

The words of the jury in their private meeting were later published as follows:

The Individual Verdicts of the Most Honourable Jury

Mr. Blind-man (Foreman): I see clearly that this man is a heretic.

Mr. No-good: Away with such a fellow from the earth.

Mr. Malice: I agree with Mr. No-good, for I hate the sight of him.

Mr. Love-lust: I could never endure him.

Mr. Live-loose: Neither could I, for he would always condemn my ways.

Mr. Heady: Hang him! Hang him!

Mr. High-mind: He is a sorry scrub.[21]

---

[21] A *scrub* is a stunted tree and is here used as an insult towards Faithful. Rather than come up with an alternate insult, I kept *scrub* in this sentence since archaic insults are quite a lot of fun!

Mr. Enmity: He makes me so mad!

Mr. Liar: He is a rogue!

Mr. Cruelty: Hanging is too good for him.

Mr. Hate-light: Send him away!

Mr. Implacable: If I were offered the entire world to be friends with this man, I would not do it! Let us immediately declare him guilty of death!

We didn't have to wait long for them to reach their verdict, and they filed out from their Deliberation Room with hatred in their eyes, glaring at both of us, but Faithful especially.

Lord Hate-good, once they had seated themselves, asked them if they had reached a decision as to Faithful's guilt, and they stood as one and condemned my friend. Lord Hate-good smiled and ordered that Faithful be immediately taken from his place to a place where he could be put to the cruellest death anyone could imagine, according to their law.

A soldier grabbed my arms as if afraid I might come to my friend's aid, and I watched in horror as they pulled Faithful from beside me and dragged him out the door. Soldiers roughly pulled me along after the mob, and by the time I reached the streets, Faithful's shirt lay on the ground, torn from his body, his hands tied to a post. Unable to do anything but trust the Lord in this moment, I prayed for my friend as they whipped him, then beat him before a crowd desperate to satisfy their bloodlust.

When the beating stopped, they lanced his flesh with knives, then picked up stones and threw them at him while I wept, unable to do anything but pray, and pray I did as they drew their swords and stabbed him.

With the torture of my dear friend Faithful coming to an end, they tied his body to a stake, placed branches and logs at his feet, and burned his body to ashes, thus ending the life of my close friend and companion on this journey along the path.

I remained on my feet the entire time, an act to stand with my friend in his final moments. As the fire died, and he was gone, the crowd grew quiet and calmed, satisfied that they had gotten what they wanted. Some men set out immediately to clean up the mess, but before they took me away, as I stood there in my grief, I saw what no others could see. Behind the multitude of people, while Faithful was beaten and while he suffered, a chariot and two horses sat, waiting patiently. The chariot was fit for a king, designed with beauty in mind, but also ready for battle, the designs and armouring worked in gold and steel, the horses strong, snorting, stomping their feet, eager to charge forward wherever they might go.

This chariot and horses sat waiting for Faithful, sent by the One who loves us to retrieve my friend. At the moment the men who killed Faithful thought they had found victory over him, Faithful himself was taken up into the chariot, and immediately it carried him into the sky and through the clouds, with the sound of a trumpet proclaiming his passage, taking him through the nearest and most direct way to the Celestial Gate.

Brave Faithful, bravely done in word and deed;
Judge, witnesses, and jury have, instead
Of overcoming thee, but shown their rage:
When they are dead, thou'lt live from age to age.[22]

---

[22] In the New Heaven and New Earth {footnote from one edition}.

I watched as long as I could, and as I lost sight of Faithful's chariot in the clouds, I felt strong hands roughly grab my arms yet again and pull me back through the crowds. Instead of going back to the courtroom, however, for my own trial, they took me to my prison cell. They threw me inside, and I landed hard. Pulling myself up to a seated position, I turned around and watched as they slammed the door shut, locking it securely.

As I sat there in the cage alone, I could not help but think of my missing friend, but I found comfort in Christ as I prayed, seeking the Lord, my refuge, in my time of trouble.

The days wore on with no more abuse from the Judge or the leading men of the town. Instead, most seemed pleased to ignore me, and in time, he who overrules all things, having even the power of their rage in his own hand, brought about a day in which I escaped my little prison.

Once out, I quickly went on my way, and as I went, I sang,

> *Well, Faithful, thou hast faithfully profest*
> *Unto thy Lord; with whom thou shalt be blest,*
> *When faithless ones, with all their vain delights,*
> *Are crying out under their hellish plights:*
> *Sing, Faithful, sing, and let thy name survive;*
> *For though they kill'd thee, thou art yet alive!*

I made my way out of the town of Vanity, away from Vanity Fair and all its worldly temptations. At first, I struggled with the thought that I would travel alone, but then I found myself joined by another.

This young man went by the name of Hopeful, receiving that name after watching Faithful and my words and behaviour in our sufferings at the fair. He joined me, and once we had entered a brotherly covenant, he told me he would be my companion on the way.

Though I had lost one friend in his testimony to the truth, so another friend rose out of the ashes to be a companion on the path. Hopeful even encouraged me greatly, telling me that there were many more in the fair who would, in time, follow after.

10. Hopeful

I glanced back over my shoulder. The town of Vanity was still within sight behind Hopeful and me as we trudged on, but I turned back to focus on the road ahead, moving toward the place I had loved and sought for so long, and the place which Hopeful had only just come to seek. I struggled, however, to concentrate on the path as my heart and thoughts remained with Faithful, but I knew I could trust my Lord, and I knew as well that Faithful remained safe, having reached our destination before me.

Hopeful, the young man who had just joined me, was all smiles, yet I could see the apprehension in his eyes. Everything was so new and exciting, yet this was such a change. The Lord would care for him, though. I knew that for sure.

We pushed on for another hour, and before long, we overtook another man, going the same way as us. His name, we came to understand in time, was By-ends, but at first, he seemed unwilling to tell us this.

"Where are you from?" I asked. "And how long have you been on this path?"

The man smiled and spoke in a calm, deep, pleasant voice. "I come from the town of Fair-speech," he replied, "and I'm going to the Celestial City." I couldn't help but notice he left out his name.

"Fair-speech!" I said with a laugh. "Is there anything good that comes from that place?"[1]

"Yes," By-ends replied quickly, "I certainly hope so."

"And what may we call you?" I asked.

"Oh, I'm a stranger to you, and you to me. If you're walking this path, I'd be happy to walk with you, but if not, I'll be okay."

I found it interesting that he didn't tell us his name but decided to ask another question instead. "I've heard of this town of Fair-speech. If I remember right, it's a wealthy place."

"Oh, that it is!" By-ends confirmed. "I have many rich family members there."

"Who is your family, if I may ask?"

"Well," he replied with a laugh, "almost the whole town, actually! But some of my close family members are Lord Turn-about, and Lord Time-server. I'm also related to Lord Fair-speech himself, and, of course, the town itself was named after his ancestors. There's also Mr. Smooth-man, Mr. Facing-both-ways, Mr. Any-thing, oh, and the pastor of our church, Mr. Two-tongues—he was my mother's brother; they shared the same father." He smiled for a moment and gave a look of humility before adding, "To tell the truth, I myself have become quite a respected man in the town, although my grandfather was merely a

---

[1] Prov. 26:25.

waterman, looking one way and rowing another, and I've built up most of my wealth in the same occupation."

"Are you married?" I asked.

"Absolutely! My wife is a very moral woman, the daughter of a moral woman herself, Lady Feigning's daughter, actually. She comes from a very honourable family and is from such good heritage that she knows how to act around anyone—whether prince or peasant." He smiled again, but this time, it was more confident. "Now, it's true, we don't exactly follow along with a strict form of religion. In fact, we disagree with those who do, but only in two minor points. First, we never fight against the wind or the tide, and second, we prefer religion when it's in style... if I may, I mean to say that we prefer religion when it goes about in silver slippers.[2] We like to be in the thick of things with the people when they like religion, when it's easy, comfortable, and everyone cheers when we follow it."

Upon hearing this, I stepped a little closer to Hopeful, just out of earshot of our new companion. Whispering to my new friend, I said, "I suspect this is Mr. By-ends of Fair-speech. If this is true, we have perhaps the most dishonest man in the area walking with us."

"Well," Hopeful whispered back, "ask him. I can't imagine he'd be ashamed of his name."

I suspected that might be true, so I stepped back towards Mr. By-ends as we continued along the path. "Sir, you talk like you know more than the rest of us, and if I'm not mistaken, I think I know of you. Are you Mr. By-ends of Fair-speech?"

---

[2] The original speaks of religion that goes about in silver slippers which seems to mean a religion that's "cool", or better said, a religion that's currently in style. I've kept the *silver slippers* reference but adjusted the sentence to try to explain it better as this is not a common phrase for us today.

By-ends scowled at me and shook his head in disgust. "That's not my name! It's a nickname, given to me by people who don't like me." He took a deep breath and shook his head slowly yet again. "Sadly, I must be content to carry it around as a mark of shame as other good men have had to bear such things before me."

"You mean you've never given a reason for people to call you that?" I asked.

"Never!" By-ends growled. "The worst thing I've ever done that might have given them reason was that I always had the good fortune to figure out what's popular, whatever that might be at any point in time. It's served me very well. But if insults are cast on me because of this, I count them a blessing. I won't let malicious people get me down."

I nodded to myself, unsurprised by what I heard, and said to By-ends, "I thought you were him, and to be honest, I think this name fits you better than you think."

"Well, if that's what you believe, I can't do anything about it, but I think you'll still find me to be good company on the path." He frowned again and glanced sideways at me before adding, "If you'll put up with me."

I took a deep breath and laid it out for him. "If you travel with us, you must fight against both the wind and the tide! But... I think that's not the kind of thing you like to do, By-ends. You must also embrace religion not only when it's in style, as you say, when it wears silver slippers, but also when it wears nothing but rags. You'll need to stand by it, too, not only when it walks the streets to the sound of applause, but when it's bound in chains, hated by all."

By-ends shook his head vigorously. "Don't force your ways and opinions on me!" he growled. "And don't you look down on my personal faith! Leave me to my freedom to live out my beliefs as I see fit… and let me walk with you along this path."

I came to a halt and shook my head. I would not play those games. "Not one more step, By-ends, unless you're willing to walk this path as we walk it."

By-ends clenched his fists and stomped his foot. "I will never desert my principles! They're harmless, and they give me what I want. If I can't travel with you, then I must travel as I did before you caught up to me, by myself until someone catches up to me who enjoys my company!"

"And in that, we agree," I said. I nodded to Hopeful, and we left him behind, moving on so his compromise would not burden us.

But as we travelled, after another hour or so, Hopeful looked back and saw three men following behind Mr. By-ends. When they reached him, By-ends bowed deeply to them with great formality, and they also returned the gesture.

Although they walked much too far behind us to hear their words, I later learned who they were and what they spoke of with one another.

The men who joined By-ends were named Mr. Hold-the-world, Mr. Money-love, and Mr. Save-all. All these men had known each other previously, for when they were children, they had attended the same school, taught by Mr. Gripe-man, a schoolmaster in Love-gain, which is a market town in the county of Coveting up in the north.

This schoolmaster taught them the art of getting what they want, whether by violence, deceit, flattery, lying, or by pretending to be religious. And these four students of his learned a great deal from him, so much so that each of these men could have become schoolmasters themselves.

And this is the conversation I learned they had with one another:

The four men greeted one another, and then Mr. Money-love asked Mr. By-ends, "Who are those people ahead of us?"

"They are a couple of foreigners who, in their own way, are on pilgrimage."

"Oh, that's too bad that they're so far ahead," Mr. Money-love replied. "Why didn't they stay back so they can walk with us? It might have been nice to travel together, since we're all on a pilgrimage."

By-ends shook his head. "We're all on a pilgrimage, that's for sure, but the men ahead of us are rigid in their beliefs. They love their own ideas and look down on what everyone else thinks. They believe no one's godly enough to walk with them unless they agree with them in everything."

"I'm sorry to hear that," Save-all said. "But we've read of that kind of thing. There are those who are so overly righteous that their rigidness leads them to judge and condemn everyone except themselves. What things did you disagree on, and how many things?"

By-ends laughed. "They're so headstrong. They think the right thing to do is to rush forward on the path in any kind of weather." He smiled and shook his head. "As for me, I'm more for waiting for wind and tide—I don't want to push myself on in rain or snow or darkness. They're for risking all for God at any moment, but I'm more for taking advantage of everything I can to keep

170

myself and that which I own safe and secure. They're for holding onto their ideas and beliefs, even when everyone else disagrees, but I like a religion that fits with the times, one that allows me to be safe and secure." He laughed again. "They're even for religion when it leaves them in rags and when they have to suffer the contempt and hatred of other people! Can you imagine that? That's not for me! I'd rather stick with a religion when it goes about in silver slippers, when it's fashionable and in style. I like religion when it moves forward in the sunshine and leads everyone to cheer when we follow it."

"Wow! I agree with you completely!" Mr. Hold-the-world exclaimed. "And don't you budge on any of that, Mr. By-ends. In my opinion, a man's a fool if he can keep what he has but is so unwise as to lose it. Let us be wise as serpents. It's best to make hay when the sun shines. You see how the bee lies still all winter and then only rises when it can enjoy the weather while making honey! God sometimes sends rain and sometimes sunshine. If they are such fools that they wish to go through the first, let us be content to take the fair weather. Personally, I like religion that stands with the security of God's blessings. I mean, anyone with half a brain can reason that if God gives us good things, we should keep them for God's sake! Abraham and Solomon grew rich in religion, and Job says that a good man will lay up gold as dust.[3] But a good man should never be like those men ahead of us, if they're the way you described them."

Save-all smiled and patted By-ends on the shoulder. "I think we're all together on this issue, so we don't need to keep on about it."

"I agree," Money-love added. "We can drop the matter. Those who neither believe Scripture nor reason don't know their own freedom or care for their own safety.

---

[3] Job 22:24-25.

We have both Scripture and reason on our side. Let's be content with that."

"My friends," By-ends replied with an enormous smile, "we're all on this journey together, pilgrims on the same road. To help get our eyes off the bad things, let me ask you all a question." He took a deep breath and collected his thoughts before laying it out for his friends. "Suppose there's a man, a minister, or a tradesman, or whatever, and he has an opportunity, a chance to grab hold of the good blessings of this life. But, as he examines the opportunity, he realizes that the only way he can get what he wants is to, at least on the surface, become very zealous, very driven in some areas of religion, areas he'd never even gotten involved in before. Can he still maintain his integrity if he uses these means—to pretend to be zealous—to gain what he wants? Will he still be an honest man?"

"I see where you're going with this," Money-love replied, "and if the others are okay with it, I'll try to answer." When no one objected, he launched into his response. "Just to comment first of all about this issue specifically regarding the minister you mentioned, suppose this minister, an honourable man, serves in a church where they simply don't pay him well, and the home they give him to live in is small.[4] This minister, however, has his heart set on a larger wage and home, and he figures out how he can get it. All he needs to do is study harder, preach more frequently and passionately, and because the people want him to, adjust some of his principles. Personally, I don't see any reason he shouldn't do this, provided God has called him to that church. In fact, I think he can do a lot more than that and still be an honest man. Here are four reasons I think this is so:

---

[4] The original refers to a *benefice*, which are the benefits such as a property or income attacked to a position in a church (pastor/vicar).

First, his desire for a larger wage and property is lawful—you can't disagree with that—since it's set before him by Providence, God's provision and care. Because of that, he can pursue and get it if he's able without hurting his conscience.

Second, to add to this, his desire to have a greater income and property leads him to be more studious and a more zealous preacher, which means he's an all-round, better man. It actually makes him improve himself, which is what God wants.

Third, if he changes some of his principles to serve his people better and fit with what they want, it shows that he's a self-denying person, he's a likeable guy, and he's definitely a good fit as a minister.

Fourth, to bring it all together, for a minister to set aside the small benefit for the great benefit should never cause him to be seen as a covetous man, instead since he's improved himself and his work, he should be perceived as one who pursues his calling, going after the opportunities that lie before him!

"And now, to the second part of the question, about the tradesman you mentioned… suppose he has a poor job. Now, this tradesman realizes that by becoming religious, he can fix his job situation, maybe get a rich wife, and get better customers—and more of them. I don't see any reason he can't properly do this, and here are three reasons I think that:

First, to become religious is a good thing, a virtuous thing. It doesn't really matter why.

Second, it's also not illegal to marry a rich woman, nor is it bad to find new customers.

Finally, someone who gets these things by becoming religious, gets good things by becoming good himself! So, he gets a good wife, good customers, and good gain… all of this by becoming religious, which is also good. Put it all together and you see that to become religious and to get good things is, simply put, good."

Everyone smiled and agreed with Money-love, seeing it as exactly the answer they wanted, and pleased to know that this kind of thing was good and beneficial. Figuring no one could possibly disagree or raise any arguments against it, they agreed to challenge Hopeful and me, since we were still within sight, with the question, as soon as they could catch up to us—especially since we had opposed Mr. By-ends earlier.

So, they called after us, and we stopped, waiting for them to catch up. But as By-ends and the others rushed forward, they decided that By-ends should not be the one to raise the challenge, thinking that there might be some left-over animosity between By-ends and the two of us. Instead, Mr. Hold-the-world was to bring forward the question.

Hopeful and I waited patiently for By-ends and his three new companions to catch up. I didn't know what to expect from them, but if they were anything like By-ends, their hearts would not be humble towards the Lord of the City to which we travelled.

When they reached us, they quickly offered a greeting, and then one man, Mr. Hold-the-world, asked if he could ask a question, challenging us to answer if we could.

We agreed, and he smiled before saying, "Suppose there's a man, or two men, rather. One is a minister, the other a tradesman. Suppose these men have an opportunity to grab hold of the good blessings of life, but the only way to gain them is to become zealous in certain aspects of religion. Can these men still maintain their integrity as honest men if they use this means to gain what they want?"

I nearly shook my head in disappointment, but took a deep breath, paused, and got right to it. "Even a brand-new believer could answer ten thousand questions like this. If it's wrong to follow Christ for bread, as we see in the sixth chapter of John, how much more wicked is it to make yourself and your faith nothing more than a pretense of genuine belief to gain the world? No one, other than heathens, hypocrites, devils, and witches could think such a thing! Let me explain why:

First, consider the heathens, Hamor and Shechem. They had their eye on the daughter of Jacob and on his cattle. Seeing that there was no way to get what they wanted except to become circumcised, they said to their companions, 'If every male among us is circumcised, just as these people are circumcised, won't their cattle, their things, and every beast they own be ours?' So, they wanted Jacob's daughter and his cattle, and they used Jacob's religion as a means to get what they wanted. You should read the entire story![5]

Second, consider the hypocritical Pharisees as well! They also took this approach to religion. They set out to take widows' houses, and they tried to get them by long prayers. Their judgement was greater damnation from God![6]

Third, Judas, the devil, also tried this! He was religious so that he could get the money bag, taking from

---

[5] Gen. 34:20-23.
[6] Luk. 20:46-47.

what was inside, but he was lost, cast away, and was the very son of perdition![7]

Fourth, Simon, the sorcerer,[8] was of this religion as well. He tried to get the Holy Spirit in order to gain money, and Peter sentenced him according to his sin![9]

Fifth, anyone willing to take up religion so that he might gain the world will just as quickly throw it away, also for the world. Just as Judas walked away from the world in his attempt to be religious, so also did he sell his religion and his Master for the world."

As I came to a stop, I shook my head at the men, all lost in their deception. "To think you can do this, Mr. Hold-the-world, as I believe you do, and to think that such a practice is authentic faith is heathenish, hypocritical, and devilish." Looking intently at the man, I poked my finger right into his chest and declared, "Your reward will be according to your works."[10]

The four men stared at one another in shock, and not one had it in them to respond. As they stood there at a loss for words, Hopeful stepped up next to me, nodding his agreement with what I said.

Finally, I turned with Hopeful, and we walked on. Glancing back, I saw By-ends and his friends resume their journey, but they stumbled as they walked, falling well behind, leaving Hopeful and me to move on beyond them.

Turning to Hopeful, I said, "If these men can't stand up to the sentence of men, what will they do when God sentences them? If they're speechless when vessels of

---

[7] John 12:6; 17:12.
[8] The original calls Simon a *witch*.
[9] Acts 8:19-22.
[10] 2 Cor. 5:10.

clay put them in their place, what will they do when rebuked by the flames of a devouring fire?"

We moved on, grateful to leave such stubbornness behind.

11. Doubting Castle

e walked on, happy to be away from By-ends and his friends. The path ahead continued in its straight line through this area, as it always did, but small hills rose throughout this area, leading us to climb up and down as we followed the path. We carried on like this for the rest of the day, and it wasn't until late morning on the next day that the land levelled out and opened into a new area.

We stepped out onto a beautiful grassy plain, the ground mostly flat before us and to the left and the right. The sun shone brightly that morning, hummingbirds alighted onto the branches of small bushes, and bees hovered over the plentiful flowers blanketing the land. The peaceful plain before us had been named Ease, and that it certainly was, providing a welcome respite after so much difficulty.

With each step through this land, our smiles grew larger, and I felt every tense muscle in my body slowly relax. The ground felt soft beneath our feet, and the air was sweet and calming. Sadly, we crossed the entire narrow plain in less than two hours, finding ourselves leaving the area sooner than we wanted.

As we came to the end of that short but welcome time, we came upon a hill named Lucre, just off to the side of the path.[1] I had heard of that hill and much about it. In that hill, a mine had been dug, a silver mine. The entrance to the mine was a little way off the path itself, just out of sight, unless you left the path and moved around the side of the hill.

The mine had been there for many years. Since it was such a rare thing, this silver mine, some pilgrims travelling along the way had stepped aside to see it, to take a quick look, but each one suffered for it. As they had approached the pit leading down into the silver mine, the ground, being weak in that area, crumbled. Many of those who fell died in that place, while others were maimed, unable to move and walk on their own ever again.

As we passed by the area of the path where many men had left to see the mine, we caught sight of a man, just by the mouth of the mine. His name was Demas, meaning one who is a gentleman, and he often made a habit of calling to pilgrims, which he did that day as we passed by.

"Hello there, friends!" Demas called. "Hello there, Pilgrims! Why don't you come over here so I can show you something?"

I stared at the man in shock, standing far off our path, and asked the only thing I could think of. "What could possibly be so great that it would lead us to step off the path?"

"Well," Demas replied with a laugh, "that's easy! It's a silver mine, and you can dig here for treasure. If you come, it won't take much work, and you'll be rich!"

---

[1] *Lucre* is a word for money, but especially for money gained through improper means.

Hopeful smiled and took a step forward, a look of desire on his face. "Let's go check it out!"

I shook my head and put my hand up, hoping to make him rethink. "Not me. I've heard of this place. Many people have died here. Besides, treasure, riches, wealth… it's all a trap for those who go after it. It hinders them along the path." Calling out to Demas, I asked, "Isn't this place dangerous? Hasn't it hindered many on their pilgrimage?"[2]

Demas laughed again. "No… not dangerous at all, except if you're careless!" But as he spoke, his face blushed a deep shade of red.

Turning to my friend, I put my hand on his arm. "Hopeful, let's stick to the path and keep on our way."

Hopeful nodded quickly, but added, "I bet By-ends, when he reaches this point, will step aside if invited to do so."

"No doubt," I replied. "His principles lead him in that direction, and I bet a hundred to one, he'll die there."

"Won't you come?" Demas cried out again as we spoke to one another.

I turned back to the man and shouted, "Demas! You're an enemy to the holy ways of the Lord of the path! You've already been condemned for turning aside by one of his Majesty's judges,[3] so why try to bring us into your own condemnation? Besides, if we turn aside, our Lord and King will hear of it, and when we hope to stand boldly before him, he'll put us to shame."

"But," Demas called back, "I'm one of your brothers! I'm a pilgrim too! If you only stay for a short while, I'll walk with you!"

---

[2] Hos. 14:8.
[3] 2 Tim. 4:10.

"What's your name?" I called back. "It's what I've been calling you, isn't it?"

"Yes, my name is Demas. I'm a son of Abraham."

"I know you! Gehazi was your great-grandfather, and Judas your father, and you have walked in their ways.[4] This is a devilish thing you do, Demas, in trying to pull us away! Your father was hanged as a traitor, and you deserve nothing better. Know this for sure, when we reach our King, we will tell him what you're doing."

We turned away from him and moved on, leaving that treacherous man behind.

By this time, By-ends and his friends had nearly caught up to us, and when they reached that area, they heard Demas's call. At the first invitation, they went over to him, seeking what he offered.

Now, I don't know if they fell into the pit by looking over the edge, or if they went down to dig, or if at the bottom of the pit the mists that commonly arise in those places smothered them, but one thing I know, after that day… no one ever saw them again on the path.

Then I sang the following song:

> *By-ends and silver Demas both agree;*
> *One calls, the other runs, that he may be*
> *A sharer in his lucre; so these do*
> *Take up in this world, and no further go.*

We pushed on, grateful to have passed temptation, but struggling as well, knowing the pull towards wealth and the riches of the world was strong.

On the other side of the hill named Lucre, rocks, ruts, and potholes littered the path ahead, along with loose

---

[4] 2 Kings 5:20-27; Matt. 26:14-15; 27:1-5.

gravel. With the plain called Ease behind us, there seemed to be no relief for our feet with the hard rock path, the loose stones, and the rise and fall of the land. The sun also beat down on us, and we found ourselves not only sweating terribly, but the back of my neck felt like it was burning under the sun's hot rays.

With the hill named Lucre far behind and the path still difficult and hard on our feet, we came to something new. An old monument stood just on the side of the path.

We both stopped on the path, staring open-mouthed at what stood before us. The shape and design… the builders had formed it in an unusual manner, and both our hearts felt troubled by what we saw.

It appeared to be a pillar of some sort, but one that had once perhaps resembled a woman. However, as much as we each stared at the object, and despite how long we examined it, we couldn't seem to make sense of what it was.

"Wait, what's that?" Hopeful asked, stepping forward, his eyes focused on some point high on the pillar. He stretched out, pushing himself up on his toes as if to get as tall as he could, and he put his hand to his forehead to shield his eyes from the sun's glare.

"What do you see up there?" I asked, stepping up close to him.

"Up there," he said, pointing to the top of the monument. "Right up above what I think might be her head. It's a plaque, but the wording is strange and…" He shook his head and laughed, "I'm no scholar Christian. You've spent a great deal of time studying in years past. Can you make it out?"

I copied my friend, standing on my toes to get a little closer to it, and shielded my eyes from the sun as I looked for it. Sure enough, I saw it. The wording was indeed strange, but after a few moments, I managed to put it together. "It reads…" I said slowly, going over the words one more time to be sure, "Remember Lot's wife."

"Ahh," Hopeful said loudly. "So that's it! This was Lot's wife. She was turned into a pillar of salt because she looked back with a heart full of coveting as she fled to safety from Sodom!"[5]

My mouth dropped open as understanding flooded my heart. "Wow! This is well-timed! And just after Demas tried to pull us away from the path to pursue the wealth of this world!" I closed my eyes in gratitude to the Lord for his grace and whispered, "If we'd fallen to Demas's temptation—as you had wanted to, Hopeful—we might have been turned into a monument just like this woman. Everyone who passed by this way would have seen us as the warning not to fall away."

Hopeful's shoulders dropped, and he hung his head in shame, remaining silent for a moment. I hadn't meant to hurt him, but we needed to be careful. If nothing else, this sight proved that very well.

When he finally spoke, his voice came out with humility. "I am sorry, Christian. I was foolish. Very foolish. It's a wonder that I didn't end up just like Lot's wife. Truly, what's the difference between her sin and mine? She only looked back, but I wanted to go see." My friend turned to me, the tears in his eyes a testament to his repentance. "I love God's grace, for I have no hope without it. I'm ashamed that this desire even entered my heart."

I put my hand on his shoulder and squeezed tightly. "We both must pay attention to what we see here, Hopeful. This is a good thing for us, something to help us as we continue along the path. This woman escaped one

5 Gen. 19:26.

judgement, the destruction of Sodom, but she was destroyed by another, turned into a pillar of salt."

"I agree," Hopeful said. "She can be an example to us, but also a reminder, a grave warning for the future. We must turn away from her sin, or we'll become a sign for others, a sign of judgement for those who don't pay attention to this warning. You know, this reminds me of Korah, Dathan, and Abiram, and their two hundred and fifty men. They all perished in their sin and became an example to others."[6]

I could see he had more to say, but he hesitated. Something bothered him, but differently than his failing and even the warning itself. "What is it, Hopeful?"

He took a deep breath. "It's… it's just this, Christian. Beyond all of that, there's something I don't understand."

"What is it?"

"It's Demas and his friends…" He looked back toward the hill named Lucre and frowned, his eyes full of grief. "How…" he began, but then stopped. When he spoke again, his voice shook with his grief. "How do they stand there so confidently, looking for that treasure, when this woman, who only looked behind her—in fact, from what we read in Scripture, she didn't step even one foot out of the way—was turned into a pillar of salt? And to add to it, they stand within sight of this pillar, the proof of the judgement which overtook her, making her an example. They just have to glance over here to see the judgement that befell this woman, yet… they aren't punished like her, nor do they have any fear!"

"It certainly makes you wonder," I replied slowly. "I think… I think it suggests that their hearts have grown

---

[6] Num. 26:9-10.

desperate in their desire for wealth. To be honest, I can't figure out who to properly compare them with. It's like a pickpocket stealing in the presence of a judge, or maybe a cutpurse, robbing people under the gallows. It's said that the people of Sodom were extreme sinners because they were sinners before the Lord, even though he'd shown such kindness to them in making the land of Sodom like the garden of Eden.[7] Because of this kindness shown to them, his wrath was even greater in that they pushed him to jealousy, and he made the judgement as hot as the fire of the Lord out of heaven could make it! I think, then, Hopeful, that it makes sense that men such as Demas and his friends who sin, despite the example of someone like Lot's wife continually set before them, warning them not to do this… I think you'll find, in the end, these men will receive the most severe judgement."

"I know you're right," Hopeful replied. "It's a mercy, a great mercy, that neither of us—especially me—are made an example like this. This definitely gives us reason to thank God, to fear him, and to always remember Lot's wife!"

I wrapped my arms around Hopeful and gave him a tight squeeze, hoping to encourage him before we set out again. After a few moments, I let him go, smiled at him to remind him of the Lord's grace, and we left the monument behind while keeping its warning close to our hearts.

As we walked on, we left the riches of the world behind and set our sights on what lay ahead.

Now, not far from the pillar, the path smoothed out, the ground becoming level with fewer rocks to stumble over. Once again, we found ourselves walking along a pleasant path next to a river. The water flowed gently in this area, pure and clear as glass. As we walked,

---

[7] Gen. 13:10, 13.

we stopped and drank from the water, finding strength and encouragement in its refreshment. David himself had called that river "the river of God," but John had called it "the river of the water of life."[8]

We enjoyed our time there greatly, not only because of the river but also because of the trees. On either side of the path, green trees grew, and on them we found many kinds of fruit—even the leaves were good for medicine. So, we enjoyed ourselves as we ate the fruit, and used the leaves to ease our various aches and pains from the long journey.

On either side of the river lay a meadow filled with beautiful lilies. The meadow remained green all year long, and we took advantage of its beauty, lying down and resting, and even falling asleep among the flowers, knowing that in that place we were safe.

When we awoke, we didn't return to our journey, not immediately. Instead, we drank from the river, gathered fruit, and then laid down to sleep yet again.[9] When we awoke the second time, we still didn't carry on, but remained. In the end, we stayed for several days and nights.

Our hearts satisfied and filled with joy, we sang this song:

> *Behold ye how these crystal streams do glide,*
> *To comfort pilgrims by the highway side;*
> *The meadows green, beside their fragrant smell,*
> *Yield dainties for them; and he that can tell*
> *What pleasant fruit, yea, leaves, these trees do yield,*
> *Will soon sell all, that he may buy this field.*

After many days, we found ourselves fully rested and ready to get back on our journey. In fact, more than

---

[8] Ps. 65:9; Rev. 22; Ezek. 47.
[9] Ps. 23:2; Isa. 14:30.

just ready, we were excited to travel the path again, moving steadily closer to our goal, the Celestial City.

So, we ate and drank again and then set out, travelling along the path, the beautiful, pleasant river running along beside us. We enjoyed those days. The calming sound of the water gently flowing by as we walked along was a constant gift from the Creator, leaving us refreshed and ready to move on to what the Lord of the way had next in store for us.

Sadly, it wasn't long before the river turned away from the path. The moment I saw this, I silently grieved to lose not only the beauty, but the chance for constant refreshment. Although we wished to stay by the water, neither of us were willing to leave the path, so we pushed on, leaving the river behind us.

The ground eventually grew rockier, and the soil under our feet was no longer soft. I felt my foot slip just a little on the uneven ground and steadied myself by grabbing Hopeful's shoulder.

With each step, more ruts, cracks, and stones added to the journey's difficulty, and my feet once again ached. A quick glance at my friend let me know I wasn't the only one struggling with sore feet. As the day wore on, hour after hour of a hard path, our discouragement only grew,[10] and although we wished for a better path to walk, nothing would stop us from continuing forward.

In this area of difficulty, on our left, a stone wall ran alongside the path, solid and thick, and just low enough for us to look over, but too high to climb. Now and then I leaned up against it for support, but eventually, I stretched up on my toes enough to see what might be on the other

---

[10] Num. 21:4

side, more out of curiosity than anything else. What I saw caught my attention immediately!

On the other side, a beautiful meadow spread out for miles, flowing over low, rolling hills, covered with flowers. When Hopeful saw me staring open-mouthed at the sight, he stretched up as well to see, and he pointed out a herd of deer, grazing peacefully in the distance without fear or concern.

We smiled at the sight but returned to our journey. As much as we enjoyed the beauty and the peace of what we saw, we had more important things on our minds.

Our feet, however, continued to ache on the rock-strewn path, and the terribly uneven, difficult path ahead only made our journey worse as the longing grew for softer ground. With each step, the peaceful meadow on the other side of the wall felt more attractive. I wiped the sweat from my forehead yet again, and nearly complained, when the words caught in my mouth.

Ahead, a small structure sat, built up against the wall. I picked up my pace in my curiosity, nearly hobbling by this point, with Hopeful calling after me, trying to find out what had caught my attention.

When I reached it, I couldn't help but smile. It was just what we needed.

"What is it, Christian? Is there danger?"

I pointed at the steps built right up against the wall, leading up and over, into the well-named By-path Meadow.

"Hopeful! It's a stile, leading into the meadow! We can climb over here and walk along the path, just on the other side of the wall." I took the first step up and peered over to get a better view. "Look! A path runs on the other side, just like ours. It's exactly what I was hoping for! This will be much easier. Let's climb over!"

Hopeful took a step back and furrowed his brow. "But what if this other path leads us out of the way?"

I laughed. "Not likely! Look at it! It runs parallel with our own path, straight as an arrow!"

Hopeful hesitated for another moment, but then smiled, agreeing to go over. I felt it was certainly the most reasonable option, and I was pleased to see him on board with it. I scrambled over to the other side, and my friend quickly joined me.

Once on the other side, I immediately felt so much better, and my feet on this new path didn't hurt as much. We also made good progress, and it wasn't long before we found another traveller who had taken the easier path as well.

He was not far ahead of us, so I called out to him and asked, "Sir, what's your name?"

"Vain-confidence," he called back.

"Where does this path lead?"

The man smiled back at us and replied, "To the Celestial Gate!"

Turning to Hopeful, I matched Vain-confidence's smile. "See? Didn't I tell you? Now we know for sure that we're on the right path!"

So we followed the man at a distance, content to walk just the two of us for a time, enjoying the beautiful meadow, the easy path, and good company.

After a few hours, the light faded, but we pushed on. We found our journey on the soft grass to be so easy, it was not difficult to keep going. When the sun finally did set, however, the moon and the stars offered little light for us, and we found ourselves nearly blind in the dark, so much so that it wasn't long before we couldn't even make out Vain-confidence ahead in the darkness.

"Careful of your footing here, Christian," Hopeful said to me in the dark. We held hands so we wouldn't lose sight of one another as we walked, but in the dark, we had no other option but to push forward. Next to me, I heard Hopeful say, "I can't see Vain-confidence anymore."

"Neither can I," I began. "I wonder if he…"

A terrible scream stopped us in our tracks as it echoed out across the meadow in the darkness, cutting off my words. Without a doubt, I knew it was the sound of Vain-confidence falling into a deep pit.[11] We dared not move, unsure of what to do in the darkness.

Later on our journey, I learned that the Prince of that land had dug that pit on purpose to catch arrogant fools, and I also learned that poor Vain-confidence was dashed to pieces in his fall, but at the time, we knew nothing more than he'd fallen.

But there, in that meadow, standing in the darkness, unaware of all that had transpired, with my heart beating so hard I was sure Hopeful could hear it in my chest, we held our ground, afraid to take another step out of fear of what lay ahead. Calling out, hoping for a response, I cried, "Vain-confidence? Vain-confidence? Are you okay? Is all well?"

We waited, leaning forward in the dark, hoping we might catch a reply, but all we heard was a distant groan of a man in agony.

"What…?" Hopeful began. At first, he sounded like he couldn't even come up with a question to ask. After a few deep breaths, in a sad voice filled with regret, he

---

[11] Isa. 9:16.

asked the very question growing in my mind. "Where are we?" he whispered.

Shame washed over me, and I couldn't even open my mouth to answer. I had not only led my friend into danger, but away from our King's path.

While we stood there in silence, unsure of where to go or what to do, a great thunderstorm arose. The rain beat down in sheets, filling our boots almost immediately, and lightning flashed so brightly, it lit up the sky and all around us. The wind picked up, too, and the water quickly flowed around our feet, rising higher and higher. We had to act quickly or else we'd be swept away in the flood!

"Oh," Hopeful groaned, barely audible above the storm, "if only I'd stayed on the path!"

"Who could have known?" I replied, nearly shouting to make myself heard. "Who would have imagined this meadow would lead us away from our own path?"

"I was afraid of this," Hopeful shouted back. "Right away when you spoke of it, I was afraid. That's why I gently cautioned you." He groaned and then added. "I would have been blunter, but you're older than I am."

I hung my head, the rain pouring down my neck and the water rising around my feet. "My brother, please don't be angry. I'm so sorry. I'm so sorry that I led you out of the way and that I've put you in such danger. Please forgive me, Hopeful. I wasn't trying to do anything wrong."

"It's okay, Christian," Hopeful shouted as he put his hands firmly on my shoulders and squeezed tight. "Relax. I forgive you. And… I trust this will turn out for good."

192

I felt a weight fall off my shoulders and smiled at Hopeful, only visible because of a flash of lightning. Shouting to get above the growing storm, I called, "I'm glad I have you, Hopeful. I'm glad I have such a merciful brother like you with whom to walk this path." But standing up straight, I felt the floodwaters around my feet and remembered our situation. We didn't have the time to stand around and talk. "Hopeful! We can't stay here! Let's try to make it back to the path!"

"Let me go first," Hopeful said, offering to take the risk of travelling that dangerous road in the dark.

"No," I replied. "If you'll let me, I'll go first. If there's any danger, I should be the one to face it." With an embarrassed laugh, I added, "It's my fault we're in this mess and that we've left the path."

Hopeful shook his head, firmly telling me, "No! You won't go first. You're upset. You could easily end up leading us out of the way again."

As much as I didn't like it, I saw the wisdom in what he said, but before we could set out, the Lord, the Master of the way, encouraged us with these words, echoing out above the wind and the rain: "Consider well the highway, the road by which you went. Return!"[12]

So, we set out, with Hopeful in the lead, and me, following close on his heels.

In the dark, Hopeful struggled to keep on the way, and with the water flowing up and over our feet, path or meadow or uneven ground all looked the same. The waters had risen enough that it had passed the height of our boots, but still we pushed on, the danger increasing by the second as the water rose, bit by bit, threatening to pull us down and under with every step.

---

[12] Jer. 31:21.

"I see now, Hopeful," I shouted to be heard above the sound of the wind. "I see… I understand."

"What do you understand, my brother?" Hopeful shouted back as he pushed forward. Despite how hard he hollered, I still struggled to make out his words.

"I understand now, Hopeful, that it's easier to leave the path and go out of the way when we are on it than to go back once we've left."

Hopeful didn't reply, but I wasn't surprised. It was difficult enough to keep our footing without the conversation.

We pushed on for a little longer, but in the darkness, with the floodwaters gathering higher and higher, we knew we'd never make it back to the stile that night without drowning nine or ten times over! So we looked for shelter, somewhere out of the rain and rising water. At first, we couldn't find anything, but then, in one of the flashes of lightning, Hopeful spotted a small hill with an outcrop of rock hanging out and over the ground.

We rushed towards it as fast as we could, nearly losing our footing again and again against the rising water until we reached the bottom of the hill. I pushed Hopeful up the first few steps, and once he had solid footing, he reached back and pulled me to safety. Once out of the flood, we scrambled up the side of the slippery rock until we reached the outcrop, hanging over the hill just enough to give a little shelter from the rain. We crawled under and held close to one another, trying to warm ourselves and fight down the shivers.

As the storm raged on, seemingly without end, we had no other choice but to settle in there for the night, waiting until morning, huddled out of the rain. As we sat there, we tried to stay awake, fighting hard to keep our eyes open, but the exhaustion quickly overtook us, and we each fell asleep.

Unfortunately, in hindsight, we learned the problem was much bigger than we had thought. Sure, we had strayed from the path, and now our lives were in danger from the storm, but another threat existed, another danger. Unknown to us, we had trespassed on the land of a wicked and dangerous man.

No… that wasn't true. Not a man. He was certainly *not* a man.

"WAKE UP!"

I jumped and hit my head on the rock above and knocked over an equally startled Hopeful. Focusing on what lay before me, I saw a large man, towering above us, three times the height of either Hopeful or myself. He wore thick, rough clothing, alternating between dingy woolens and leathers, scuffed, torn, and dirty. His tunic clung tightly to his enormous belly, and his massive hands were gnarled and rough, as if he'd been in countless fights. His face matched his clothing, with a ragged beard and rough skin surrounding a mouth formed in a toothy snarl.

"Who are you, and why are you on my land?" he hollered, his booming voice echoing across the plains.

"We're pilgrims," I exclaimed in my fear, blinking my eyes awake. "We've lost our way and are trying to find our path again."

He ground his teeth and shook his head. "You've trespassed on my property, trampling my fields and lying on my land." Pausing, he examined us each closely as his frown slowly turned into a smile. The change in expression felt far more terrifying to me. In a quiet, deep voice, he said, "Because of your trespass, you'll be coming with me!"

Without another word, he grabbed us and pushed us ahead of him, not back toward the path, but deeper into the giant's land. Hopeful and I wanted to challenge him, but we couldn't think of anything to say, because the truth was, we were at fault.

In time, we learned we had trespassed on the land belonging to Giant Despair. He owned a castle, quite far from where we'd slept, and in the early morning, he'd gone out to walk through his fields. That was when he found us sleeping on his land.

He shoved me hard, and I stumbled forward. Our march with the Giant behind us felt like it lasted for hours as we ran, fell, helped one another up, and continued on, all to the sound of the Giant's threats. At no point during our trek did we see any opportunity to escape, and certainly no chance for rest. The giant growled and roared with each step and allowed no time to even catch our breath as he pushed us up and over hill after hill and down into valley after valley.

It was upon the top of one of the taller hills that we first caught sight of what would soon become our prison. A stone castle, dark, old, covered in vines and moss, stood less than a mile from us, and upon seeing his home, the giant pushed us even harder.

When we reached the gate, he grabbed us, one in each hand, and shouldered his way through the door into a large courtyard overgrown with weeds, thorns, and thistles. He dragged us through the courtyard, and on the other side, he kicked open a door and half carried, half dragged us down stone steps until we had descended deep into the earth. The smell of mould, filth, and rotting flesh filled our nostrils, and I gagged while Hopeful coughed. At the bottom of the stairs, he took us through an open doorway and threw us onto a pile of old clothes and bones before, without so much as a word, he turned and left, pulling the door closed behind him. A moment later, we heard a loud *click*.

With the door locked tight, we were plunged into darkness in a nasty place reeking of death and decay. Our spirits immediately fell, lost as we were in darkness.[13]

In our cell, we lay from Wednesday morning until Saturday night, without bread, water, or light. No one came to see us in all that time, not even to confirm how we were doing. I couldn't even write in my journal, as I didn't have enough light to see my hand before my face, let alone the quill and paper. Under so much earth and darkness, we felt the weight of our terrible plight, without friends or even acquaintances aside from one another.

Laying in that dungeon, I felt far worse than Hopeful. Not that his situation was any better than mine, but I knew it was because of my poor leadership that we were left in such a place.

The pilgrims now, to gratify the flesh,
Will seek its ease; but oh! how they afresh
Do thereby plunge themselves new griefs into!
Who seek to please the flesh, themselves undo.

Now, Giant Despair had a wife named Diffidence,[14] and when the men had been in the dungeon for over three days, he told his wife all about them while they laid in bed at night. He explained how he had taken two men prisoners after they had trespassed on his grounds.

As they spoke, he asked her for her advice, how to harm them more and punish them for their crime. As she considered her response, she asked him where they'd come from and where they were going. She asked as well what sort of men they were, and he told her everything.

She nodded slowly to herself as she considered her thoughts, and finally counselled him to beat them without mercy in the morning.

The next morning, he took her advice and found himself a crab-tree cudgel.[15] Taking his new weapon with him, he made straight for the dungeon.

Early Sunday morning, we laid there in the darkness, just as we had the last four days, unsure what our future held, or if it held anything at all beyond living out our lives in endless darkness. In the silence, even one another's company was not much comfort, especially for me, as I still felt the weight of my guilt for placing us there.

---

[14] *Diffidence* today means shyness that flows from a lack of self-confidence, but when this was written it appears to have meant *a lack of trust or even a lack of faith*. A strange name, perhaps, for the wife of a Giant, but perhaps appropriate for the wife of Despair.

[15] It was once common to use crab-tree wood for sticks and cudgels as it was strong, hard, knotty, and the bark could be quite rough. I don't think I'd like to be hit with a cudgel, but a crab-tree cudgel adds misery to an already horrible experience. A cudgel is a short stick used as a club for beating people.

This was, by far, worse than the time the people of Vanity Fair held Faithful and me prisoner. Although we spent the time ridiculed and abused, at least we were there because of the Lord's leading. This time, however, we had no such comfort.

But that morning, as we lay there, I heard something different—a sound other than the slow drip of water or the scratching of mice or rats as they worked their way through small holes into and out of our little prison.

The sound grew louder by the second, a thumping… footsteps. This new sound brought with it no sense of relief, and we both tensed as we feared who might approach.

The door burst open, and I instinctively covered my eyes, the glare of the lantern too bright for my eyes. Peeking through my fingers, I could just barely make out the large, enraged face of Giant Despair standing over us, a cruel club in his hand. I feared the worst, but instead of a beating, he insulted and criticized us, tearing us down, telling us we were worthless and speaking of all the wicked and foolish things we had ever done.

The insults came at us repeatedly, and for a time, he seemed to have no end of cruel words to throw at us. But even so, despite the onslaught, we refused to speak back to him in such a manner.

When he eventually ran out of insults, the thing I feared the most happened. He used his club and used it mercilessly. He beat us and beat us as if he had no thought of ever ending until the two of us lay on the ground, unable even to turn ourselves over from our backs to our sides or to our bellies. And when the Giant saw how badly beaten we were, he finally relented and left us there to sympathize with one another and to mourn over our situation.

I listened to his feet stomping on the steps outside our prison, growing quieter by the second. I wanted to call out to Hopeful, but all I could do was sigh and groan. The only reason I knew he still lived was because I also heard his groans, somewhere off to my right.

We laid there all day, doing nothing but groaning in our misery and crying out in our pain and grief.

"And how are they now?" Diffidence asked her husband as they crawled into bed. "Are they still alive?"

Giant Despair growled and shook his head, pulling the thick wool blankets right up to his chin. "They... stubborn! They just won't die! Even after so long in my prison and after such a beating!" He growled and twisted the blankets in his giant fists. With a pout in his voice, he mumbled, "Those wretched souls!"

Diffidence slid close to him and said, "Then I recommend you give them advice, dear husband."

Giant Despair looked at his wife in surprise. "Advice? What sort of advice?"

"Isn't it obvious?" she asked. "Tell them to kill themselves—to do away with themselves to save future pain!"

Her counsel, seeming good to him, sat well in his heart, and he decided to do just that the next day.

The next morning, I awoke with a start, the pain shooting across my back and shoulders. If anything, our aches and pains had grown worse, and every movement drove me, at the very least, to tears. When I heard the thumping noise again, I could do nothing but groan.

The door crashed open, just like yesterday, but I didn't have the strength to cover my eyes this time, only close them to shield them from the bright glare of the Giant's lantern. When I opened them again, the Giant leaned over me, examining my wounds and cuts and bruises from the day before.

Once finished, he moved on to Hopeful, examining him as well, until he appeared satisfied with Hopeful's condition.

Moving back to the doorway, Giant Despair growled at each of us before saying, "Listen, trespassers! You'll never make it out of here. Never! You'll live out your days in this darkness. Your only way forward, your only hope of escape, is to kill yourselves. You can use a knife, or poison, I don't care, BUT YOU SHOULD END IT! Why should you choose to live, seeing that life comes with such bitterness?"

"Please, sir," I pleaded in just above a whisper. "Please… let us go."

Giant Despair's face filled with rage. Seeing that we weren't taking his advice, he screamed and raised his ugly cudgel in the air once again. As he charged towards us, I thought for sure we were to be attacked yet again, and I didn't think we'd survive another beating. Instead, just before he reached us, he fell to the ground and convulsed. I didn't know it at the time, but Giant Despair often fell to seizures when the sun shone on a beautiful day.

When he calmed down, he struggled to pull himself upright, and only just managed to hold the cudgel under his left arm. His right hand hung limply at his side, and his face was filled with his own despair. Without another word, he gathered up the lantern as best he could and made his way out of our prison, locking the door behind him.

I listened to his uneven footfalls on the stairs as he stumbled his way up and away from us, grateful that we escaped a beating that day.

"Brother?" I spoke into the darkness. I hated to admit it, but the Giant's advice sounded good to me. "Brother? Hopeful? What should we do? This life is horrible!" I took a few breaths to settle my racing heart and added. "Hopeful, I don't know which is better, to live like this or to die by our own hands. 'I would choose strangling and death rather than my bones.'[16] Should we just continue here and be ruled by the Giant?"

"It's pretty bad," Hopeful agreed, his weak voice just barely loud enough to hear. "No doubt about it. Death would certainly be more welcome to me than a life like this. But… Christian… consider this: the Lord of the country to which we are going has told us to do no murder. If that's the case toward another, how much more does he not want us to take the Giant's counsel to kill ourselves?"

I heard a shuffle, the sound coming from my friend's direction, and felt his hand on my arm. "Christian, the one who kills another kills that man's body, but to kill ourselves, we kill the body and the soul all at once! You talk about ease in the grave, but have you forgotten about hell? That's where murderers go, right? No murderer has eternal life!"[17] I heard him groan beside me, caught up in a wave of intense agony. Once it passed, he calmed his breathing before saying, "Listen, my brother, remember

---

[16] Job 7:15.
[17] 1 John 3:15.

that the law is not in Giant Despair's control. Others have been taken by him, as far as we understand, and they've escaped out of his hand. Who knows, the God who made the world may even kill Giant Despair! Or perhaps the Giant might forget to lock the door. Or maybe he'll even have another seizure here in the prison and lose the use of all his limbs. If that ever happens, personally, I'm going to take up my courage and do everything I can to get away!" I heard him sigh in the darkness before he continued. "Christian… I was a fool not to run the last time he had a fit, but my brother, be patient and endure. The time may come when we find our happy release, but let's not be our own murderers."

I closed my eyes. Hopeful's words were just what I needed, calming my mind and heart. With the strength the Lord gave through my dear friend's reminder, we continued together in the dark for the rest of that day, laying there in our agony.

Nearing the end of the day, we heard the terrible thumping of the Giant's feet yet again as our captor came down to our little prison. The door swung open and, once my eyes adjusted to the light of the lantern, I saw a look of surprise on his face. In a quiet voice filled with shock, he whispered, "You're still alive?"

I wanted to say, "Just barely…" but I dared not speak. Between the wounds we'd received and the lack of bread and water, we couldn't do much more than lie there and breathe as he stood over us.

The sound of his teeth grinding together scared me as much as the growl growing in his throat. He began to shake, and when he looked like he couldn't stand it anymore, he stomped his feet and howled at us in his rage, "Since you disobeyed my counsel and are still alive, it'll be worse for you than if you'd never been born!"

I wept, tears streaming down my cheeks, unable to take much more… not much more at all. I tried to pull away, but then, without even a single blow, in my fear and distress, I passed out.

I opened my eyes to see nothing… nothing but a deep, disorienting darkness. The light was gone from the Giant's lantern, and I knew he was as well.

He hadn't beaten us that time, for which I was grateful, but once again, I wanted to take his advice, to end it all. "Hopeful?" I whispered. "Hopeful. We should do it. We should just kill ourselves and be done with it all."

"My brother!" he replied in the darkness, his scratchy voice pleading with me in my grief. "Don't you remember how courageous you've been so far on this journey? Apollyon couldn't best you, nor could anything you saw, heard, or felt in the Valley of the Shadow of Death! The Valley of the Shadow of Death, Christian! As horrific as it was, you still made it through! Think of all the things you've survived, all the difficult times, the terror… all of it![18] And now you're overcome by fear? You know I'm here in this dungeon as well, right? And I'm nothing compared to you! You have always been so much stronger. This giant… he's beaten me, too. He's kept food and water from me, and I hate to be without the light, just like you!" I heard him try to pull himself closer to me and then felt his hand on my arm. "Christian, please. Let's have a little more patience. Remember how you stood strong against the judge at Vanity Fair and didn't fear the chains or the

---

[18] The original includes the words *the amazement* in this list, but in modern English, that doesn't make sense to us in this context.

cage or even a violent death? If for no other reason than to avoid the shame that a Christian shouldn't carry, let's be patient."

Now, once night had come, the Giant went to his bed, and he and his wife again discussed the prisoners.

"Have they finally taken your advice?" Diffidence asked. "Did they take their lives?"

"They're scoundrels," the Giant replied, "but they are strong! They seem willing to put up with whatever I do to them rather than kill themselves."

She paused for a moment, considering the matter. Finally, she said, "Then here is what you should do, my dear. Tomorrow, take them into the castle-yard and show them the skulls and all the bones and all that remains of those you have already killed—those who came before them! Then, make them believe that you'll do the same to them, that you'll tear them to pieces within a week!

The next morning, we awoke to find ourselves in the same darkness. Neither of us had the strength to move, but only to wait for what might come next. Our stomachs ached, and our mouths felt like fire, our tongues dry and swollen. Every word spoken hurt as it came out of our parched throats.

When we heard the uneven thumping of the giant's footsteps on the stairs, neither of us could hold back our groans, fearing that what might come would be worse than anything we had faced so far.

The door swung open, and I still couldn't raise my hand to block the light of the Giant's lantern, but before my eyes could adjust, I felt my body wrenched upwards, and then found myself on the stairs, the giant pushing and shoving us up and up and up.

Hopeful and I gasped for air with every step, and within seconds, I even yearned for the peace and quiet of our little cell rather than have to endure more in the giant's presence. At the top of the stairs, he pushed us through a large, solid doorway into the castle-yard, and despite my weakness, I couldn't help but gasp. Beside me, Hopeful cried out in his shock.

At our feet and spread across the ground, as far as the castle-yard stretched, to the north, the south, the east, and the west, the thorns and weeds grew thick, growing up and through and around nothing but skulls and bones—all that remained of countless other men and women, spread out before us, bleached white from the sun's rays.

My strength melted, but I dared not fall to my knees and land on the remains of another pilgrim—one of my brothers who had gone before and fell prey to this wicked monster.

"These," the giant's mocking voice began, slow, deep, and loud, "were pilgrims, just like you. Once, that is." He laughed, and then added, "And they too trespassed on my ground, just like you. And when I saw fit, I tore these men and women to pieces, and they could not resist me…" I felt the large hand of Giant Despair wrap around my neck, and he spun me around towards him, pulling Hopeful in next to me with his other hand. Our captor bent down, bringing his ugly face in close, and in a half-whisper, half-growl, he told us, "And you won't be able to resist me either! Within ten days, I'll do the same to both of you."

With a laugh, he tossed us back through the doorway and began to beat us as he chased us down the stairs to our cell. Once inside, we huddled together against the wall as Giant Despair pulled the door closed behind him. We listened to the thumping of his feet fade away, along with his laughter as he returned to his castle above.

The two of us lay there all Saturday, mourning our situation, but unable to see any way out.

"How are the prisoners now?" Diffidence asked that evening as they settled into bed.

Giant Despair shook his enormous head slowly and ground his teeth. "Same!" he snarled. "Same as before! Nothin's changed! I can't beat them into killing themselves, and I can't counsel them into killing themselves!"

"I fear," Diffidence began, "that these men live in hope. Perhaps they hope someone will come and rescue them; or perhaps they have lock picks hidden in their clothes and expect to use them at some point."

Giant Despair furrowed his brow and stared intently at his wife. "You think so? That could be a real problem. Well, in that case, I'll search them in the morning, and we'll see if they're hiding anything!"

At around midnight, Hopeful and I did something we had done little of the last while. Something we had grown to neglect.

As we laid in the darkness alone, beaten and discouraged, we turned our hearts upward, and we prayed.

We prayed hour after hour, crying out to God for help, for comfort, to save us from such a wretched place. We lost ourselves in prayer, seeking God through the rest of the night and until almost the break of the new day.

And it was in that moment, just before sunrise, that my mouth dropped open. "I've been a fool!" I whispered.

Hopeful stopped praying immediately. He paused for a moment before asking, "What are you talking about, Christian?"

"I've been a fool!" I repeated. "A complete fool! I've just laid here in a stinking dungeon when I can simply walk free!" Reaching out in the dark and grabbing hold of Hopeful, I shook his arm and said, "I have a key, Hopeful! I have a key! It's here in my breast pocket. A key named Promise! I... I believe it'll open any door in Doubting Castle!"

"That's great news!" Hopeful cried, excitement filling his voice. "Pull it out and try it in the door!"

I reached into my breast pocket, my hands shaking both from the shame at forgetting the key was there, and from the anticipation that it might be God's way out of that prison.

I hobbled to the door, and with each step, the possibility of escape flooded me with fresh energy. The aches and pains from the beatings faded from my mind as I reached the door. The key itself was small and unimpressive, but the weight told me it was built of solid and expensive material.

It slid into the lock as if made especially for that place, and the bolt gave way. My heart raced as the door swung back into our cell, and we stepped out. The light in that area was not bright at all without the Giant's lantern, but having been used to the darkness of our cell, even the little we could see brought joy to our hearts as we climbed the stairs. At the top, we used the key again on the outer door, leading to the castle-yard, and once again, it opened easily. In a few moments, we were across the castle-yard and at the iron gate.

The lock on the iron gate was the first one to give us trouble. I struggled with it for a few minutes, doing my best to turn it, hoping and trusting it would win out against the difficult, old, rusted mechanism. When it finally did, I grinned like a fool, and Hopeful let out a small laugh of joy.

"Help me with the gate," I whispered to Hopeful, and each of us grabbed an iron rung and pushed as hard as we could.

But this gate not only gave us trouble with the lock, but no one had greased the hinges, perhaps for many years. The gate gave such a groan and such a creak that we knew the Giant would hear even before we heard his roar! "Push harder!" I hollered, and Hopeful and I shoved with all our strength. The opening grew large enough for us to fit through, and Hopeful squeezed out first, followed immediately by me.

"Run, Christian!" Hopeful cried, and we took off as fast as we could back toward the King's Highway. Our strength was low after so long without food and water and after the beatings we'd received, but the Lord's grace was strong, even for two foolish and wayward pilgrims such as us.

As we ran, a loud crash behind us got our attention. I looked back just long enough to see Giant

Despair lumbering after us. "He'll be on us in a few seconds," I cried out, but then a loud thump followed by a groan drew my attention.

I spun around and cheered. Giant Despair had suffered another seizure and his limbs had failed him again, but this time, not even his feet would work. He thrashed around on the ground as we ran hard and quickly left him behind. The soft, lush grass of the Giant's meadow no longer held any attraction for us as we ran across it, not like before. Now, we longed only for the straight, true path.

When we reached the stile, we quickly scrambled up and over, and, on the other side, we each wept for joy to be back on the King's Highway, safe from Giant Despair as we were now finally out of his control. We collapsed on the ground, laughing and praising the Lord.

But neither of us could stop thinking about the stile, the means by which we entered Giant Despair's land.

"What should we do about it?" Hopeful asked. "We can't let others fall into the same trap!"

I thought good and long on the question. There had to be a way to protect other pilgrims. Finally, an idea came to me, and I smiled before saying, "A pillar."

"Pardon?" Hopeful asked.

"A pillar!" I said with a smile. "Let's erect a pillar! On the side facing the road, we'll engrave a warning on it. Perhaps something like this,

OVER THIS STILE IS THE
WAY TO DOUBTING CASTLE.
THAT PLACE IS KEPT BY
GIANT DESPAIR. HE
DESPISES THE KING OF
THE CELESTIAL COUNTRY
AND SEEKS TO DESTROY
HIS HOLY PILGRIMS.

Hopeful agreed, so we set to work building the pillar, hoping to protect future pilgrims from a similar fate. It took us most of the rest of the day, but even in our weary state, we persevered by the grace of God until finished.

Years later, we learned this pillar had in fact saved many from falling into the same sin as we had. For that, I am very grateful.

When we had finished the pillar, we went on our way rejoicing, singing the following hymn:

Out of the way we went, and then we found
What 'twas to tread upon forbidden ground;
And let them that come after have a care,
Lest heedlessness makes them, as we, to fare.
Lest they for trespassing his prisoners are,
Whose castle's Doubting, and whose name's
Despair.

12. Shepherds and Wisdom

We started along the straight path once again, the pillar raised behind us and the joy of being back on the path pushing us on. Not far from that spot, we found a small river flowing by the path, along with some fruit trees, and we stopped to refresh ourselves after so long without food.

The path in that area continued to run over rocky, uneven ground, but the difficulty was a joy for us compared to our suffering in Doubting Castle.

In time, the rough terrain gave way to a bit of grass, then a few small rivers, then, coming over a rise, we saw a copse, followed by the sight of a deer, grazing in a meadow. The path itself grew a little smoother, and our spirits were quickly refreshed.

The path led us along until we reached the Delectable Mountains. They rose high into the sky, their gentle slopes covered in thick, green grass. All along the hills and inclines, we saw dozens and dozens of flocks of sheep grazing on the healthy green grass under the careful watch of their shepherds.

Hopeful and I, with joy, climbed the mountains. We wanted to see the gardens and the orchards, the vineyards and fountains of water. And as we wandered through the area, those who lived on the mountains encouraged us to drink and wash ourselves and even eat of the vineyards.

While wandering the area, we approached the shepherds feeding their flocks as they stood along the side of the path, hoping to find some answers to questions heavy on our hearts.

We came to a halt and leaned on our walking staffs as any weary pilgrim might when they stop to talk, and the shepherds smiled at us, making us feel quite welcome. "Whose Delectable Mountains are these?" I asked. "And who owns the sheep feeding here?"

Mountains delectable they now ascend,
Where Shepherds be, which to them do commend
Alluring things, and things that cautious are,
Pilgrims are steady kept by faith and fear.

One of the shepherds, a tall, sun-darkened man, lean, but strong, smiled warmly at me. "These mountains are Immanuel's Land, dear Pilgrim, and it is within sight of his city. The sheep themselves belong to him. They're the ones for whom he laid down his life."[1]

I returned the shepherd's smile, grateful to be among friends, even family, brothers and sisters, brought together by the Lord of the way. "Is this the way to the Celestial City?" I asked.

"You are just on your way."

---

[1] John 10:11.

"How far from here?"

The shepherd leaned forward a little, holding tight to his staff. "Too far for anyone but those who will truly reach that place."

I nodded slowly and asked, "Is the way safe or dangerous?"

"Safe for those for whom it is to be safe, but the transgressors will stumble along the way."[2]

"Is there," I asked, "in this land, any relief for pilgrims who are weary and faint from their journey?"

As we spoke, the other shepherds gathered around, and the tall shepherd said, "The Lord of these mountains has commanded us not to forget to entertain strangers. Because of this, the good you see before you is yours to enjoy!"[3] The shepherd turned his head slightly, as if examining Hopeful and me a little more intently. "You are pilgrims, are you not? Pilgrims journeying along the path?"

"We are," Hopeful replied.

Upon hearing that we were followers of their Lord, they asked us questions such as, "Where do you come from?" and "How did each of you get onto the path?" and "What have you experienced so far on your journey?" As we spoke, they explained to us that few who begin their journey along the path reached the mountains.

When they heard our answers and were pleased with them, the shepherd smiled and said, "Welcome to the Delectable Mountains!"

We learned the shepherds were named Knowledge, Experience, Watchful, and Sincere. These

---

[2] Hos. 14:9.
[3] Heb. 13:1-2.

men were wise and helpful, filled with encouragement and kindness, and they took us by the hand and led us to their tents. Once there, they fed us with whatever they had on hand.

We enjoyed their company and found them to be wonderful hosts. The shepherds even invited us to stay awhile, so we could get to know them better, and to find comfort in the pleasant land of the Delectable Mountains.

Upon hearing this, Hopeful and I were thrilled and quickly accepted their invitation. That night, we slept in tents, comfortable, dry, safe, and happy to have a time of refreshment after such an arduous journey.

"Hello in there!"

I opened my eyes slowly, unsure at first where I was. The tent around me was large, and the ground under my bedroll was soft.

"Hello?" the voice came again.

"Yes... good morning... we're awake," I called back, remembering where we were. I felt so rested and refreshed, it was hard to wake up.

Hopeful sat up on the other side of the tent, wiping the sleep from his eyes, and we crawled out of our blankets and packed up before stepping out into the early morning light. The sun felt warm on my neck as we met the smiling shepherds before setting out with them for a walk through the beautiful mountains to begin the day.

We walked up and over hills, enjoying the breeze and the warmth of the rising sun on our backs and the company of new, but good friends. At the top of one of the larger hills, a shorter, older shepherd stopped and turned to the others. He asked, "What do you think? Should we show them some sights?"

The other shepherds nodded their heads without hesitation, so the older shepherd led us along to a mountain named Error. When we reached the top, we found the edge dropped off steeply on the far side, and the men encouraged us to look down to the land below. My mouth dropped open at the sight, for at the bottom of the cliff, I saw the bodies of several men, dashed to pieces by the fall.

"What…?" I began. "What does this mean?"

The older shepherd stepped up next to me and leaned over the edge just a little. As he stared down at the sight below, he asked, "Haven't you heard of those who fell into error by listening to Hymeneus and Philetus, men who said the resurrection has already happened?"[4]

"We have," I replied.

He pointed down at the scene below and explained, "The men you see lying dashed to pieces at the bottom of this mountain are those who fell into that error. Their bodies have lain there all this time unburied, as an example to others to take heed when they climb too high or come too near the edge of this mountain."

I quickly stepped back, careful not to get too close and saw Hopeful did the same. We had made our own fair share of mistakes, sins, and foolish choices. We didn't need one more to add to it.

"Come with us," the older shepherd ordered.

We walked down off the mountain named Error and up onto a different mountain, this one named Caution.

---

[4] 2 Tim. 2:17-18.

When we reached the peak, the men encouraged us to look far off into the distance. I strained to see, and after a few moments, Hopeful pointed out men wandering among the tombs. Even from such a distance, I could see from the way they moved that they were blind. They stumbled this way and that, over and around the tombs, unable to find their way out.

"And what does this mean?" I asked.

"Did you see a little below these mountains, back along the path, a stile? It led into a meadow on the left-hand side of the way."

I glanced sheepishly at Hopeful, and he in turn back at me. "Yes, we saw it," I said quietly.

"From that stile," the shepherd explained, "runs a path which leads directly to Doubting Castle, held by Giant Despair. Those men you see," he explained, pointing to those among the tombs, "were once on pilgrimage, just as you are now, until they came to that same stile. But because the way was rough in that place, they crossed over into the meadow, and Giant Despair took them, casting them into Doubting Castle." The shepherd's face filled with grief as he told us, "After the Giant kept them in the dungeon for a long time, he put out their eyes and then led them to the tombs, leaving them there. They have remained there, wandering to this very day so that the saying of the wise man might be fulfilled, 'One who wanders from the way of good sense will rest in the assembly of the dead.'"[5]

Tears streamed down my face, and I turned to Hopeful. He too wept, but we were grateful to the Lord of the way for his mercy. We did not, however, say anything to the shepherds, but kept our shame to ourselves.

_____

[5] Prov. 21:16.

"Come," the older shepherd said. "We have more to show you."

We followed them down off the mountain named Caution and to a valley, right up to a door in the side of a hill. One of the younger shepherds opened the door, and they told us to look inside.

We approached cautiously, unsure of what to expect. The inside of this passageway was dark and smoky, and a revolting smell wafted up from the depths. We dared not enter, but we thought we heard a rumbling noise from deep within and the agonized cry of tormented souls.

"Is that brimstone?" Hopeful asked, wrinkling his nose at the smell coming from the other side of the doorway.

The shepherd didn't answer, so I asked, "What does this mean, sir?"

He paused as he stared into the darkness for a few moments, but then eventually explained in his deep, quiet voice, "This is a by-way to hell. It's a doorway for hypocrites, specifically those who sell their birthright, like Esau, or those who sell their master, like Judas, or those who blaspheme the gospel, like Alexander, or those who lie and conceal the truth, like Ananias and Sapphira."[6]

Hopeful frowned, deep in thought. "I suppose that each of them appeared to be on a pilgrimage, just like us."

"Yes," he said, turning his gaze to Hopeful, "and they held to the way for a long time, too."

---

[6] Gen. 25:29-34; Lk. 22:47-53; 1 Tim. 1:18-20; Acts 5:1-11.

Hopeful gulped and glanced at me before asking, "How far, Sir? How far did they travel on their pilgrimage before they were eventually cast away?"[7]

"Some made it farther than these mountains," he replied, "and some not as far."

I shook my head and suspected Hopeful struggled with the same fear which moved through my heart and soul. I said to my friend, "We need to cry out to the Strong One for strength!"

"Ay," the shepherd replied, "and when he gives you strength, you will need to use it!"

By this time, Hopeful and I were ready to get back on our journey. The shepherds felt we should as well, so they walked with us, leading us out of the Delectable Mountains. When we reached the edge of their territory, the shepherds agreed to show us one more thing. They wished to show us the gates of the Celestial City, although they wondered if we might not have the skill to use the telescope.[8]

We gratefully accepted the offer, so the shepherds led us to the top of a high mountain named Clear. At the top, they gave me their looking glass.

I raised it to my eye to see, but all I could think of was the last thing the shepherds had shown us. The smell of brimstone, still in my nose, and the memory... the thoughts... the fear... the knowledge that others had been on pilgrimage just like Hopeful and me... and yet their

---

[7] This particular statement was quite difficult to put into modern language. Here is the original... perhaps you can see what caused the difficulty. "How far might they go on in pilgrimage in their day, since they notwithstanding were thus miserably cast away?" My personal response, from one author to another, is to ask John Bunyan, "What have you done???"

[8] In the original, the term *perspective glass* is used.

hypocrisy led to their doom… The thought of it all made my hands shake. I tried to hold them steady, but the more I tried, the more the tremors increased.

I thought I could, however, despite my shaking hands, make out what appeared to be a gate, and I thought perhaps I might have even seen some of the glory of the place. When I handed the telescope to Hopeful, I noticed he struggled the same as me, and when he finally lowered it and returned it to the shepherds, I saw the same disappointment in his eyes as I felt in my own heart.

Yet, what we saw, what we could make out, was beautiful and gave us hope. As a result, we left that hill singing this song:

> *Thus, by the Shepherds, secrets are reveal'd,*
> *Which from all other men are kept conceal'd.*
> *Come to the Shepherds, then, if you would see*
> *Things deep, things hid, and that mysterious be.*

When we were ready to leave, a shepherd gave me a note for the way, directions for us on the path. Another warned us to beware of the Flatterer. A third warned us not to sleep on the Enchanted Grounds, and the fourth wished us God-speed.

In the heart of a dreamer, the dreamer awoke. He awoke to consider the things of which he dreamed, but then lay down again, falling asleep, and dreaming of more. A dream of travellers, pilgrims, a journey, a path. A dream in which his two pilgrims

travelled down the mountains, along the highway,
towards the beautiful city.[9]

As much as we may have wanted to stay, we left the Delectable Mountains behind. We were pilgrims on our journey to the Celestial City and could not settle until we had reached our destination.

Now, below the mountains, on the left-hand side of the road, lies the country of Conceit. And as we approached the border of Conceit, we saw in the distance, someone coming towards the road. He came from that direction and reached the road right about the point where we walked, coming along a very crooked path.

The man was young, impetuous,[10] and went by the name of Ignorance. Since we were all travelling together, we engaged him in conversation as we walked along the path.

"Where do you come from?" I asked. "And where are you heading?"

"Sir," Ignorance replied, "I was born in the country just over there to the left, and I'm going to the Celestial City."

I frowned at that, unsure if he understood what he was saying. "How do you expect to get through the gate when you reach the City? You might find that difficult."

_____

[9] This is the point in Bunyan's story where he writes that he awoke from his dream before he fell asleep again.
[10] The original description of this young man is that *he was a very brisk lad*, which seems to mean, from the use at the time, that he was abrupt, thoughtless, and uncaring.

"I'll get through the same way everyone else does," Ignorance replied.

"But…" I began, concerned for the young man, "what do you have to show at the gate to make them let you in?"

Ignorance smiled confidently as we walked along. "I know what my Lord wants, and I've lived a good life. I give to everyone what they deserve, and I pray, fast, pay tithes, and give to the poor. To add to all that, I've even left my country behind to reach the Celestial City."

"But…" I began, glancing over at Hopeful. "You didn't come in at the wicket-gate at the beginning of the path! You came in through that crooked path. Because of that, I worry that no matter how well you think of yourself, when the day of reckoning comes, you'll have proven yourself to be a thief and a robber and won't be allowed into the city!"

Ignorance put his hands up and smiled condescendingly at me. "Gentlemen," he said politely. "You are both strangers to me. I don't know either of you. Why don't you just follow your beliefs, and I'll follow mine. I think that'll work well. As for the gate that you mentioned, the wicket gate, everyone everywhere knows it's a long way from my country. In fact, I'm not sure that anyone from my own country even knows the way to it! Not that we need to reach that gate, since you can see we have a perfectly fine, pleasant green path that comes down from our country, leading right into this path here!"

I didn't respond to Ignorance right away. He was wise in his own eyes, so instead I whispered to Hopeful, "There is more hope for a fool than for him." I sighed and added, "'Even when the fool walks on the road, he lacks sense, and he says to everyone that he is a fool.' What do you think we should do? Should we talk some more with him or walk on ahead and let him think about what I told him? Maybe we could stop and ask him more about it later on in the hope that we can help him bit by bit."[11]

Hopeful replied with a poem:

> *Let Ignorance a little while now muse*
> *On what is said, and let him not refuse*
> *Good counsel to embrace, lest he remain*
> *Still ignorant of what's the chiefest gain.*
> *God saith, those that no understanding have,*
> *Although he made them, them he will not save.*

He also said, "I don't think it's good to say everything he needs to hear all at once. Let's move on ahead, if you're willing, and talk to him again in a little while. At least as much as he's able to bear."

So, we both moved on, and Ignorance came along behind us. Once we had moved on a decent distance, we entered an area of the path where the walls on either side had been built high and huge trees had grown up, their branches reaching over the path. The leaves on those trees grew so thick, we walked with very little light.

As we walked in the darkness, we could just make out shapes in the distance. Someone, or something, approached from ahead. At first, all I could make out was what looked like a giant spider or creature with many legs, but as it grew closer, I saw it was something far, far worse. A man, bound with seven strong cords, carried by seven devils. They carried him towards us, heading back the way we had come. Neither Hopeful nor I had to ask where they were taking him. Somehow, we knew. They were en route to the door in the hill, the one we saw back with the Shepherds.

---

[11] Prov. 26:12; Eccl. 10:3.

They were on their way to the by-way to hell.[12]

Once again, I began to tremble, as did Hopeful. As the devils carried him past us, I looked to see if I recognized the man. I wasn't sure, but he appeared to be someone I knew... a man by the name of Turn-away. He dwelt in the town of Apostasy. But... I didn't see his face all that well, for the man had hung his head like a thief who had been caught.

Once they were fully past us, Hopeful looked back and examined the man from behind, seeing a note stuck to the man's back. He took a step to follow just long enough to read the inscription. It read,

WANTON PROFESSOR AND DAMNABLE APOSTATE[13]

We did our best to calm ourselves as we watched the devils disappear into the darkness, and I tried my best to slow my breathing after such a sight. When I had caught my breath, I waved for Hopeful to follow as we started along the path again, forcing ourselves to move on.

While we walked, I shared something on my mind. "I remember being told once of something that happened to a good man. He was named Little-faith, but he was a good man. He lived in the town of Sincere." I frowned and shook my head. "At the place where you enter this path,

---

[12] Prov. 5:22; Matt. 12:45.

[13] This is the phrase in the original. I think, perhaps, we might 'translate' this as "Immoral professor and condemned rejector of the faith." The idea seems to be that he professes to know Christ, yet his immoral life denies it, that he has ultimately rejected the faith, leading him to be someone who is easily condemned to hell.

there comes down from Broad-way Gate a road called Dead Man's Lane. It's called that because of all the murders that happen there. So, Little-faith was on pilgrimage, as we are now, and he happened to sit down and fall asleep right in that area. By chance, at that moment, three strong thugs came down Dead Man's Lane, coming from Broad-way Gate. The names of the thugs were Faint-heart, Mistrust, and Guilt. They were brothers, and when they saw Little-faith, they ran at him as fast as they could!"

I paused for a moment to collect my thoughts before I continued my story. When I was ready, I said, "Now, the good man, Little-faith, had just awakened from his sleep, and was standing to go on his journey. But they reached him and threatened him, preventing him from going anywhere. Now, Little-faith, he just went as pale as can be and didn't have the strength to fight or to run.

"Faint-heart then ordered Little-faith to hand over his wallet, but Little-faith didn't want to, of course, and with all of it, he didn't move quickly enough, so Mistrust came right up close to him and shoved his hand in Little-faith's pocket, pulling out a bag of silver. That's when Little-faith cried out, 'Thieves! Thieves!' and Guilt hit Little-faith in the head with the large club he carried.

"The blow knocked the poor man flat on his back where he lay bleeding, and bad enough that he could have bled to death! So, as Little-faith lay there on the ground, the thieves just stood there. I guess they had nowhere else to go, and who knows how long they would have remained, but then they heard someone else on the road, so they ran. They thought it might be Great-grace, a man who lives in the city of Good-confidence. So, they took off and left the poor man to care for himself. Now, after a little while, Little-faith awoke and got up, doing all he could to stumble along on his way."

Hopeful took a moment to collect his thoughts and then asked, "But did they take everything? I mean, everything he'd ever had?"

"No," I replied, shaking my head. "They didn't find the place where he kept his jewels, so they were safe. But from what I was told, the good man struggled terribly with his loss, because the thieves took most of his spending money. They didn't get his jewels, as I mentioned, but he had little extra money left, barely enough to make it the rest of his journey.[14] In fact, if what I heard was true, he had to beg to provide for himself as he walked the path just to keep himself alive, because he wasn't willing to sell his jewels. He begged and did what he could as he travelled along, going hungry often for much of the rest of the way."

Hopeful remained silent for a few moments as we walked, taking it all in. Finally, he said, "It's a surprise they didn't take his certificate, the one he needs to get through the Celestial Gate."

"It is, but they didn't. They missed it, but not because he hid it well. He was too scared and didn't have the strength or skill to hide anything. So, it was more by good providence that they missed it than by anything he did."

"He must have at least been happy that they didn't get his jewels," Hopeful added.

"You know, it might have been a comfort to him, if he'd used them as he should, but the people who told me the story said he didn't really use them much at all for the rest of the journey. Because he was so upset about losing his money, he rarely even thought of the jewels. In fact, when he would think of the jewels and feel better about things, he'd remember once again about the loss of his

---

[14] 1 Pet. 4:18.

money, and then he wouldn't be able to think of anything else."[15]

"Poor guy," Hopeful whispered. "He obviously struggled with a lot of grief."

"Absolutely!" I replied. "I think we'd have dealt with the same thing. To be hurt like he was, robbed, wounded... and in a strange place like that, too? It's a wonder the grief itself didn't kill him! I was told he did nothing but complain bitterly the rest of his journey, telling everyone who overtook him on the path about it as he travelled along, giving details about how he was robbed, who did it to him, what was lost, how he was wounded, and how he barely escaped with his life!"

Hopeful shook his head slowly. "You know, it's a wonder that just the sheer poverty didn't drive him to sell or pawn his jewels, just so he could find a bit of relief along the path."

"You're talking like you still have a shell on your head!"[16] I said in shock. "What would he pawn them for? Who do you think he would sell them to? Those jewels were worthless in that land, and he didn't want the relief he'd find from selling them for a little extra money! Besides, if he'd shown up at the gates to the Celestial City without them—and he knew this—he would have lost his inheritance there. And that, Hopeful, would have been worse to him than the sight and cruelty of ten thousand thieves!"

"Why are you snapping at me, brother?" Hopeful said, stepping back indignantly. "Esau did just that! He sold his birthright for a little stew, and that birthright was his

---

[15] 1 Pet. 1:9.
[16] This concept likely refers to a newly born chick that runs around with the shell still on its head, suggesting a high degree of youth and ignorance of the world.

greatest jewel! If he could do that, why shouldn't Little-faith?"[17]

"Well, you're right, Esau sold his birthright," I replied. "And so do many others. But by doing so, they exclude themselves from the true blessing, just as wicked Esau did! But you must understand the difference between Esau and Little-faith, and also between what they owned. Esau's birthright was of this world, but Little-faith's was not. Esau's belly was his god, but Little-faith's belly was not. Esau was driven by the desires of his flesh; Little-faith was not. And Esau couldn't see past the fulfilling of his desires. In fact, he said, 'I am about to die; of what use is a birthright to me?'[18] But with Little-faith, even though it was his lot in life to only have a little faith, the little faith he had kept him from going to such extremes. It also made him see his jewels and value them so much that he would not sell them like Esau sold his birthright.

"Hopeful, you don't read anywhere in Scripture that Esau had faith, not even a little! It's no surprise that someone who's driven only by their desires—such as a man who can't resist because he has no faith—if he sells his birthright, his soul, and everything to the devil! With men like that, they're just like a donkey in heat—relentless![19] When men driven by lust set their mind on something, they will get what they want, no matter the cost. But Little-faith wasn't like that. He set his mind on divine things. His life was about the spiritual and about things from above. What would it benefit someone like that to sell their jewels for no other reason than to fill his mind with empty things—even if he could find someone to buy them? You think you can convince a man to buy hay to fill his belly? Or do you think you can convince the turtle-dove to

---

[17] Heb. 12:16.
[18] Gen. 25:32.
[19] Jer. 2:24.

eat the flesh of dead animals like a crow? While faithless men can pawn, mortgage, or sell all they have and even themselves for carnal lusts, those who have faith, saving faith, even if it's only a little, can't. That, Hopeful, is where you are mistaken."

"I see that, Christian, but your reaction towards me almost made me angry." His voice was sharp, and he spoke quickly.

"Why?" I asked. "I only compared you to some birds that are thoughtless, running around where no one else runs, still with the shell on their heads.[20] But set that aside. Consider the matter we're discussing and everything will be fine between us."

Hopeful shook his head. "But Christian, these three men, the thieves, I'm convinced they're a bunch of cowards! If they weren't, why would they have run at the sound of someone coming up the road? And why didn't Little-faith gather up his courage? I can't help but think that he could have stood up against them at least once and only given in when there had been no chance of victory."

"Many have accused these men of being cowards, but few find they can say that on the day they meet them. As for having courage, Little-faith had none. I think, my brother, if you had been in that situation, you would have stood for a bit, then given in. It's easy to feel this way about the situation since the men aren't anywhere near us, but if they stood next to you like they stood before Little-faith, you might have second thoughts. But keep this in mind, these men are experienced thieves, employed by the king of the bottomless pit. If need be, their king himself will

---

[20] Christian's description of the bird here is that it is of the brisker sort which seems to point back to the description of Ignorance a few pages earlier. It suggested back then that Ignorance was abrupt, impatient, impetuous, and now Christian seems to accuse Hopeful of something similar.

come help them, and his voice is like the roaring of a lion![21] I was once in that kind of situation, just like Little-faith, and I found it a horrible experience! Those three men came at me, and as soon as I resisted like a Christian should, they called out and their master came running!" I looked at Hopeful with shame for a moment and admitted, "I would have given my life for a penny in that moment. However, by God's grace, I was clothed with tested armour." I frowned and looked down. "Even so, Hopeful, I found it very difficult to stand strong, to keep my courage. No man, Hopeful, knows how he will react in battle until he finds himself in the fight."

"But those men, the thieves, they ran as soon as they thought Great-grace was on the road!" Hopeful replied.

"That's true," I said. "But they have often run and so has their master... when Great-grace shows up." I laughed at that. "It's no surprise that they run! He's the King's champion. But I think you must remember there's a big difference between Little-faith and the King's champion. All those who serve the King are not his champions, nor can they all fight like Great-grace. Is it proper to think a child could face off against Goliath as David did? Or that a wren could be as strong as an ox? Some are strong; some are weak; some have great faith; some have little. Little-faith was one of the weak, and therefore he failed."[22]

"I wish Great-grace had been the one to approach, that he had caught up with those men!" Hopeful said.

"If it had been Great-grace," I replied, "he would have had his hands full! Great-grace is an excellent swordsman and can fend them off—and has before—if he

---

[21] 1 Pet. 5:8.
[22] In the original, Bunyan uses the idiom *went to the wall*. In this context, it seems to refer to failure.

can keep them at sword's length from himself. But if they can get past his blade, they're likely to knock him over. And… well… when a man's down, there's not much he can do!

"Hopeful, if you ever meet Great-grace, you'll see the scars and cuts on his face that prove what I'm saying. I heard once that while in combat, he said he despaired of life itself![23] Those strong, wicked men made David groan, mourn, and roar! Even Heman and Hezekiah, champions in their times, were forced to take a stand when attacked by those men. And it wasn't easy for them! Oh, and Peter! We can't forget him. He faced off against those wicked men, and even though he is called the prince of the apostles, those men pushed him around so hard that they made him afraid of a servant girl![24]

"Besides," I continued, "their king is just a call away! He's never so far that he can't hear them. If they ever face anything they can't handle, he, if at all possible, comes in to help. It's said of their king, 'Though the sword reaches him, it does not avail, nor the spear, the dart, or the javelin. He counts iron as straw, and bronze as rotten wood. The arrow cannot make him flee; for him, sling stones are turned to stubble. Clubs are counted as stubble; he laughs at the rattle of javelins.'[25] It's true that if a man could always have Job's horse and had the skill and courage to ride him, he might do remarkable things. 'Do you give the horse his might? Do you clothe his neck with a mane? Do you make him leap like the locust? His majestic snorting is terrifying. He paws in the valley and exults in his strength; he goes out to meet the weapons. He laughs at fear and is not dismayed; he does not turn back from the sword. Upon him rattle the quiver, the flashing spear, and the javelin.

---

[23] 2 Cor. 1:8.
[24] Mar. 14:66-72.
[25] Job 41:26-29.

With fierceness and rage he swallows the ground; he cannot stand still at the sound of the trumpet. When the trumpet sounds, he says "Aha!" He smells the battle from afar, the thunder of the captains, and the shouting.'[26]

"For soldiers such as us, we should never desire to meet an enemy, nor should we ever boast as if we could do better when we hear that others have failed. We should never be so enamoured with thoughts of our own strength! Those who do often fare poorly when faced with battle. Consider Peter, whom I mentioned earlier. He boasted and his vain heart pushed him to say he would do better than others and stand strong for his Master beyond all others. But who has been beaten as badly as Peter by these wicked men?

"When we hear, Hopeful, that a robbery has happened on the King's highway, we should do these two things:

"First, go out prepared for battle and be sure to take a shield along. For without that, it doesn't matter how hard you fight against Leviathan, he will not back down. If you don't have a shield, he won't fear you at all. Because of that, one man who had skill said, 'In all circumstances take up the shield of faith, with which you can extinguish all the flaming darts of the evil one.'[27]

"Second, it is good that we ask the King to have someone go with us, especially to have him go with us himself! That's what made David rejoice in the Valley of the Shadow of Death. And Moses, he would rather have died where he stood than take one step without his God. Oh, my brother! If God will go with us, we don't need to

---

[26] Job 39:19-25.
[27] Eph. 6:16.

fear ten thousand enemies! But without him, the proud 'fall among the slain.'[28]

"I, for one, have been in the fight before today. And even though I am still alive because of him who is better than all, yet I can't boast of my own strength. In fact, I'll be happy if I never have to face another battle, although I doubt we're beyond all danger. However, since the lion and the bear have not yet devoured me, I hope God will also deliver us from the next uncircumcised Philistine!"

When I had finished saying all this, I sang this song:

> *Poor Little-faith! Hast been among the thieves?*
> *Wast robb'd? Remember this, whoso believes,*
> *And gets more faith, shall then a victor be*
> *Over ten thousand, else scarce over three.*

---

[28] Exo. 33:15; Ps. 3:5-8, 27:1-3; Isa. 10:4.

13. The Flatterers

The path in this region continued to be relatively smooth, but it was a while before the trees parted enough for the sunlight to shine through brightly.

Behind us, Ignorance trailed along. Ahead, the path, continuing straight as an arrow, just as it had from the start, was a constant reminder of where we were going.

As we came out of the dark area of the path, something new and unexpected happened. A new path, one very much like this current section of the road, lay before us. We came to a halt and looked at each other with worry. If this had been like all the other paths we'd faced, coming in from the side, crooked, running along next to us, or anything else, I suspect we would have just ignored it, but this one...

It was not like the others.

This new path, as far as we could see, lay straight as an arrow. It appeared to go so much in the same direction as the proper path and looked so much like it that it was hard to tell which one was the true path!

"Which... one?" Hopeful asked.

I didn't reply. Truly, I had no idea how to answer him. Both paths looked the same, yet they led in different directions, if only slightly.

As we stood there, considering this, a man approached. He stood tall, a full head higher than either of us. He was attractive, had a friendly smile, dark skin, and wore a very light robe. "Why are you standing here?" he asked in a voice that immediately put me at ease.

"We're going to the Celestial City," I replied, "but we don't know which of these paths to take!"

He laughed, but not mockingly. Instead, he offered a friendly smile and said, "Follow me. That's where I'm going."

So, the man led us along one of the paths. It felt good to move again and to have some clear direction. We were on a journey, and we couldn't get where we were going by standing still!

We continued along for a while, content to follow this man, but what we didn't realize until later, what we didn't quite see, was that the path began to turn. Not by much, but just by a little. In fact, it didn't just turn once, but it turned bit by bit until we, unknown to us, were heading in the complete opposite direction!

Yet… we still followed the man.

Now and then, if we slowed at all, he would put us at ease with his winning smile and calm manner, promising us we were heading the right direction. As the three of us journeyed together, he walked just far enough ahead that we could follow him easily.

Suddenly, the man came to a stop and turned around. We had fallen behind a little as he had a larger stride than us, so we rushed to catch up to him. When we were just about upon him, however, he reached down to the ground and grabbed a rope. Pulling on it, he smiled as my feet came out from under me!

I landed hard on the ground and crashed into Hopeful beside me, twisting around and crying out in pain. I then felt both of us rise quickly into the air. When my vision settled, my friend and I were hopelessly tangled in a net, hanging well about the height of the man.

I struggled and twisted, trying to get myself upright. "You okay?" I gasped.

"I… I'm fine," Hopeful replied.

Peering out of the net, I turned my attention to the man who had led us there. At first, he just stared at us with an enormous smile, all kindness now gone from his face, but then he broke out in laughter as he tied the rope to a tree. Turning his back to us, he cast off his light robe, the one he had used to deceive us into thinking he was a man we could trust. Without another word, he turned and walked away, doubtless looking for someone else to ensnare.

I struggled desperately to pull the ropes off or to reach for any sharp object I could find to cut us free, but my hands and arms were so entangled, I could do nothing but hang there. Hopeful, sadly, caught in the same net as me, faced the same problem. Despite our inability to get out, we struggled hard for a long time, desperate to get out of that trap! Yet, try as we might, in time, all we could do was to break down and weep.

"This is my fault," I cried. "The shepherds warned us to watch out for the flatterers! We've just found out that the saying of the wise man is true: 'A man who flatters his neighbour spreads a net for his feet.'"[1]

---

[1] Prov. 29:5.

Hopeful took a deep breath and added meekly, "They also gave us a note, directions for the path. It was given so we could find our way, but we forgot to read it, didn't we? We haven't kept ourselves from the way of the violent. David was wiser than we were in this. Remember how he said, 'With regard to the works of men, by the word of your lips I have avoided the ways of the violent.'"[2]

So, we hung there, unable to move, unable to free ourselves, regretting our foolishness.

After a long time, in the distance, I caught sight of someone. A man approached—a Shining One. He came towards us, carrying a whip made of a small cord. Coming right up close, he called up to us, "Where have you come from, and what are you doing up there?"

"We are poor pilgrims," I replied. "We are going to Zion, but a dark-skinned man, clothed in white, led us out of the way. He said he was going to Zion and told us to follow him."

"That was Flatterer!" the man declared. "He is a false apostle who pretends to be an angel of light!"[3]

The Shining one moved to the place where the Flatterer had tied off the rope and undid it, lowering us to the ground. Once down, we lay there, still unable to help ourselves, and the Shining One came close. He grabbed the net and, with his strong arms, ripped the net open, then pulled us out.

"Follow me, and I'll take you back to the path."

Without another word, he turned and took us back the way we had come when we followed the Flatterer. The path led us around by the long-way, forcing us to retrace

---

2 Ps. 17:4.
3 Prov. 29:5; Dan. 11:32; 2 Cor. 11:13, 14.

our steps, and eventually we reached our path—the true path.

When we had come to a halt, he spoke again. "Where did you stay last night?"

"With the Shepherds in the Delectable Mountains," Hopeful replied.

The Shining One frowned and asked, "Did they not give you a note? One which would give you direction for the path?"

"They did," I said.

"And did you," he asked, "when you were unsure of the way to go, read that note?"

I hung my head and shook my head. "No."

"And why not?"

"We forgot," I replied quietly.

"And did the Shepherds remind you to beware of the Flatterer?"

"Yes," I said, still with my head hung low, "but we just didn't think that this well-spoken man could be him."[4]

"Lie down!" he ordered.

We immediately obeyed, lying down on the ground at his feet. The man walked around us and then took his whip and beat us with it until we hurt terribly. He did this to teach us the good way to walk, and as he whipped us, he said, "Those whom I love, I reprove and discipline, so be zealous and repent!"[5]

When he finished, he helped me to my feet, and then did the same for Hopeful. We stood there, feeling the

---

[4] Rom. 16:18.
[5] Deut. 25:2; 2 Chron. 6:26,27; Rev. 3:19.

aches and pains from the whips, but also feeling sorrow that we had fallen so far and for such a deception.

"You may continue now," he said to us, "but be sure to pay close attention to the other directions of the shepherds!"

"Thank you, Sir, for your kindness" I said, and Hopeful added his thanks as well.

When the man left us, we continued along the proper path, singing the following song:

> *Come hither, you that walk along the way;*
> *See how the pilgrims fare that go astray.*
> *They catched are in an entangling net,*
> *'Cause they good counsel lightly did forget:*
> *'Tis true they rescued were, but yet you see,*
> *They're scourged to boot. Let this your caution be.*

We rushed down the path, making good time, both of us happy to be back on the right course. Our hearts, filled with joy, looked forward to the Celestial City, the very place we had our sights set on! I longed to finally see my Saviour face to face, knowing we would find peace there in his presence.

"Who is that?" Hopeful asked, pulling me from my thoughts.

I strained to see ahead and could just make out the shape of someone in the distance. As we drew closer, we saw he walked calmly and all alone along the path towards us. "Look!" I said. "A man with his back to Zion coming to meet us."

"Let's be careful with this one," Hopeful warned. "He might be a flatterer, just like the other man."

We walked on, and the man drew closer and closer until we finally reached him. When we greeted him, he told us his name was Atheist and asked us where we were going.

"We're going to Mount Zion," I replied.

At that response, the man laughed. Not just a small laugh, but a deep, belly laugh. He laughed and laughed and laughed, and it didn't take long before we could see he was not laughing out of joy, but he was laughing at us.

I frowned at Hopeful, then turned back to the man. "Why are you laughing?"

Atheist calmed himself down a little, but still chuckled as he spoke. "I laugh because you two are so… so ignorant! I mean, you're taking on such a tiresome journey, and the only thing you'll get out of all your pain is the actual journey!"

"Why?" I asked. "You think they won't welcome us in?"

Atheist broke into laughter again. "Welcome you in?" He put his hands on his belly and laughed even harder. "To where? There's no such place as you're dreaming of in all this world!"

"But there is in the world to come," I explained.

He smiled at me condescendingly and shook his head. "When I was at home in my country, that's what I heard as well. So, I went out to see." Shaking his head again, he continued, "I've been searching for twenty years! But now, after all this time, I still haven't found anything more than I did on the first day I set out!"[6]

"We've heard it's there," I said. "And we both believe it!"

---

[6] Jer. 22:12; Eccl. 10:15.

"If I hadn't believed while still at home, I never would have come this far! But I've been searching all this time and found nothing. I should have found something, because I've been a lot further along the path than either of you!" He laughed yet again at us and shook his head. "I'm going back home, and I'll enjoy the things that I gave up, now that I see that what I hoped for doesn't exist."

Turning to Hopeful, I asked, "Is it true? Is what this man said really the way it is?"

Hopeful grabbed my arm and stared intently into my eyes. "Watch out, Christian! This is one of the flatterers! Remember what it's cost us so far listening to this kind of person. Think about it! No Mount Zion? Didn't we see the gate of the city from the Delectable Mountains? And aren't we to walk by faith? Let's go on," Hopeful urged, "before the man with the whip comes back. You should have taught me this lesson, but I'll be the teacher now. 'Cease to hear instruction, my son, and you will stray from the words of knowledge.' Watch out, my brother. Don't listen to this man. We need to have 'faith and preserve our souls.'"[7]

I smiled at Hopeful. "My brother, I didn't ask because I doubted the truth, but to test you, to get an honest glimpse of your heart. As for this man, I know he's blinded by the god of this world. Let's move on, knowing that we believe the truth, and 'no lie is of the truth.'"[8]

Hopeful laughed, not like Atheist, a mocking, arrogant laugh, but one filled with joy. "Now I rejoice in the hope of the glory of God!"

So we moved on and left Atheist to return to his home. The man continued on his way, laughing at us as he disappeared out of sight.

---

[7] 2 Cor. 5:7; Prov. 19:27; Heb. 10:39.
[8] 1 John 2:21.

The path led us along through different lands, some grassy and smooth, others rocky and rough, but always straight, and always towards our goal of the Celestial City. In time, we found the land changed to beautiful, flowing, flowered fields filled with small copses sprouting up here and there.

The air in this land smelled sweet, and we both found ourselves relaxed and feeling more comfortable. Hopeful, beside me, stumbled just a little, and I caught his arm. His eyelids were heavy with sleep, and he smiled at me. "I'm exhausted, Christian. I can barely keep my eyes open. Let's lie down here in one of these beautiful meadows and take a nap."

I squeezed his arm tight and shook it a little. "No way!" I said. "We could fall asleep and never awake again!"

"Why, brother?" Hopeful asked. "Sleep is good for those who work hard. We'd feel a lot better after taking a nap."

"Don't you remember?" I asked. "One of the shepherds warned us to watch out for the Enchanted Grounds! He meant we shouldn't fall asleep! 'So let us not sleep, as others do, but let us keep awake and be sober.'"[9]

Hopeful's face fell, and his mouth dropped open. "Oh, Christian, that's my fault! I'm so sorry." He turned and looked down at the ground, at the soft grass and the flowered fields. In a quiet voice, he said, "If I'd been here all alone, I would have risked death by sleeping! It's true what the wise man said, 'Two are better than one, because they have a good reward for their toil.'[10] Having you here with me is a real mercy, Christian."

---

[9] 1 Thess 5:6.
[10] Ecc. 4:9.

I smiled and let go of his arm. "Well, Hopeful, to keep ourselves awake in this land, what do you think about having a discussion?"

"That sounds great to me!" Hopeful replied.

"Where should we begin?"

Hopeful thought for a moment and then smiled as an idea hit him. "Why don't we begin where God began with us? But you start us off."

"Well then, first, I'm going to sing you a song."

When saints do sleepy grow, let them come hither,
And hear how these two pilgrims talk together:
Yea, let them learn of them, in any wise,
Thus to keep ope[11] their drowsy slumb'ring eyes.
Saints' fellowship, if it be managed well,
Keeps them awake, and that in spite of hell.

"Let me ask you a question," I began. "How did you first come to this way of thinking?"

"Do you mean," Hopeful asked, "how I first considered my soul's need?"

"That's what I'm asking!"

"Well, for a long time," Hopeful said, "I continued to delight in the things you could see and buy in Vanity Fair. I mean… that's where I grew up, my whole life spent in that place. I desired all those things that I now believe if I'd continued in them, they would have drowned me in hell and destruction."

"What kinds of things?"

---

[11] An archaic version of *open* as in "Why did you leave the fridge ope?" or as a dentist might say, "Ope wide."

"Things like the treasures and riches of the world. I also really loved to take part in rioting, revelling, drinking, swearing, lying, uncleanness, Sabbath-breaking, and more... all those things that destroy the soul. But I eventually found through considering the things of God, things I heard from you and our beloved Faithful, who was put to death for his faith and righteous life at Vanity Fair, that 'the end of those things is death.' And I learned that 'because of these things, the wrath of God comes upon the sons of disobedience.'"[12]

"And did you immediately fall under the power of that conviction?"

Hopeful shook his head. "No! Not at all! I wasn't willing, at first, to recognize how evil sin was, nor was I willing to admit the damnation that follows when you commit that sin. So, when I was first confronted with the Word, I set out to close my eyes to the light of the truth."

"But why did you carry on with your sin," I asked, "when the Spirit of God began to work in you?"

"Well, there were many reasons, Christian. First, I really didn't know or understand that it was the work of God in my heart. I never thought that God would begin the conversion of a sinner by opening their eyes to sin![13] Second, sin was still very attractive to me, and I really hated the idea of giving it up. Third, I couldn't figure out how to step away from my old friends because I enjoyed them so much along with what they were doing. And fourth, the times when I felt conviction... those times were so horrible for me and bothered my heart so much that I couldn't stand even thinking of those times!"

---

[12] Rom. 6:21-23; Eph. 5:6.
[13] Author's Note: Personally, I find this one of the most powerful and eye-opening statements in the book.

"Then," I asked, "there must have been times when you weren't feeling convicted, right?"

"Absolutely! But then it would hit me again—all the conviction—and I'd be in as bad a situation, or worse, than I had been before."

"What would remind you of your sins?"

"Many things," Hopeful explained. "When I'd meet a good man in the streets, or when I heard anyone read the Bible. When I had a headache, or were told one of my neighbours was sick, or when I heard the bell toll for the dead, or when I thought of my own death, or when I heard of someone who died suddenly... any of those things! But especially when I thought I would soon face judgement!"

"Was there any way you could ease the guilt you felt whenever these things came to mind?"

"Nope! Not at all." Hopeful took a deep breath, then let it out slowly before he continued. "If I tried, the conviction would come on me even quicker! And if I thought, at any time, of going back to sin, even though my mind had hated it, it would be like double the torment!"

"And how did you manage?" I asked. "What did you do?"

"Well," Hopeful said, "I figured I had to fix up my life! In fact, I figured if I didn't, I was sure to be sent to hell."

"And did you do it?" I found myself fascinated by his story and couldn't wait to hear how God had worked all this in his life. "I mean, did you try to fix up your life?"

"Yes, for sure! I not only ran from my sin, but sinful friends as well. I took up religious works such as prayer, Bible reading, crying over my sin, telling the truth to my neighbours, and more. There were so many things I did… too many to list."

"And did you feel you were good, then?"

"For a little while," Hopeful said with a frown. "But in the end, all the conviction for sin came crashing down on me again, even on top of my life changes!"

"How come?" I asked. "You'd reformed your life!"

"Well, several things brought the conviction back on me, especially certain Scriptures. Passages like, 'all our righteous deeds are like a polluted garment,' and 'by works of the law no one will be justified,' and 'when you have done all you were commanded, say, we are unworthy servants,' and many more Scriptures like that. So, I reasoned it all out, thinking, if all my righteous deeds are like a polluted garment, and if by the works of the law no one can be justified, and if when we have done everything we were commanded to do, we are still unworthy, then it's foolish to think of working your way to heaven! And then I thought if a man has a debt of a hundred dollars, but then pays for everything he buys after that, if the debt still isn't paid, the man to whom he owes the money can still sue him and throw him into prison until he pays it all back!"[14]

"Okay," I said, "then how did you work all this out in your own life?"

"I thought about how I've run myself deep into God's debt with my sins, and now by changing my ways, I still won't pay off the original debt. So, I figured I should continue with the way I've changed my life, but I knew I still needed to be freed from the condemnation that I'd put myself under by my former sin."

---

[14] Isa. 64:6; Gal. 2:16; Luke 17:10.

"Okay, that's some good reasoning. Please, Hopeful, go on."

"Another thing weighed on my heart. I realized that if I looked closely at what I was doing since I changed my ways, I still saw sin, new sin, mixing itself with the best of what I did. From that, I knew that even without my former love of myself and my wicked choices, the bit of sin that was in even one new good work was enough to send me to hell—even if my former life had been perfect!"

"What did you do then?"

"Do?" Hopeful laughed, but not with joy. "I had no idea what to do! At least, until I poured out my heart to Faithful. He and I knew each other quite well. He told me that unless I could obtain the righteousness of a man who had never sinned, nothing righteous I could do or even the righteousness of the entire world could save me."

"And do you think he was right?" I asked.

"If he'd told me this when I was happy with my own change of life, I would have called him a fool for all his pain. But once I saw my sin and the sin that stuck to my most righteous actions, I felt I had no choice but to agree."

"But, when he told you this, did you think there was any man anywhere who had never committed sin? Anyone who was righteous enough?"

Hopeful shook his head. "I have to admit, when he first said it, it sounded pretty strange, but after talking to him a bit more and spending time with him, I became fully convinced."

I nodded. It was a hard truth to accept, but by the grace of the Lord, eyes could be opened to see and understand. "Did you ask him who that man was and how you could be justified by him?"

"I did!" Hopeful exclaimed. "And he told me it was the Lord Jesus, the one who dwells at the right hand of the Most High. He said I needed to be justified by him, trusting what he did while living on the earth and suffering on the cross. So, I asked Faithful how that man's righteousness could be so effective as to justify another before God." Hopeful smiled, and this time, there was joy. "He told me Jesus was the mighty God, and did what he did, even dying, not for himself but for me! He did it so that his good and worthy work could be imputed[15] to me, if I believed in him!"[16]

"And what did you do then?"

"I argued against believing, for I figured there was no way Jesus would save me."

"What did Faithful say to you then?" I asked.

"He told me to go to Jesus and find out for myself! Now, I thought that would be pretentious of me—there's no way someone like Jesus would want to see me! But he told me I was invited to come. Then he gave me a book of Jesus's writing to encourage me to come, and Faithful told

---

[15] *Imputed* may be an unfamiliar word to many, although we might hear or read it now and then. Even if it may be unfamiliar, I still wanted to keep this word the same as it's a powerful theological term that is important for Christians to know. Christ's righteousness is imputed to us. That's not so much that his righteousness is given to us as, much as his righteousness is written *on us* and *in us* as our very own—his righteousness is credited to us. This is important because we are not *just* cleaned up sinners, we actually stand before God as having the righteousness of the perfect, holy, Jesus Christ because we have *his* righteousness *imputed* upon us! Do you see that? Because Jesus's righteousness is imputed to you, you are seen by God as having Jesus's righteousness, not because of you, but because of Jesus! And that, my friends, is imputation! Isn't that worth knowing and understanding?

[16] Heb. 10; Rom. 6; Col. 1; 1 Pet. 1.

me that in that book, every single little letter[17] stood firmer than heaven and earth. So, I asked him what I needed to do when I came before Jesus, and he told me I needed to plead on my knees with all my heart and soul for the Father to reveal him to me. Then I asked him how I should make my humble request, and he told me to go to Jesus and that I'd find him on a mercy-seat, where he sits all year long to pardon and forgive anyone who comes. I then told Faithful that I didn't know what to say when I faced him, and he told me to say, 'God, please be merciful to me, for I'm a sinner. Make me to know and believe in Jesus Christ, for I see that if he had not been righteous or if I do not have faith in that righteousness, I will be utterly cast away! Lord, I've heard that you are a merciful God, and you have declared that your Son, Jesus Christ, should be the Saviour of the world, and also, that you will place him upon such a poor sinner as I am—and I'm definitely a sinner! Lord, take this opportunity and magnify your grace in the salvation of my soul through your Son, Jesus Christ. Amen.'"[18]

"And did you do it? Do what Faithful told you to do?"

Hopeful nodded and gave me a little smile. "I did... over and over."

"And did the Father reveal his Son to you?"

"No, not at first." He laughed and shook his head. "Nor at second, nor third, fourth, or fifth. Not even on the sixth time."

"Well, what did you do?"

---

[17] The original referred to every *jot and tittle*. I changed it to something more contemporary, but the concept is that even the seemingly small and unimportant things of Christ's words will never fail as long as heaven and earth stand!

[18] Matt. 11:28, 24:35; Ps. 95:6; Dan. 6:10; Jer. 29:12, 13; Exo. 25:22; Lev. 16:2; Num. 7:89; Heb. 4:16.

"What did I do? I didn't know what to do!"

Nodding, I smiled at my friend. I understood. I understood how difficult it could be. Coming to Jesus was both the easiest, simplest thing to do, and the most difficult. "Did you consider just not praying at all?"

"A hundred times. Two hundred times, even!"

"And why didn't you stop praying then?" I asked.

"Because," Hopeful replied, "I believed what I had been told, that without the righteousness of Jesus Christ, all the world couldn't save me! So, I thought that if I just gave up, I would die, and I didn't want to die at the throne of grace. But then these words of Scripture came to mind: 'If it seems slow, wait for it; it will surely come; it will not delay.'[19] So, I continued praying until the Father showed me his Son!"

"And how was Jesus revealed to you?"

"Well, I didn't see him with my physical eyes, but with the eyes of my understanding. I was really struggling with it all—I was really sad, actually. In fact, I think I was sadder at that point than at any other time in my life! This sadness came on because of a fresh new understanding of how great and vile my sin is. And so, as I sat there, thinking about how I had nothing to look forward to other than hell and the eternal damnation of my soul, I suddenly saw the Lord Jesus Christ looking down from heaven on me, and he said, 'Believe in the Lord Jesus and you will be saved.'[20]

"And what did you do?"

"I answered him! I said, 'But Lord, I'm a great sinner—very great!' And he said to me, 'My grace is sufficient for you.' Then I said, 'But Lord, what is

---

[19] Hab. 2:3.
[20] Eph. 1:18, 19; Acts 16:30, 31.

251

believing?' And in that moment, I understood the saying, 'Whoever comes to me shall not hunger, and whoever believes in me shall never thirst.' And that's when I understood that believing and coming were all part of the same thing. The man who comes to Jesus, who runs after salvation by Christ in his heart and affections, that man definitely believes in Christ! When I realized this, my eyes filled with tears, and I asked, 'But Lord, can you accept such a terrible sinner like me? Can you save me?' And I heard him reply, 'Whoever comes to me, I will never cast out.' And then I said, 'But Lord, how do I think about you when I come to you so that my faith will be properly placed upon you?' He simply told me, 'Christ Jesus came into the world to save sinners,' and he 'is the end of the law for righteousness to everyone who believes.' He 'was delivered up for our trespasses and raised for our justification,' this very Jesus, 'who loves us and has freed us from our sins by his blood.' He is, for us, a 'mediator between God and men,' and 'he always lives to make intercession for' us."[21]

"And what did you make of all that?" I asked.

"Well, from what I gathered, I saw I needed to look for righteousness in Jesus and satisfaction for my sins by his blood! What he did in obedience to his Father's law and in submitting to the penalty of that law was not for himself, but for everyone who will accept it for his salvation and be thankful!"

Hopeful laughed. In his excitement over his testimony of Christ's work in his life, I don't think he realized that he had picked up speed as we moved down the path, leaving me to nearly jog to keep up with him. As we rushed along, I watched the joy on his face and with each step he took.

---

[21] 2 Cor.12:9; John 6:35-37; 1 Tim. 1:15; Rom. 10:4, 4:25; Rev. 1:5; 1 Tim. 2:5; Heb. 7:24-25.

He laughed once again before continuing. "So, my dear friend, my heart was full of joy, my eyes were full of tears, and my affection was filled—no... not filled... running over! Filled and running over with love for the name, people, and ways of Jesus Christ!"

"What a revelation of Christ to your soul!" I said with a laugh as I put my arm on his to slow him down a little. "But tell me, Hopeful. What effect did this have on your spirit?"

"It made me see and understand many things. It made me see that despite all the righteousness that is in the world, everything—EVERYTHING—is condemned! It made me see that God the Father, though he is just, can justly justify the sinner who comes to him. It made me terribly ashamed of how vile my former life was, and it left me shocked by how ignorant I had been, since before that moment, there had never entered my mind any thought of how beautiful Jesus Christ is! It made me love holy living and long to do something for the honour and glory of the name of the Lord Jesus." His voice then grew serious as he told me, "I knew at that moment that if I had a thousand gallons of blood in my body, I would spill it all for the sake of the Lord Jesus!"

Hopeful finished and walked on with joy while I tried my best not only to keep up with him, but also to take in everything he'd told me. I followed along with an enormous grin on my face, grateful for what the Lord Jesus had done in my friend's life.

14. Ignorance

We reached the top of a small hill.

Well, it had looked small from the bottom, but both Hopeful and I were left gasping for air by the time we reached the peak. I paused there on the path to catch my breath while Hopeful took the time to look around to see the lay of the land. When he turned around to face behind us, he paused. After a moment, he said, "Look at Ignorance back there! He's fallen so far behind."

"I see him," I replied with a chuckle. "He doesn't really like being around us."

"No," Hopeful replied, "but it wouldn't have hurt him to stick close."

"That's true, but I'd guess he'd think otherwise."

"I think you're right," Hopeful said, "but let's wait for him anyway."

I agreed, and we remained where we were while we waited. Ignorance took his time catching up, but when he reached us, I asked, "Hey Ignorance, why do you walk so far behind us?"

The man slowed down as he approached and came to a stop not far from us. With a frown, he said, "I like to be by myself, walking alone. I prefer it over company, unless the company itself is something I like more than solitude."

I grimaced, hearing the message loud and clear. Leaning over to Hopeful, I whispered, "Didn't I tell you he doesn't enjoy being around us?" I took a deep breath and added, "However, this is a solitary place. Let's chat with him." To Ignorance, I said, "How are you, Ignorance? How are things between you and God now?"

"I hope all is well," Ignorance replied, "for I always have good thoughts and get great ideas while I walk."

"Like what?" I asked, waving for him to follow. Hopeful and I started up, and after a moment's hesitation, Ignorance moved forward.

When he caught up, he said, "I think of things like God and heaven."

I glanced at Hopeful, then back at Ignorance. "So do the demons and all the condemned souls."

"But I think of them and desire them."

"So do many who are never likely to get there. 'The soul of the sluggard craves and gets nothing.'"[1]

"But I think of them and leave everything to get it."

"That I doubt," I replied. "Leaving everything is very difficult, much harder than most people know. But what would make you think you've left everything for God and heaven?"

---

[1] Prov. 13:4.

"I know this in my mind."[2]

"The wise man says, 'whoever trusts in his own mind is a fool,'"[3] I replied.

"But he's talking about an evil mind. My mind is good."

I frowned at that comment. "How can you prove that?"

Ignorance returned the frown with one of his own and said, "My mind comforts me with the hope of heaven."

"That could be because of its deceitfulness. One's mind may comfort them in the hope of something for which he has no reason to hope."

"But my mind and my life agree with one another," Ignorance explained. "Because of that, my hope is solid."

"What makes you think your mind and life agree?"

"I know it in my mind."

"Ask Hopeful if I'm a thief!"[4] I said in my shock. Shaking my head, I mumbled under my breath, "You know it in your mind…" Taking a deep breath, I added, "If the Word of God doesn't witness to it, Ignorance, all other testimony is worthless!"

"But don't good minds have good thoughts? And isn't a life that is lived according to God's commands a good life?"

---

[2] The original uses the phrase, "My heart tells me so," but I changed it to *mind* due to the ESV's use of the word *mind* in Prov. 28:26 which Christian quotes in his reply.

[3] Prov. 28:26.

[4] The original says, "Ask my fellow if I be a thief! Thy heart tells thee so!" The thrust of it seems to be suggesting that another's testimony is worthless, even on the matter of whether or not Christian himself is a thief. All that matters is the Word of God's testimony.

"Yes," I replied, "a heart that has good thoughts is good, and a life lived according to God's commands is good, but it is one thing to have a good heart and life, it's a totally different thing to only think you do."

"Then tell me, what do you think are good thoughts?" Ignorance asked. "And what is a life lived according to God's commandments?"

"There are many good thoughts, Ignorance. Some good thoughts have to do with us, some with God, some with Christ… and with other things."

"What are good thoughts that have to do with us?"

I smiled at the young man and said, "Thoughts that agree with the Word of God."

"And when do our thoughts of ourselves agree with the Word of God?" he asked.

I took a deep breath. I hoped that this was a sign that Ignorance's heart might soften towards the truth. "Our thoughts agree with the Word of God when we judge our hearts the same way that the Word does. What I mean is, the Word of God says of the natural man, 'None is righteous, no one does good.' It also says that every intention of the thoughts of man's heart is only evil continually. And 'the intention of man's heart is evil from his youth.' So, Ignorance, when we think this way of ourselves, understanding this to be true, then will our thoughts be good thoughts, because they are according to the Word of God."[5]

Ignorance scowled and shook his head. "I'll never believe that my heart is that bad!"

"Then, my dear Ignorance, you have never had one good thought about yourself your entire life!" Before he

---

[5] Rom. 3:10-12; Gen. 6:5, 8:21.

could reply, I put up my hands and said, "But… let me continue. As the Word of God judges your heart, so it judges your ways, and when the thoughts of your heart and your ways agree with the judgement given on each by the Word of God, then both are good, because they agree with the Word of God!"

"Explain that to me," Ignorance asked.

"The Word of God, Ignorance, says that a man's ways are crooked—not good, but perverse! It tells us that our ways are naturally far away from the righteous path, and that our ways haven't even known the righteous path! Now, when a man thinks this way about his life, I mean, when he thinks in a sensible, reasonable way with a deep humility, then his thoughts of his own life are good, because his thoughts agree with the Word of God."[6]

"And what are good thoughts concerning God?" Ignorance asked me.

"It's very much the same thing as I told you regarding our thoughts about ourselves. When our thoughts of God agree with what the Word says of him, when we think of who he is and what he is like in the same way that the Word teaches, then we have good thoughts of him. Of course, I can't go into detail about what that looks like right now. There's a lot in the Word of God about this! But, if we consider him regarding us, we have good thoughts of God when we think he knows us better than we know ourselves and can see sin in us when and where we see none. When we believe he knows our deep thoughts and that even our hearts are open to him, like a book, at all times, then we have good thoughts concerning God. And when we know and believe that all our righteousness is rotten and stinks to him, and that he can't stand to see us

---

[6] Ps. 125:5; Prov. 2:15; Rom. 3.

259

place ourselves before him with self-confidence,[7] even at our best, then we have good thoughts concerning God."

"Come on, Christian!" Ignorance growled, his eyes filled with disgust and his mouth in a sneer. "Do you really think that I'm such a fool as to think God can't see anything more than I see? Or that I could try to impress God with my actions?

"Well then," I said, "tell me how you think of God."

"To be blunt and to the point, I know I must believe in Christ to be justified."

I stopped there on the path, raised my eyebrows, and turned to look Ignorance right in the eye. "You think you need to believe in Jesus, yet you can't see your need for him? You see neither your original sin nor your actual sin! Instead, your view of yourself and of what you do shows you to be someone who has never seen the need for Christ's own righteousness to justify you before God! How, then, can you say you believe in Christ?"

"I believe enough to get what I need," Ignorance said with a frown.

"And what do you believe?" I asked.

"I believe Christ died for sinners, and that I will be justified before God from the curse because of his gracious acceptance of my obedience to his law. You see, Christ makes my religious work acceptable to his Father by virtue of his own merit. Because of this, I will be justified."

---

[7] The original simply uses the word *confidence* here, but to distinguish this from Heb. 4:16 where we would understand a biblical confidence (boldness) as coming from Christ's work and his grace offered, I have changed this word to *self-confidence* to pull out the concept of confidence based on our own effort and/or opinion of ourselves.

I frowned at the young man, disappointed by his stubbornness, but not surprised. Turning back to the path, I started up again, and Ignorance took his place beside me, waiting for my response while Hopeful trailed a little behind.

After a few minutes, I said, "Ignorance, let me respond to your confession of faith... let me challenge it.

"First, you believe with an imaginary faith. This faith you speak of is described nowhere in the Word. Second, you believe with a false faith because it takes justification from the personal righteousness of Christ and applies that justification to your own. This faith doesn't make Christ a justifier of you as a person, but of your works, and then it justifies you as a person for the sake of your work, which is false. Therefore, your faith is deceitful. In fact, it will leave you facing wrath on the day of God Almighty. True justifying faith puts the soul, one which is aware of its condition by the law, in a place where it flees, seeking refuge in Christ's righteousness. This righteousness of Christ is not an act of grace by which he makes your obedience justified, acceptable to God. Instead, Christ's righteousness is his personal obedience to the law in doing and suffering for us in the way that we should have obeyed and suffered! This righteousness is the kind that true faith accepts. The soul who then stands under that righteousness and is covered by it is presented as spotless before God. That soul is accepted by God and freed from condemnation!"

"What?" Ignorance said with a laugh, incredulity filling his voice. "You would have us trust what Christ himself has done without any work on our part? That kind of conceit would loosen the reins of our lust and allow us to live however we want! What does it matter how we live if we can be justified from all sin by Christ's personal righteousness, simply because we believe it?"

"Ignorance is your name, and that's definitely who you are! Even your answer demonstrates what I've said. You are ignorant of what justifying righteousness is, and ignorant of how to save your soul from the overwhelming wrath of God through the faith of justifying righteousness! You are even ignorant of the true effects of saving faith in the righteousness of Christ, which is to win over the heart to God in Christ, to bow the heart to him! It is to bring a soul to love his name, his word, his ways, and his people, which is not at all what you ignorantly imagine!"

When I finished, I was met with silence. Deep inside, I hoped perhaps he might consider what I said, but I knew this was not the case. The look in his eye was not one of humble acceptance, but of stubborn ignorance.

Stepping up next to me, Hopeful whispered, "Ask him if he's ever had Christ revealed to him from heaven?"

The sound must have carried as Ignorance scoffed and said, "What? You go for those revelations? What you and everyone else who believes that kind of thing says is nothing more than the result of a distracted mind!"

"Why is that?" Hopeful replied calmly. "Christ is so hidden in God from our natural ability to perceive him he cannot be seen in any salvific manner unless God the Father reveals him to us."

"That's what you believe," Ignorance said, derision dripping from his lips. "Your faith, not mine. My beliefs are as good as yours, although I don't hold to so many... creative ideas as you."

"If you don't mind me stepping in again," I said with a shake of my head, "you shouldn't talk down about this issue. I can confidently say, just as Hopeful has, that no one can know Jesus Christ unless the Father reveals him. Even faith, which is the very means by which the soul takes hold of Christ, if it is true faith, it must come by the exceeding greatness of his mighty power. I think, Ignorance, the working of this faith is something of which you are ignorant." As we continued, I turned my head to him to make eye contact, hoping one last time that God might soften his heart. In a pleading voice, I urged him, saying, "Wake up, Ignorant! See your own wickedness and run to the Lord Jesus. By his righteousness, the righteousness of God, for he is God, you can be delivered from condemnation!"[8]

My heart sank as Ignorance took a deep breath, yawning as if he felt tired, although I could see he was not. He came to a halt and put his hands up. "Christian, Hopeful, you travel too fast for me. I just can't keep up with you. Why don't the two of you go on ahead, and I'll walk behind you for a bit."

Disappointed, but not surprised, we said our goodbyes and moved on. There was little to nothing we could do for the young man. Instead, we spoke these words:

> *Well, Ignorance, wilt thou yet foolish be,*
> *To slight good counsel, ten times given thee?*
> *And if thou yet refuse it, thou shalt know,*
> *Ere long, the evil of thy doing so.*
> *Remember, man, in time, stoop, do not fear;*
> *Good counsel taken well, saves: therefore hear.*
> *But if thou yet shalt slight it, thou wilt be*
> *The loser, (Ignorance), I'll warrant thee.*

Turning to my friend and companion on the path, I said, "Well, let's move on, Hopeful. I think we'll have to walk by ourselves again."

---

[8] Matt. 11:27; 1 Cor. 12:3; Eph. 1:18-19.

So, we moved on again with Ignorance limping along the path behind us,[9] but he continued to weigh on my heart. "I pity him, that poor man," I said to Hopeful. "It's certainly not going to go well for him at the end."

Hopeful put his hand encouragingly on my shoulder. "There are many where we came from who are like him. Whole families, even entire streets, who are like him—even pilgrims, walking along the path! And if there are so many in the towns where we came from who are like this, imagine how many there are where he was born!"

I shared his concern. My heart ached for so many lost souls. "The Word says, 'He has blinded their eyes… lest they see with their eyes.'"[10] There was not much else we could say about Ignorance, but desiring to speak of the one issue a little more, I said, "Now that we're by ourselves, what do you think of those who are spiritually blind? Do you think they never feel conviction for sin and then never fear that they're in a dangerous position?"

Hopeful laughed. "No, dear Christian, you answer that question yourself. You're older, the more mature between the two of us."

I smiled, unsure if that was a compliment or a friendly jab at my age. "Well then, this is what the old man thinks," I said with a laugh. "I suspect they may sometimes feel conviction and fear their standing before God, but they are also naturally ignorant and because of this, they don't understand that those convictions are good things. Because of their ignorance, they desperately try to stifle them, and

_____

[9] In the original, Bunyan writes, "and Ignorance he came hobbling after." While there doesn't seem to be a physical injury that would point to this need to hobble, it's interesting to see this in light of the allegory: his refusal to trust in saving grace and hold to true faith left him hobbling/limping along the path.
[10] John 12:40.

then presumptuously flatter themselves in the way their hearts want to go."

Hopeful nodded. "I believe as you do, that fear is helpful and good for a person, and to set them on a right path at the beginning of a pilgrimage."

"It absolutely does, if it's proper fear. In fact, the Word says, 'The fear of the Lord is the beginning of wisdom.'"[11]

"And how would you describe proper fear?" Hopeful asked.

I pursed my lips for a moment while I collected my thoughts. When I spoke, my words came out slowly. "True, right, or proper fear is revealed in three ways. First, by the way it rises in our hearts, being caused by a saving conviction for sin. Second, it drives the soul to grab hold of Christ for salvation. And finally, it brings about in the soul a great reverence for God and causes the reverence to continue. This reverence is not only to God but also to his word and his ways, and it keeps the soul soft, making it afraid to turn away from these things, either to the right or to the left toward anything that might dishonour God, break the soul's peace, grieve the Spirit, or give reason for the enemy to accuse."[12]

"Well, that's a good explanation," Hopeful said. "I think that makes sense, and I believe you've spoken well." Looking around as if noticing the area for the first time, he asked, "Do you think we're almost past the Enchanted Ground?"

---

[11] Prov. 1:7, 9:10; Job 28:28; Ps. 111:10.
[12] The original used the word, *reproach* here, instead of accuse. However, in a contemporary retelling, I think "accuse" fits better here as the context would suggest that he's speaking of preventing the enemy from rightfully criticizing.

"Why? Are you bored with our conversation?" I asked with a teasing laugh.

"No," he replied with a chuckle. "Honestly, I just want to know where we are."

"We have about two miles left until we're out of this area," I told him, "but let's continue with the topic." I took another moment to collect my thoughts before continuing. "Those who are ignorant don't know that these convictions that raise fear in their hearts are for their good. Because of that, they try to stifle the convictions."

"And how do they stifle them?" Hopeful asked me.

"Well, first of all, they think the devil brings those fears about, even though they come from God. Thinking this, they resist them as things that they believe will destroy them. Second, they think these fears spoil their faith, even though these poor men have no faith at all. Because of this, they harden their hearts against the fear. Third, they assume they should never fear, and then they allow their confidence to grow beyond what is proper, considering how little they understand.[13] And finally, they see their fears take away their own pitiful sense of self-holiness, and because of that, they resist it with everything they have!"

"I know a little of that," Hopeful said. "Before I knew the gospel, it was that way with me."

That didn't surprise me since it is the story of so many of us who walk the path, but I felt it was time to change the subject. "Let's leave Ignorance behind and talk about something else. Something also profitable to our faith."

"I'm all for that, Christian! You start us out!"

---

[13] The original here says, *wax presumptuously confident.*

"Okay. Tell me, did you know… maybe ten years back… a man by the name of Temporary? He lived in your part of the country and was a prominent religious man."

"Did I know him?" Hopeful replied with a laugh. "Oh, I certainly did! He lived in Graceless, a town about two miles outside of Honesty, and he lived right next to a man named Turnback."

"Right," I said. "Actually, he lived in the same house as Turnback. Well, Temporary, as far as I believe, was once spiritually awakened, and had some understanding of his sin and the coming penalty."

"Yes, I would agree with your assessment of him. I lived only about three miles from him, and he would often stop by my place, usually weeping when he arrived. I felt so sorry for him and actually had a lot of hope for him. But, as we often see, not everyone who cries, 'Lord, Lord…'"[14]

I grimaced, knowing Hopeful spoke the truth. Continuing with my story, I explained, "He once told me he had decided to go on pilgrimage, as we are now, but then he met a man by the name of Save-self, and suddenly it was like he was a complete stranger to me."

"Well, since you brought him up, why don't we dig into the reason for sudden backsliding of people such as Temporary?" Hopeful suggested.

"That's a great idea! But please, Hopeful, you begin the conversation."

"Okay, well, in my opinion, Christian, there are four reasons for backsliding:

"First, even though the conscience is awakened, their minds are not changed. So, when the power of the

---

[14] Matt. 7:21.

guilt wears off, the motivation for becoming religious simply ends, so they naturally turn to their old path. You see this lived out when a dog is sick from what it has eaten. As long as the sickness holds on, it vomits everything up. It doesn't do this by choice (if we say that a dog has a mind to choose), but because its stomach is upset. When the sickness is over and its stomach has settled—its tastes obviously not at odds with vomit—it turns around and eats it all back up again. It's just as the Scriptures say, 'The dog returns to its own vomit.'[15] So, if their desire for heaven is intense, but only because of the sense and fear of hell, then, when the sense of hell and fear of damnation calms down, so will their desire for heaven and salvation. Then it comes to pass that when their guilt and fear are gone, their desires for heaven and happiness pass away, and they return to their own path.

"Second, another reason is that they have fears that drive them to slavery, and these fears become their masters. I'm thinking specifically of their fear of mankind, for 'the fear of man lays a snare.'[16] So, even though they appear to intensely desire heaven as long as the flames of hell are burning around their ears, yet when the fear fades away, they reconsider it all. Mainly, they think it is good to be wise and not risk losing everything for things they're not really sure about, or at the very least, not to risk unavoidable and unnecessary trouble. Because of this, they fall back into the world.

"Third, the shame that often goes hand in hand with religion is also a hindrance to them. They are proud and arrogant, and religion, in their opinion, is something to look down on. So, when they lose their sense of hell and the wrath to come, they return to their former path.

---

[15] 2 Pet. 2:22.
[16] Prov. 29:25.

"And finally, guilt, and to meditate on fear, are bad things to them. They don't want to know what miserable things might lie ahead of them until they face them. Although, perhaps at first seeing the danger, they might be inclined to run to the same place righteous people run and find safety, but because, as I mentioned, they turn away from thoughts of guilt and fear the moment those feelings of fear and the wrath of God pass, they gladly harden their hearts. In fact, they even choose paths that will harden their hearts more."

I nodded my head, considering all that Hopeful had just shared. "I think you've just about nailed it, Hopeful. In the end, they are lacking an actual change in their mind and will. They're like a criminal who stands before a judge, shaking and trembling. While there, he seems to repent entirely, but it's really all about the fear of prison,[17] not about a hatred for the crime he's committed. In fact, the moment he's given his freedom, he turns around and continues to be a thief, still living as a criminal. If his mind is changed, however, he would stop his wicked ways."

"Okay," Hopeful replied, "now that I've shared some thoughts on why people backslide, why don't you tell me your thoughts on the matter?"

"Certainly!" I said. "I would say there are nine reasons:

"First, they stop thinking, as much as they are able, about God, death, and judgement to come.

"Second, they set aside, bit by bit, all their spiritual disciplines such as private prayer, fighting down their lusts, watching and grieving for sin, and things like that.

---

[17] In the original, it speaks of a fear of the *halter* which is a rope placed around the neck. Since hangings aren't common practice today, I went with *prison* instead.

"Third, they push away the company of genuinely passionate and loving Christians.

"Fourth, once this is done, they dislike serving and seeking the Lord, such as hearing the word, reading the word, the gathering of the church, and so on.

"Fifth, they poke holes in the lives, actions, and choices of the godly for no other reason than to justify tossing religion away.

"Sixth, they hang around and cling with sinful, undisciplined, and immoral people.

"Seventh, they have sinful and immoral conversations in private and are happy when they see anyone who is considered honest having similar conversations. They use that as a justification for doing it more boldly.

"Eighth, at this point, they play with minor sins openly.

"And finally, their heart becomes hard, and they show themselves openly and proudly for who they are."

Wrapping it all up, I explained, "Once thrown into such a miserable state, they fall into eternal death in their own deception, unless, of course, a miracle of grace happens."

With that, we both fell silent. The topic, being well talked through, was well enough to leave alone for a time.

We moved on in our journey along the path, straight as an arrow, heading to the very place we longed to be.

I smiled more and more with each step. One thing I knew for sure… it wouldn't be long.

Soon I would see my Saviour.

15. The River

The beauty of the Enchanted Grounds, all that made Hopeful and my eyes heavy, all the attractive things throughout it, faded away. Though the Enchanted Grounds had been beautiful, I was happy to leave that treacherous place behind. And so with joy, we ventured into a new land.

Taking a deep breath, I smiled. Beside me, Hopeful also grinned from ear to ear. The air itself was sweet—although a different sweetness than in the Enchanted Grounds—and just to breathe this air put my heart at ease. The ground here was softer than it had been on many parts of our journey, and our path led directly through this beautiful country, a land known as Beulah.

In this land, we found comfort from our tiresome journey by enjoying rest and taking our time to savour the peace we found. Each day, we listened to the music of the birds and their gentle songs, enjoyed the beauty of the flowers growing in the meadows, and even heard the voice of the turtledove in the land.[1]

---

[1] Song of Sol. 2:12.

In this country, the sun shone day and night, and we found peace as we rested in the safety of this land. We had reached a point beyond the Valley of the Shadow of Death and were out of reach of Giant Despair. From this land, we could not even see Doubting Castle!

But what we could see was the city to which we were going. We even met the Shining Ones in this land, for the inhabitants of the Celestial City often walked these fields as it was on the border of heaven itself. And in this land, the covenant between the bride and bridegroom was renewed, for "as the bridegroom rejoices over the bride, so shall your God rejoice over you." In this land we even heard voices coming from the city, loud voices, calling out, "Say to the daughter of Zion, 'Behold, your salvation comes; behold, his reward is with him, and his recompense before him.'" And the inhabitants of the country called them, "The Holy People, The Redeemed of the Lord... Sought Out."

Here we had no lack of food and felt no hunger, as we had plenty of corn and wine. This land held an abundance of everything we had longed for in our pilgrimage. Here, we were well cared for.[2]

Hopeful and I could not help ourselves; we rejoiced and praised the Lord, crying out with joy, and in this manner, we made our way along. In fact, in all our journey, in all the good times and all the difficulties, there was no point where we rejoiced as much as we did in this land.

And as we continued along the path, drawing close to the city, we began to see it more clearly. The city was built with pearls and precious stones. The streets within were paved with gold, and the beauty was almost too much to bear.

---

[2] Isa. 62:4; Song of Sol. 2:10-12; Isa. 62:5-12.

With each step, I felt the longing in my heart grow, longing to reach our future home. The city itself was so beautiful, and built with such precious materials, that the natural glory of the place and the reflection of the sun off its structures left me feeling sick with desire. Even Hopeful felt the same, and the longing for it drove us to the ground, groaning from the pain in our gut, and crying out, "If you find my beloved… tell him I am sick with love."[3]

We lay there for a time, struggling with our yearning, but could not move until we had rested. Climbing to our feet, we pushed on, strengthened enough to bear with our sickness.

Along the edge of the path, well-cared-for stone walls lined both sides, with gates now and then along the way. Each of the gates stood wide open, and as we passed, we turned to look and saw beautiful orchards, vineyards, and gardens, ripe with fruit and ready for picking.

"Who's that?" Hopeful asked, pulling me away from admiring the large bunches of purple grapes hanging from the many vines in the vineyard we passed.

A man stood before us, a gardener, leaning on a large staff. He wore rough clothing, dirt covering his knees, and he held his staff in his strong hands. On his head, he wore a large-brimmed hat, shading his cheerful eyes and enormous smile.

"Welcome," he called out to us as we came close.

"Thank you," I replied. The man's smile grew, and I found I couldn't help but like him. "Who owns these beautiful vineyards and gardens?"

"They belong to the King!" the man replied with a loud laugh. "They are planted for his own delight, and for

_____

3 Song of Sol. 5:8.

273

the comfort of his pilgrims." He paused for a moment before turning to the side. "Follow me."

He led us slowly through one of the gates into a large vineyard. Rows upon rows of vines led off into the distance, and each one was full of clusters of ripe grapes. Leading us right up to one of the closest, he raised his hand to point and said, "Enjoy! They are for you to take as much as you wish."[4]

Hopeful and I picked the grapes and ate our fill, careful to take what we wanted, but not more than we could eat at that moment. When we had eaten our fill, the gardener took us along paths and walkways, places where the King himself walked, and showed us the arbours where our Lord enjoyed sitting, relaxing, and admiring the beauty of the land.

As the day grew late, though the sun never set, we felt tired and took the opportunity to rest. With no need of a shelter, we simply laid down on the grass near one of the beautiful arbours and fell asleep to the sounds of the bird's songs and to the smell of the lilies growing all around the arbour.

We lay there for some time; I'm not sure how long. I slept, then I awoke, then I fell asleep again, resting in such peace. Whenever I awoke, Hopeful remained asleep, but in his sleep, he talked more than at any other time during our journey together. I suspect the same was true of me while I slept.

At one point, we both awoke at the same time and asked the gardener about how we spoke in our sleep, as we thought it was quite unusual. He merely said, "Why do you think it's so unusual? It's the nature of the grapes of these

---

[4] Deut. 23:24.

vineyards. They go down sweetly, and make people talk in their sleep!"

I laughed at that thought and then settled down with my journal while Hopeful dozed off to sleep yet again.[5]

My eyes pop open, and I stare up at the clouds for a moment before sitting up. As I do, my journal slides off my chest and onto the soft, green grass. I smile contentedly to myself, climb to my feet, and stretch. Beside me, Hopeful stirs from our latest nap in this beautiful country.

Crouching down, I open my pack to slide my journal away, along with my quill and ink, but my journal slips out of my hand, falling onto the grass. Before my last nap, I had finished journalling our story up until that moment.

With a big smile on my face, I think about how good it feels to be caught up on my journal, the entire journey until now recorded completely.

I catch sight of the gardener, not far from me. He's humming as he tends to the grounds, clipping back some bushes near the gates to this garden. I grab the journal from the ground where it had fallen and shove it away in my pack. Somehow, I know, this close to the end, that I won't

---

[5] I have written this book until this point as though Christian has been recording everything in his journal. However, from here on out, he no longer records the journey. As such, the tense changes here from past tense (the notes in the journal) to present tense (as they are experiencing it). If you are not prepared for a change in tense, it can be jarring at times, but I feel it is helpful at this point to carry the pilgrims through their final days.

be writing in my journal anymore. From here on out, we face it all without record. Only the Lord of the way will know.

"Time to move on, do you think?" Hopeful asks with a yawn.

I laugh. I can't help it. So close to the city, in such a peaceful place, nothing but joy fills my heart. "Yes, Hopeful. Time to move on. Let's complete our journey." With a smile, I add quietly, "We're almost there."

We say our goodbyes to the gardener and leave through the open gate. Ahead stands the great city, but with the reflection of the sun upon the golden streets and the buildings made of pearls and precious stones, we find we can't look directly at it, unless we use a special instrument given to us by the gardener.[6]

With our eyes shielded, and grins on our faces, we push on, cheerful and full of gladness, knowing that the Lord of the way is not far away.

"Hello there!"

I look ahead to see the source of the voice, still shielding my eyes from the radiance of the city. In the brightness, I make out the shapes of two men standing on the road, their clothes shining like gold, and their faces shining like the light itself.[7]

"Where do you come from?" the man on the right calls out.

"I come from the City of Destruction," I reply, "and my friend Hopeful comes from Vanity Fair."

"I see," the man says slowly. "And where, might I ask, have you stayed along the way? What difficulties and

---

[6] Rev. 21:18.
[7] 2 Cor. 3:18.

dangers have you faced, and what comforts and pleasures have you met on the path?"

I take the time to tell our story to the two men, and Hopeful shares a great deal as well. When we finish, Hopeful grabs my arm and nods at my pack. I know what he's suggesting. I pull off my pack, drop it to the ground, and fish out the journal, along with the quill and inkwell. With a smile on my face, I offer it all to the two men, and they take it, returning a smile.

It's probably best to pass it along. Here at the end, I know I won't need it from now on.

Once I hand the journal over, the one man thumbs through my notes, while the other, the one who had spoken to us at first, raises his eyes and tells us, "My friends, you have two more difficulties. Only two, but you must face them before you may enter the city."

"Will you go with us?" Hopeful asks. "For the rest of the journey, will you remain by our sides?"

"We will," the man says with compassion in his eyes, "as much as we are able, but you must reach the city by your own faith."

The two men turn toward the city, and we speed up to join them. The four of us carry on, the Shining Ones by our side offering great comfort in this last leg of the journey. The path itself, as it always has, runs straight as an arrow, and we continue over hills and through valleys until we reach the top of a large hill within sight of the city's gate.

Still, because of the glory of the city, we can't make out the details of what we so long for, but we press on anyway. Hopeful and I, with our new companions, start down the hill with our eyes set on our destination, so focused on what is ahead, that at first, we don't see what lies immediately before us.

Hopeful grabs my arm, pulling my focus away from the city. "Christian! Look!"

Before us, between where we stand and the city we seek, runs a large river, blocking our path. I search up and down the shore with my eyes, only to find there is no bridge for travellers! To make matters worse, even from where I stand, I see the river runs deep.

I stand there in shock, Hopeful beside me, still clutching my arm. My heart pounds in my chest. I can't imagine how we might get across!

I turn to the Shining Ones, my mouth hanging open, and I suspect the fear is written on my face. How can we have come so far to face such a barrier?

Before I can ask anything, One of the Shining Ones says, "You must cross it, or you cannot approach the gate."

I shake my head slowly as I turn back to face the river, the terror and stress at facing such a difficulty overwhelming me. All I can manage is a whisper as I ask, "Is there no other way?"

The Shining One takes a slow, deep breath before answering. "Yes, my friend, but there have only ever been two granted permission to take that path, only two since the foundation of the world, Enoch and Elijah. No one else may take their path until the last trumpet sounds."[8]

My heart drops out of my chest. To come so far… to go through so much… to face so many dangers, threats, challenges… yet, to have to cross that river, a trial far worse than any I'd faced till this moment. For some reason, this trial scares me more than anything else has. I turn to look

---

[8] 1 Cor. 15:51-52.

at Hopeful and see he's also struggling, but perhaps not as much as me.

Turning to the left, then the right, I search desperately for some way to escape the river, hoping, by chance, that I might not have to cross it. But there it sits before us, a final step. And as much as I look for another way, I see the path that I have followed all these years leads straight to the river's edge.

"Is…" I begin, unable to keep my voice steady. "Is the water… is it the same depth all the way across?"

"No," the Shining One says in a kind, but firm voice as he shakes his head slowly. "We cannot help you in this part. You will find it deeper or shallower, depending on your faith in the King of the place."

Everything in me wants to run. To turn and go anywhere but through that river. But then again… there's nowhere else to go. And everything I want is on the other side. I can't stop the inevitable, because this is it… this is truly the end of my journey.

"It's time," Hopeful whispers. "I'm ready."

I nod and close my eyes. Taking a deep breath, I say, "Then let's face our final breath."

We head down the hill, following the path as the Shining Ones remaining behind. Hopeful, beside me, walks with confidence, but for me, each step closer to the river causes my terror to grow. At the water's edge, Hopeful doesn't hesitate. He doesn't pull off his shoes, his cloak, anything; he just walks right in, ready to face what lies ahead.

I, however, cannot move forward with such confidence. With fear building in my heart, I take my first step, the water immediately feeling cold around my toes, my ankles, my calves. I take another few steps, terrified, and struggling with the whole thing.

One more step… and the bottom drops out beneath me, my whole body plunging into the murky depths below.

I force my way up, my head breaking the surface as I choke and gasp, spitting out the water in my mouth. "Hopeful! I'm sinking! I'm in deep waters! The waves cover my head, all his waves go over me!"[9]

I thrash about in the water, desperately trying to find my footing, anything I can use to keep my head above the water. When I sink, I find nothing, and when I come up, I gulp in lungfuls of air.

"Don't worry, my brother!" Hopeful calls to me, one of the times I resurface. "I feel the bottom. It's solid!"

Desperately pulling myself up again, I gasp for air. "My friend," I cry out as I fight against the waves. "The sorrows of death have surrounded me. I won't see the land that flows with milk and honey!"

I gasp again as darkness floods my heart, my mind, my eyes, and a deep terror, a horror, overcomes and torments my soul. I see nothing around me, not even the waves, although I feel them rushing around, filling my mouth, beating against my sides. I don't remember… can't remember anything… anything good at all! My life has been a disaster, a complete loss. I have felt no joy, no pleasure. I have lost it all! The demons come for me, and I will die in this river with no hope of entrance at the gate I so longed for.

The only thing I can see clearly, the only thing I can know and understand, is my sin. All my sins, all my wicked deeds rush into my mind, into my heart, all of them,

---

[9] Ps. 42:7.

both before I became a pilgrim and after. The weight of them is overwhelming, and I'm surrounded by evil spirits, hobgoblins. All I can do is scream out in my anguish, "Get away from me, evil spirits! Leave me, hobgoblins!"

"Christian! Christian!"

I hear a voice, a voice I recognize, but I don't know. Hopeful? Hopeful is the name that comes to mind. I sink down again, the water all around me, my mouth filling with water. When I fight my way to the surface again, I can barely keep my head up. I don't even have the strength to cough out the water in my lungs.

"Brother!"

That voice again… of one I once knew… Hopeful… that… is that his name?

"Brother, I see the gate… I see men standing by, ready to receive us!"

"No…" I cry out with the little strength I have left. "It's you, Hopeful. It's you they're waiting for. You have been Hopeful ever since I met you."

Between the roar of the wind and the waves, I hear his reply, his voice calm, sure, and at peace. "And so have you, Christian."

"My brother," I said, choking out my words. "If I were clean, he would now arise and help me. But my sins overwhelm me and have brought me into this trap. My sins will leave me here."

"My brother," Hopeful calls out, his voice faint in the storm. "You've forgotten the Scriptures where it says of the wicked, 'For they have no pangs until death; their bodies are fat and sleek. They are not in trouble as others are; they are not stricken like the rest of mankind.'[10] These

---

[10] Ps. 73:4-5.

troubles and this distress you feel, my brother, all that you go through in these waters are not a sign that God has abandoned you. This, Christian, is given to you to try you! To test you to see if you will remember in this time all his goodness given to you and cling to him in your distress!"

His words silence me, and though I struggle, fight, battle with the waves, the darkness, the wind, the terror, all of it… in that moment, my mind fills with the wisdom he's given me.

"Be encouraged, Christian! Jesus Christ is making you whole!"

A bright light catches my eye, and I twist in the water, focusing on the only thing I can make out in the darkness. "I… see him!" I yell. "I see him! Hopeful, I see him! I see my Saviour! He's… telling me something… He's telling me when I walk through the waters, he will be with me! When I go through the rivers, they will never overwhelm me![11] Oh, Hopeful! Hopeful, I see him!"

My foot strikes against something solid, and I scramble to push myself up. The firm ground holds me, and I find my footing. While still gasping, I stand on solid and sure ground as Hopeful wades over to my side. Putting his arm around me and smiling at me, he points to the water, calm as can be, and we move forward. The enemy is now as still as a stone.

Pushing through the waist deep water, I find from that moment on, the water all around me is shallow. Each step, although difficult, is no longer filled with terror and fear—only hope for what is to come!

This close to the other side, the water grows shallower with each step, and after a few more minutes, I

---

[11] Isa. 43:2.

step out of the water and onto the bank of the river with Hopeful beside me.

I turn to my friend. Neither of us can stop grinning.

We're almost home!

"Welcome," a voice calls out.

The two men, the Shining Ones, stand not far away, waiting for us.

"We are ministering spirits," the one says in a calm, kind voice. "We are sent to minister to those who are heirs of salvation." Reaching out to us, he says, "Come with us towards the gate."

We joyfully run forward and reach the two Shining Ones. Taking Hopeful and I each by the arm, they lead us forward, toward the city, the city we have journeyed towards all these long years.

The city itself sits on a large hill, high above the river. It's steep and high, and I know in my former life, such a hill would have worn me out. I would have struggled with each step. But in this place, we climb with ease, helped by the men who hold us by the arms.

My eyes drift down to my body as we climb. For the first time, I notice that although I went into the river with my cloak, my shoes, and my armour, I came out with nothing but my skin!

I laugh. Hopeful is in the same state as me, but neither of us feel embarrassed. We have left all behind. Nothing of the world has any hold on us anymore.

Because we carry nothing of the world on our persons, we feel light and free and run up the hill with no difficulty. Looking all around, trying to get my bearings, I see the foundation of the city itself is higher than even the clouds, but that will be no trouble in our present state!

As we climb the mountain, the air changing with the altitude, we speak cheerfully with one another, comforted after such an ordeal with the river, and happy to have such good new friends with us.

Now, now, look how the holy pilgrims ride,
Clouds are their chariots, angels are their guide:
Who would not here for him all hazards run,
That thus provides for his when this world's done?

As we climb higher and higher, we spend our time talking with the Shining Ones. We ask them to tell us of the glory of the heavenly city, and their response is that the beauty and glory of it is inexpressible! But they tell us some things, such as that the city is Mount Zion, the heavenly Jerusalem, and in that place are angels without number, and the spirits of righteous men made perfect.[12]

"You are now going," one of the Shining Ones explains, "to the paradise of God. There you will see the Tree of Life and eat never-fading fruits from it! When you reach the city, white robes will be given to you, and you will walk and talk with the King every day, for all of eternity! In the city, you will never see many of the things you saw when you were in the lower region on the earth. Things such as sorrow, sickness, affliction, death—those things have all passed away!" With a large smile, the Shining One continues, "You are now going to Abraham, to Isaac, to Jacob, and to all the prophets, men whom God has rescued

---

[12] Heb. 12:22-24.

284

from the evil to come, and who are now resting on their beds, each one walking in his righteousness."[13]

"And what will we do there?" Hopeful asks.

The Shining One laughed, not mockingly, but with joy. "You, dear Hopeful, will receive in this place all the comforts from all your work! You will have joy for all your sadness! You will reap what you have sown, the fruit of all your prayers, tears, and suffering for the King, all throughout your pilgrimage. In this place, you will wear crowns of gold and enjoy seeing the Holy One—every day for the rest of eternity—for here you will see him as he truly is! Here you will serve him forever with praise, with shouting, with thanksgiving, the very one you desired to serve in the world, though it was difficult because of the weakness of your flesh. In this place, your eyes will rejoice with seeing and your ears with hearing the pleasant voice of the Mighty One. And here you will enjoy your friends, those who have gone on before you. Here, you will joyfully welcome all those who come to this holy place after you. Here you will be clothed with glory and majesty and be dressed in a manner that is fit to ride out with the King of Glory. When he will come with the sound of trumpet in the clouds, as on the wings of the wind, you will come with him! And when he sits upon the throne of judgement, you will sit by him. When he passes sentence on all the workers of iniquity, whether they are angels or men, you also will have a voice in that judgement because they were not only his enemies, but yours. And, my dear Hopeful and Christian, friends, pilgrims who have finally reached home, when he will return to the city, you will return with him with the sound of trumpets, and then you will be with him forever!"[14]

---

[13] Rev. 2:7; 3:4; 21:4-5; Isa. 57:1-2; 65:17.
[14] Gal. 6:7; 1 John 3:2; 1 Thes. 4:13-16; Jude 1:14; Dan. 7:9-10; 1 Cor. 6:2-3.

I can hardly hold myself back from running with all my might. The look on Hopeful's face makes me think he desires the same thing, but we maintain our steady pace up the mountain, which is still just short of a run!

Drawing near the gate of the glorious city in front of us, I try to take it all in, but it's far more than I had ever imagined! Just when I wonder who will open the gate, the great doors swing out towards us, shining the light from within out and down the road up the mountain. A crowd, a heavenly host, all dressed in beautiful, pure garments of glory, come out, calling to us, greeting us.

One of the Shining Ones points to those from the city and explains to us, "These are the men who loved our Lord while in the world. They are the ones who left all for his holy name. He sent us to gather them, and we brought them this far on their desired journey that they might go in and look on their Redeemer's face with joy!"

Then the heavenly host, the endless crowd coming to meet us, shouts out loudly, "Blessed are those who are called to the marriage supper of the Lamb."[15]

"Look!" Hopeful cries out, pointing forward.

Through the gate stream a dozen men, all dressed in white and shining gowns. They file to the left and right of the gate, carrying trumpets of gold in their hands. I watch as they raise their trumpets to their lips, take a deep breath, and let loose with a loud and melodious sound, echoing even throughout the heavens! They blow again and again, saluting us with ten thousand welcomes from the world, and they do this both by shouting at times and blowing the trumpets at other times.

The trumpeters then surround us on every side, some going before, some behind, some on the right, some

---

[15] Rev. 19:9.

286

on the left, almost as if they are trying to guard us through the upper regions. As we approach the city, they continue to sound their trumpets with a melodious song with notes on high. To any who saw us, I suppose they might have thought that all of heaven itself had come to meet us!

We walk on together, Hopeful, the two Shining Ones, and me, surrounded by the trumpeters and the crowds of people. Now and then, as we walk, the trumpeters, while playing their joyful sound, let us know how welcome we are in their company, and how glad they are to meet us, signalling this to us with a simple raise of an eyebrow, or a smile, or even a look.

We're nearly there! We're almost at the gates, but before we can enter the city, Hopeful and I are swallowed up by the sight of angels and the sound of beautiful music. It's almost too much to bear! To add to it all, we can even see into the city itself, laid out before us!

"I think I hear bells from the city, ringing to welcome us!" Hopeful cries out with a laugh.

I put my arm around Hopeful's shoulders. My heart feels like it's about to burst with joy. "We've finally made it!" I shout, my heart warming over with the joyful thoughts about living there with these people for ever and ever.

"I'm glad I left my journal behind!" I shout to Hopeful over the music and cheers. "There is no way my tongue can describe it all, let alone can any pen tell of my joy!"

And with that, we reach the gate, the glorious, beautiful gate. Above the giant doors, written in letters of gold, I read, "Blessed are those who wash their robes, so that they may have the right to the tree of life and that they may enter the city by the gates."[16]

We come to a halt, and everyone grows silent, just before stepping through the gates. I want to run right through, but I know I must be welcomed in.

"Call out for entrance into the city!" one of the Shining Ones commands us.

"Please!" I cry out. "May we enter?"

Above the gate, I see movement, and three faces appear, three men looking down at us. Although I have met none of these men, I know who they are. They are Enoch, Moses, and Elijah.

"These pilgrims," one of the Shining Ones calls out, "come from the City of Destruction, for the love that they hold for the King of this place!"

In my possession, though we had lost all our clothing and earthly belongings, I still have my certificate, the very one I had received in the beginning. Hopeful has his as well, and we hand them over to the Shining Ones. Taking our certificates, they run through the gates, taking them directly to the King.

When they reach him, he reads the certificates and immediately demands, "Where are the men?"

"They are standing outside the gate," one of the Shining Ones replies.

"Open the gates," he orders, "that the righteous nation that keeps faith may enter."[17]

When we receive our welcome, we enter the gate, and as we enter, I feel myself… change. Not a little, either!

[16] Rev. 22:14.
[17] Isa. 26:2.

I… I am made new! Brand new!

Men come up to us as we stand there in our new bodies. They drape new garments around our shoulders, covering us, garments shining like gold! As they clothe us, two other men come carrying harps and crowns, and they give one to each of us—the harp to praise, and the crowns as a token of honour.

Then all the bells in the city ring again for joy, and a loud voice cries out, "ENTER INTO THE JOY OF YOUR LORD!"

I can't hold it in any longer! I open my mouth and cry out, with Hopeful joining in, "TO HIM WHO SITS ON THE THRONE AND TO THE LAMB BE BLESSING AND HONOUR AND GLORY AND MIGHT FOREVER AND EVER!"[18]

In the heart of a dreamer, a man found hope, a place to rest his weary soul. And in that place, he found glory. Glory and honour for all of eternity.
And the dreamer looked, and behold, the gates which had opened to welcome in the men, were beautiful, and the dreamer looked in through the gates and saw the City shining like the sun, and the streets paved with gold. In the streets walked many men and women, with crowns on their heads, palms in their hands, and golden harps with which to sing praises. The dreamer also saw those who had wings, and they answered one another, continually crying out, "Holy, holy, holy, is the Lord God Almighty."[19]
After that, they shut the gates, and the dreamer saw no more. But that brief glimpse of glory left the dreamer with a longing that he could be among them.

---

[18] Rev. 5:13.
[19] Rev. 4:8.

Now, back down the mountain, and across the river, another man approached, seeking entrance to the city. A young man, one by the name of Ignorance. He came upon the edge of the river, but did not step in, for he saw no need to endure the test of faith. Instead, he found a ferryman in that area, a man by the name of Vain-hope. This man had a boat and helped him over to the other side with little difficulty at all.

Once across, Ignorance left Vain-hope, grateful for his help, and began his climb up the mountain, all alone, of course. In time, he reached the gate, still alone, for no one had come to meet him or to offer encouragement.

When he reached the gate, he looked up to the writing above the gate, "Blessed are those who wash their robes, so that they may have the right to the tree of life and that they may enter the city by the gates,"[20] and then he knocked, assuming that he would quickly find entrance into the city.

Just as with Christian and Hopeful, men looked down from over the gate, but this time, they asked, "Where have you come from, and what do you want?"

Ignorance smiled and called back, "I ate and drank in the presence of the King, and he taught in our streets!"

"Give us your certificate!" they called back. "We will take it to the King."

Ignorance's face fell, and he looked around in fear. Reaching into his cloak, he felt around, hoping, by chance, to find a certificate in there, but found nothing.

---

[20] Rev. 22:14.

"Don't you have one?" the men called down.

Ignorance's heart raced, and he began to sweat. His hands shook, and his lips trembled, but he did not answer a word.

"Send word to the King!" a man called out.

They waited for a time for the King's response, but when it came, it was nothing like what Ignorance had hoped for. The King refused to come, but instead sent the two Shining Ones, the very ones who led Christian and Hopeful to the city.

These men, however, did not come to show kindness and encouragement to Ignorance. Instead, they bound him, hand and foot. Once he was fully secure, they hoisted him up, and flew with him into the air to the door, the one dug into the side of the hill, and cast him in there, for there was a way to hell not only from the City of Destruction, but even from the gates of heaven.

In the heart of a dreamer, the dreamer awoke. He found himself in a den, a place to rest his weary soul. The journey taken had been but a dream, a dream of travellers, pilgrims, a path; a journey that took them from this world to that which is to come. A journey now shared with you.

The Conclusion

Now, Reader, I have told my dream to thee;[21]
See if thou canst interpret it to me,
Or to thyself, or neighbour; but take heed
Of misinterpreting; for that, instead
Of doing good, will but thyself abuse:
By misinterpreting, evil ensues.
Take heed, also, that thou be not extreme,
In playing with the outside of my dream:
Nor let my figure or similitude
Put thee into a laughter or a feud.
Leave this for boys and fools; but as for thee,
Do thou the substance of my matter see.
Put by the curtains, look within my veil,
Turn up my metaphors, and do not fail,
There, if thou seekest them, such things to find,
As will be helpful to an honest mind.
What of my dross thou findest there, be bold
To throw away, but yet preserve the gold;
What if my gold be wrapped up in ore?
None throws away the apple for the core.
But if thou shalt cast all away as vain,
I know not but 'twill make me dream again.

---

[21] This conclusion has been left in Bunyan's original language.

I hope you have enjoyed this Rewalked Edition of Pilgrim's Progress! To dive in deeper on your own or in a group, don't forget to check out the Study Guide by Shawn P. Robinson!

May God bless you as you travel this path towards the Celestial City!

Pilgrim's Progress
Rewalked with Study
Guide and Helps

Pilgrim's Progress
Original Edition with
Study Guide and Helps

Pilgrim's Progress
Rewalked

Pilgrim's
Progress Online

About the Author

Shawn P. Robinson has a passion for teaching God's Word and seeing people grow in their faith and has had the privilege of serving in Christian ministry as an Associate Pastor, Lead Pastor, and as a Church Planter.

In 2017, a viral infection in his brain pulled him from pastoral ministry, changing the course of his life from a focus on ministry to trying to recover. Eventually, Shawn's health forced him to step down from his pastoral role. Amid the illness, Shawn began to write a children's book for his sons and from that grew a passion for writing fiction, which has proven to be an exciting blessing from God during a time when he can no longer serve in vocational ministry.

As Shawn continued to write fiction, learning to trust the Lord in this new direction of life, he quickly found joy both in sharing stories and in sharing gospel allegories.

In time, the Lord laid it on Shawn's heart to create a modern-day rewrite of Pilgrim's Progress, one which might not only remain faithful to the original but also be presented in a more contemporary narrative format, hopefully opening up the story to a new generation. With this, Shawn set out to provide study guides with deep and challenging questions based on a Pilgrim's Progress study he offered to his church years before.

Shawn has a Bachelor of Arts in Christian Studies from Briercrest Bible College in Saskatchewan and a Master of Divinity from Carey Theological College in British Columbia. Shawn is ordained with the Fellowship of Evangelical Baptist Churches in Ontario, Canada. Shawn and his wife and two sons live in Southwestern Ontario.

CHECK OUT THESE BOOKS BY
Shawn P. B. Robinson

Adult Fiction (Sci-fi & Fantasy)

The Ridge Series (3 books)
ADA: An Anthology of Short Stories

YA Fiction (Fantasy, Sci-fi, Dystopian)

The Sevordine Chronicles (5 Books)
Greks (2 Books)—Coming Soon
The Modder's Run (2 Books)—Coming Soon

Books for Younger Readers

Annalynn the Canadian Spy Series (6 Books)
Jerry the Squirrel (4 Books)
Arestana Series (3 Books)
Activity Books (2 Books)

Pilgrim's Progress

Pilgrim's Progress *Rewalked*
Pilgrim's Progress *Rewalked* with Study Guide
Pilgrim's Progress Annotated Original with Study
Guide

www.shawnpbrobinson.com/books

Made in the USA
Columbia, SC
09 June 2025

59102793R00190